LET
SLEEPING
DOGS LIE

DEAN KASTLE

ACKNOWLEDGEMENTS

Long is the list of friends and family who helped bring these stories to life, but I have to mention a few. Many thanks go to Ben K, authors Steve Karas, Kylie Lynne, and Lou Anders, and Dean B.—my number-one story consultant. Finally, my wife and motivator in chief, Marilyn, deserves a shout out. You have my love, appreciation, and deepest gratitude.

This one is for Benjamin, who helped work out some SERIOUS kinks!

CONTENTS

CHAPTER ONE

T imes of peace could be tricky for a man like Geth, but
gods all be damned if he wasn't going to give it a try.

"Press! Press!" He moved between pairs of soldiers, shouting encouragement and curses in equal measure. "Guard up!
Thram's balls, move your feet man! Now press!"

The clack of wooden wasters echoed off the stone walls of
Towerrock's sword-yard, the scent of woodsmoke mixed with
the honest odor of a good sweat. Fallen leaves rattled and swirled
in the corners as the sun dipped to render half the trampled turf
shaded and chill, the other half bright and warm.

Geth signaled a halt. He passed a skin of water to a young
green-cloak. "On the balls of your feet, always. Ready to press,
ready to fall back, ready to circle to either side."

"Yessir, Yardmaster."

Yardmaster. Thram and bloody Awer, how things could
change. Perhaps it was the return of autumn, or the familiar
surroundings, but the events of Geth's arrival in Umbel, specifi-
cally the Tooth, were always near the front of Geth's mind these

days. Who could have guessed a foreign outlaw would rise as far as Towerrock's second in command?

He clapped the lad on the shoulder, turned to meet his captains, Kerrel and Hack. "Keep them at it as long as there's light. Not longer though. I don't want some dumb scratch to get his ribs broke."

Hack snapped a salute of fist to heart, pimple-scarred face intense as ever. "We'll make men of them yet, Captain. You can count on it."

From his side, young Kerrel copied the gesture at an easier pace. Hack turned to holler at the soldiers, leaving Geth with the younger warrior.

"You still reading the Omnibus?" he asked.

Kerrel nodded. "The Red Book mostly."

"Good. Forget about sacrificing chickens and all that, but don't skip a page. That book is where I learned most of what I know about war."

"Not at war itself?"

Geth frowned. "Well, I suppose I did learn a thing or two in the field."

Kerrel managed to keep a straight face.

Geth shook his head and left through the gates. Hack's shouts and the thump of wasters resumed. Green-cloaks saluted as the big warrior passed, womenfolk too, baskets of laundry in hand, or foodstuffs, water jugs. A stonemason grinned and gestured to a patched-up section of the west-facing wall. A pantler handed him a fresh-baked meat-pie. But Steward Willa—the old she-devil—blocked his way at the foot of the stairwell leading up to the ramparts.

"You'll need to have a look at these." She thumped a stack of ledgers. "The harvest tallies are in, and I've never seen a sorrier list. Then again, after a few years of war and pestilence, we've got less mouths to feed anyway. I think we'll manage with some provisions bartered from your...*northern friends.*"

Her tone made clear what she thought of his 'northern friends.'

"Dried up old hag," Geth muttered under his breath.

"What was that?"

"I said *King Hadean's* northern friends won't let us down. I'll be headed that way to make sure of it soon enough."

Willa had a way of tilting her head, lips curled in a very familiar fashion, so that her eyes seemed to judge, sentence, and assign him alongside the rest of the good-for-nothings. But she knew her business when it came to running a fortress. Geth smiled, thinking of Melagus. With a quick step, he skirted wide to pass her and hurried up the stairs.

"Tomorrow then!" she called after him. "The tallies!"

Geth blew out a sigh when he reached the safety of the parapet. The air was cool up there and he took in a great deep breath. Just standing on the high ground, looking out over the folds of the land, the smooth curves of the river—it did wonders. The sun blazed bright and cheery over brown and yellow fields, grey-white fortress walls, and the thatched rooftops of Greenfell.

Autumn in Umbel, and me the Yardmaster of Towrrock. Geth shook his head. "Thram and bloody Awer." How things had come full circle.

To the east, billowing white clouds dotted the horizon. Phelan was somewhere out there, driving Eora crazy at the Oak and Heart if things had gone to plan. He was a wanted man, but Geth had no choice except to trust Eora's magicks to keep him hidden. From Palladine, Queen Lyanne, and anyone else. He'd always wanted an inn, the little man, and Geth wasn't about to stand in his way. He couldn't join him though, even if he'd wanted to. He had a baby on the way. He shook his head at the thought, started off toward the bird-keeper's loft with a purposeful stride.

But the old man shook his grey head as Geth arrived.

"Nothing?" the big warrior asked.

"Like the day before. And the day before that."

Geth pulled at his mustache, turned back toward the stairs. "Thram's balls." He sighed. "May as well see about Willa and her tallies, I reckon."

There was always work to be done in a fortress the size of Towerrock, more so with the town of Greenfell still on the mend. But as chief of it all—except on Brant's rare visits—Geth's arms weren't needed hauling lumber or swinging a hammer. Aside from the soldiers, he had a host of ministers and minders, groundskeepers, masons, smiths, and carpenters at his call. Not to mention the cooks, scullions, servers, launderers, and clothiers. And the gods only knew who else.

"Be like Hadean," he reminded himself. "Like Khyr, like Bad-Leg." He walked the walls, nodded to the men on watch. He toured the building sites, offered a thumbs up to craftsmen on the scaffolds. At lunchtime, he ate in the great hall with whoever sat the tables, no matter their station. That part wasn't hard. But by day's end, he was back on the parapets, pointed toward the bird lofts for the inevitable shake of the head from the old man.

"How long can it possibly take to have a baby?"

The old bird-keep eyed him stone-faced. "About nine months, I've heard tell."

A younger Geth might have tossed the bastard right off the walls. He smiled instead, shook his head, and started back down. That night, however, a night when the wind howled with the first frigid rumor of winter, he dreamed of the dead. The wolf-dog Eko rose, as if from slumber, in the morning-misted sword-yard.

"There you are," Geth said, like the beast had wandered off for a time and not been killed by that treasonous sonofabitch, Towdric. The big warrior kneeled and Eko came to him, licked his face and climbed half on him, paws on Geth's shoulders. He stood and the wolf ran a joyful circle around his legs then bounded out of the ward. Geth followed through the empty keep and out the grave-silent gates until he was marching toward a line of trees in the distance.

"Ilia."

He awoke with the word still on his lips. Pulling on his boots without a pause even to use the bedpan, Geth sped through the corridors and up the stairs toward the bird lofts. The old man opened his mouth, but Geth spoke before he had the chance.

"I already know."

Geth was halfway back down the stairs, note in hand, when the old bird-keep's voice reached him. "Wait!" He waved a tiny scrap of parchment. "Got this one too, from down south."

Geth frowned. "Hadean?" He took the message, cracked the seal, and read. "Thram's balls. He'll be here in just a few days."

He left the old man and hurried toward the Lord's Hall in search of Willa. Preparations would need to be made, rooms readied, a proper reception for the king and his escorts. Why they made the journey though, he couldn't say.

"Damn you, Melagus," he cursed. "Could've written a longer note."

But there it was. He kept himself busy getting ready, tried not to fret over the dream-summons to Ilia. The baby would be born healthy and strong. And he would be there soon to meet him. That was that.

In two day's time, the king and his ship were spotted rowing north on the shimmering blue surface of Vorus. Geth, Willa, Kerrel, and Hack met them down at the waterside. No one was more surprised than the big warrior to see Mother on the ship as well, standing beside Melagus and his messenger-boy, Orie.

She found him as soon the pleasantries with Hadean were done. "There he is! Lord of the town!"

"Yardmaster, Mother, of the sword-yard. Brant's the lord around here, not me."

"And where is he? Ah, left my boy in charge, lording over the town, just like I said. And doing a fine job of it, seems to me."

He accepted a hug and left it at that. Mother turned back to help Melagus over the gunwale of the ship and fussed over the lad Orie's hair as he slipped nimbly over beside the counselor.

"Still at it," Geth mumbled, shaking his head. At least the little boy looked hale, hair combed to one side to cover his missing ear.

Geth, Willa, and the welcome party led the king and his entourage across the bridge to the Tooth and their rooms. A feast would be held that evening, but Hadean and the counselor followed Geth down the close, torch-lit corridors toward the old war room first.

"You're wondering what could warrant the journey," King Hadean said, taking a chair. Willa herself arrived with a tray of cold meats, cheese, dried fruits, and nuts. She poured wine for each of them. Hadean took a long drink, sighed. "Iyngaer is troubled in the north."

Geth felt this chest loosen. "I reckon that's to be expected, my lord. Have to say, I was expecting worse."

"Thankfully, that's the whole of it. Umbel City has recovered nicely after Towdric's insurrection."

Melagus offered Geth a satisfied smirk. "Truth be told, it's almost as if it never happened."

"Forgotten already, the traitor?" Geth spit. "The gods might be just after all."

Hadean nodded. "Thanks to the both of you—" he looked from Melagus to Geth and back "the southern reaches of the realm were spared sword and fire. The harvest came in like always. There was little in need of repair."

"Less so, the north." Melagus said dryly.

Willa cleared her throat at this. "My lord king, I have the tallies from the harvest. My assessors have been clear across the northern reaches, from the edge of Witchwood all the way to the Flats. Out west, in the Tumble valley, they managed to bring in some produce. But nearer the North River, we lost everything down to the seedstock."

Hadean frowned. "Take only a small share of the harvest in taxes this year. Resell it to those in need. At a loss if needed."

Geth kept silent in this kind of discussion, but he saw Melagus watching the king with approval. Willa's head started to tilt until she caught herself, turned it into a nod. "Of course, my king. We'll be scraping the barrels this year though I'm afraid. How I'll pay the laborers and soldiers, I can't begin to fathom."

"It will be difficult, no doubt. But as long as they are fed and sheltered and kept from harm, they'll understand. I will address the people. And also the lords."

"Well spoken, my king," Melagus chimed in. "If we overtax the farmers now, we'll starve them out. And next year we'll have nothing. But if we grant leniency, tighten our belts this year, next year too maybe, we'll all rebound together."

"And there will be ships coming upriver with grain within the week," Hadean added. "Let the south now repay the north, for the sacrifices made to protect their fields and livestock."

Willa dipped her head. "I am told we may expect provisions from Ilia as well. Added to your measures, it could be enough to see us through the winter."

"It will be." Geth stood as straight as he could. "We've set up each of the boundary forts as a trading post. May as well use them for something, now the war's over."

That had been Melagus's idea. The counselor met his eye, but he let Geth have the moment. It was a damn good idea too. Even Willa looked thoughtful.

Hadean made a face though. "And that brings us back to Iyngaer. We fought hard for peace, but we'll only have it as long as the chieftain rules in Dues *and* Thiringia. Lady Pythelle tells me Agrem the Seer has been...in contact."

Magicks. Geth reckoned he'd just have to get used to it. "You say the chieftain is having troubles?"

"It started small, but it's growing. A raid here and there, rumors of discontent among the Thirings."

"Discontent, eh?" Geth swallowed a choice curse. "They had a foreign sorcerer in the big chair. Now they have a tribesman and they're discontent?"

"Some men seek out conflict," Melagus said. "It's all they know. Ceter held the Thiring tribe together through fear—we've all had a taste of that—but things aren't so simple for Iyngaer, ruling, as he has, from across the river."

Hadean rose to pace the length of the little chamber. "And now he finds it difficult to rule Thiringia at all."

Geth frowned. The king only paced when things were serious. "That bad?"

"Bad enough to warrant the journey from Umbel City," said Melagus.

"You're not thinking of going to Ilia, are you?" Geth looked from the counselor to the king.

"Well—"

"Because Agrem's been in touch with me too."

"Has he?" Melagus asked.

"Got a pigeon from Ilia on top of that. The...er...baby is almost here."

Hadean's face lit up. "Congratulations!" He stepped over to clap Geth on the shoulder, shake his hand. Melagus was smiling as well, but Geth knew it had less to do with his son.

"Just say it." He eyed the counselor flatly.

Melagus spread his hands. "Well, we could use a man in Ilia, as you say."

CHAPTER TWO

G eth couldn't get to Ilia soon enough. Willa had been growing more anxious with each report of abandoned crops or livestock lost, and Geth was ready to be on a horse, beneath an open sky. Anywhere but under her eye.

"I'll be headed to see Iyngaer before I turn west toward Ekhen Laer," he told Kerrel over an impromptu dinner. "Best we can tell, there's no getting up to Laer, not without a small army anyway. Rebels are out and about all across Thiringia."

The lad swallowed down a cooked carrot, leaned up against the counter across from Geth in the kitchens. Sauciers and scullions scurried around them, well-accustomed to their Yardmaster's intrusions by now. A hefty woman with a mole on her nose smiled at the appreciative noises he uttered each time he lifted a lid to dip into a pot.

Kerrel didn't refuse an invitation to join in. Somehow the boy got less crumbs on his shirt though, less sauce down his chin. "You think it's Vongaer?" he asked Geth.

"Has to be. He was all but settled as chieftain until we showed up to usher Iyngaer in. Must be he's found some support as well."

"I could come along if you think it'll come to a fight."

Geth shook his head. "Someone has to stay back and keep an eye on things for me. If I leave Hack, he'll grind the new recruits to dust."

Kerrel's lips went up in a smile.

"Keep them drilling at an even pace," Geth said. "Bastards like you and me, we're naturals in the sword-yard. But if there's one thing I've learned, it doesn't come that easy for most people."

"Yessir."

Geth went quiet for a moment, crunching down a heel of bread as he thought. "I'll talk to Willa, maybe call up Brant's second, Worran, to lend you a hand. Keep a few soldiers ready to march north, at a moment's notice, just in case."

"I'll have one eye on the pigeon lofts."

Geth headed to the lofts himself after that. He drafted a message for Ilia announcing his eminent arrival. Iyngaer would want to have an escort waiting for him in the boundaries, he reckoned. Doing his best to think like Melagus, Geth made sure to mention their need for provisions in the note as well.

He told the counselor his plan out in the great hall before Hadean's welcome feast.

Melagus gave a nod. "You've come a long way. A very long way. A few months ago, you would have left for Ilia with nothing but your sword and that rogue, Phelan."

Geth pulled at one end of his mustache. That's exactly what he'd done a few seasons back. "This time I'm bringing wagons. Woolens, tools, weapons, wine—whatever else the tribesmen might like to trade for. With any luck, those wagons will come back with trout and deer and turnips. We can always use more lumber if there's room. And eyfra, that spirit they make."

Young Orie burst from the door to the kitchens just then, red-faced, a stolen sweet bread in hand. Melagus wagged a finger at him, and Mother appeared to snatch it back before the boy could get more than a bite. "Save your appetite for the feast, child!"

Geth turned to the counselor. "Keeping him close these days?"

"Yes. And out of harm. Perhaps I've come a ways myself."

Geth opened his mouth, but Mother chimed in first. "You couldn't put a foot wrong if you tried." She turned to pinch Orie's cheek, earned a groan in reply. "And he's a good, sweet lad, young Orie. Aren't you, my boy?"

"Yes, Mame," Orie piped.

"Except when it comes to sweets."

The boy produced one of those guilty smiles only a child could get away with.

"A good lad," Geth said, "swiping from the larders? Sounds like your Uncle Geth at a certain age. Never did kick the habit, now that I think of it."

"Well, that's why *I'm* here." Mother rested her hands on Orie's shoulders. "To see to it the boy learns some proper manners, before he ends up like you."

"Gods forbid," Melagus muttered.

But Mother was smiling. They looked an awful lot like a married couple around that child, now that Geth was paying attention. It was no secret Mother had designs on Melagus; Geth couldn't help wondering if she'd already cornered him at some point, served up a helping of 'Lady Largess.' He shuddered.

The guests began to arrive. Aromas of cooked meat preceded a parade of mouth-watering dishes; chicken, mutton, and cooked vegetables, carried out on steaming trays by proud cooks and servers like the woman with the mole. Somehow, even the old bird-keep was among them.

Got himself right up close to the food. Geth gave the oldster a stern look, received a formal salute of fist to heart. "Ha! All respectful, now that the king's watching."

They tucked in. The last of autumn's fruit finished the meal, coupled with those sweet breads and washed down with a dessert wine. A lute sounded and a gentle melody rose just below the din of conversation, something with an exotic sound, reminiscent of the great Dominion in the distant east.

"Showing off for the king," Geth told Melagus, flicking his chin toward the lutist. "Or maybe the ladies." The counselor sat to his right, Hadean in the place of honor, central, on Geth's other side.

But he must have heard. "Mysterious creatures, to be sure," the king said. "They do like music though, I've found. And dancing."

"And how *is* the Queen? They say marriage is like strong magick; a powerful blessing, but no small thing to manage."

"The Queen is well." Hadean brightened as he said it, then frowned right after. "I'm not sure she loves Umbel City though. And I struggle to think of ways to please her."

"Ever a mystery, women," Melagus said. "Most certainly."

Geth snorted, "Well, if you're looking for advice in that department, I'm afraid you couldn't have picked worse company."

"Not if you want *good* advice," Melagus said.

Hadean smiled.

The lute strummed, the torchlight flickered. Geth got to thinking of Vriana and his child. He swallowed down his wine and called for something stronger.

Now that the trip to Ilia was finally on him, he found he was nervous. How could a man charge into swords and spears with no hesitation, but turn to the bottle for fear of a child? "Thram's purple cock..."

What was he afraid of anyway? That the child wouldn't like him? That Vriana would send him away? Or that she'd expect him to stay?

He didn't know himself. Downing a mouthful of brown Ilar liquor with a grimace, he realized he was looking forward to Iyngaer and his troubles. Rebels and war? Those were things he understood.

With the help of Melagus and Willa, Geth's wagon train to Ilia was assembled and waiting in the ward when the big warrior awoke. He took his sword and shield, a fancy knife for Vriana, and a little toy sword whittled from wood for his child-to-be. He didn't need much more. Aside from drivers and a handful of retainers, an escort of twenty riders would accompany them. Hack held Geth's reins for him as he climbed into the saddle.

"Wouldn't mind a few more men, Captain," he said. "A whole army even. March in and flatten those rebel bastards once and for all."

"I like the way you think, Hack. But it's not easy to maneuver an army under the trees. They'd see us coming from miles away. We'd be all stretched out and vulnerable, along narrow roads, surrounded by cover, plenty of places to hide. Easy meat for the sort of hit and fly campaign we threw at the tribes ourselves last winter."

Hack grumbled a curse, one hand on his hilt.

"Once we know what we're looking at," Geth told him, "we can send for more men. Don't forget that Iyngaer's got plenty of swords at his call as well. If it was so easy to root out these treacherous bastards, he'd have done it already."

That got through to the green-cloak. Geth wore a smile as he watched Hack swing onto his own mount. It would be good to have him along, someone to distract him from confliction emotions about Vriana and fatherhood, a steady voice to keep him focused on the conflict ahead.

They started out, across the rebuilt bridge, through the half-repaired town of Greenfell, northward among brown and yellow fields. A hearty autumn wind whipped Geth's cloak, chilled his knuckles, but it felt good to be on an errand again. They followed the curves of the River Road, of Vorus, the river itself, until Point-fort came into view that evening.

Crookbow met them outside the low walls of the fort. "Well, if it isn't my favorite sellsword."

"You still got that hat?"

The pardoned thief straightened the fur cap on his head, offered a mock salute. Hack growled something about 'respect' from behind Geth, but the big warrior just laughed. "I see you've got the trade-post up and running around here. Better show me how all that hard work looks once it's made it to a plate."

"Gods all be damned, you're always hungry, aren't you?"

Geth cast a glance around the place, admired the pens of Ilar short-deer, the stacks of timber, the new sheds presumably stuffed with other goods. Crookbow himself wore a fat ring on his thumb now, but Geth didn't begrudge him the ostentation, as long as he continued to run his fort well.

"Everything moving along?" Geth asked as men tethered their mounts, milled about with the Point-forters, exchanging news and drinks.

"The trade part, sure," Crookbow said. "We couldn't have stopped it if we tried. The regular folk out there, they don't care for war. They couldn't wait for it to be over. They need things. The Ilars too, not just our boys. Soon as word got out that there would be safe trading at the forts, they started pouring in."

"More than a few started trickling out too though," Crookbow went on. "Where there's travel, trade, there's opportunities for a certain type."

"Thieves." Geth reckoned he should have expected as much. "How many men have you lost?"

"A good dozen. Cald's friends, as you might've guessed. And there were bandits out here already."

"Guess that makes sense. Lot of land, not so much law. And a lot of empty stomachs."

Crookbow nodded. "They've hit a few homesteads, a few merchants on the road, cattlemen, the like. We're on it though, chief, don't worry. We'll get them rounded up. Or scared off at least."

Geth spit, looked toward the horizon as if he might catch sight of a bandit he could chase down right now. Keeping the north of Umbel safe was his charge after all, be it from traitors, tribesmen, or common thieves.

But standing there with the thief-turned-soldier reminded Geth of the battle they'd won together, and the man they'd defeated. "I need a favor, Crookbow. You still got that horse I gave you?"

"The one you called Palladine?"

Geth wanted to spit again, just thinking of the lily captain. "Yeah, that one. I need that horse back."

"Well, that's a damn fine animal. I won't love losing him. And who needs him more than me anyway?"

Geth's eyes were turned north, toward the forest. "I can think of someone."

As expected, Iyngaer had sent escorts to meet Geth's party at the edge of the forest. The sun shined down on a half dozen tribes-men as they waved from horseback, their long hair whipped by a stiff autumn wind. All but one, his short locks jutting out in every direction, greying spikes held firm by some unknown magick.

"Agrem!" Geth dismounted to embrace the Seer. "I got your message. The part about coming to Ilia anyway."

"Mmmm." The Seer nodded. "There is more. But Iyngaer will tell it."

They climbed back into the saddle, each of them. With the clop of horse hooves and the creak of wagon wheels, the company passed under the trees and into Ilia. Agrem said nothing, but the hunch of his back spoke volumes. They rode in silence until Geth couldn't take it anymore.

"Gods all be damned, 'Grem, what is it?"

Agrem breathed a sigh. "Mmmm."

"You know I can't tell what that means."

"It is war, Geth et Trusla. Always war these years." He shook his head. "I was thinking we won. I was thinking it was over. I was wrong."

Geth frowned. "Isn't that the way of it? We never can be happy, seems like. Someone's always got to rile things up."

"Mmmm."

There was something more on the Seer's mind, but Geth didn't press. There wasn't any point, he'd only tell it when he was ready.

At least the travel passed without incident. It was a fine season in Geth's opinion, autumn-red oak and yellow birch flashing like jewels against the backdrop of proud green pines. It was cold, sure, but their campfires were merry each night, even if the tribesmen at watch seemed especially wary.

They veered from the River Road along paths barely wide enough for the wagons, chittering black squirrels rustling the leaves overhead. The first homesteads appeared, then the first villages, and finally a broad, grassy valley opened up before them, snaked through by a tributary of great Vorus, and overshadowed by the town and fortress of Dues on its hill.

The timber palisades yawned open to admit them and hails rang down. 'Truslata!' they called. And even 'Gethe' Govendi!'

Geth shook his head as they passed the gatehouse and entered the town. "Does that mean what I think it means?" he asked Agrem. "Running a fortress is enough to make a chief these days?"

The real chief, Iyngaer Lonega, waited for them up the gravel path between rings of longhouses, beside his hall. Stretched hide banners on their crosses rippled in the wind and the tall chieftain's white bearskin flapped about his broad shoulders. He cut an imposing figure, crutches gone, expression stoney as ever.

But a hint of a smile split that russet beard as the big warrior slid from the saddle and started toward him. "Geth-et-Trusla."

"Iyngaer Govendi."

Geth dipped his head in a bow. When he looked up, the chieftain reached out to clasp his hand, gestured him warmly toward his hall. "Come."

They started down the length, toward the central fire. Memory of his trial, of all the ordeals at the chieftain's hands, flashed through Geth's mind from first sight of the great animal skull nailed above the lintel. He'd nearly died before earning the right to join the Ilar Misa. Then again, following behind the chieftain, he reminded himself that he was the man that had given Iyngaer that ponderous limp. A fair exchange maybe. Much had passed since then, and by some fickle working of the gods, these days they were friends.

Hails from the leather-clad warriors standing in twos and threes under the high timber roof emphasized how much had changed. Someone pressed a skin of eyfra—forest fire, as Phelan called it—into his hands. The chieftain led him to a seat beside the crackling fire. Iyngaer eased himself into his great wooden chair, something from the south he'd adopted even before his injury.

"I brought you a gift," Geth told him. "It's a horse. A beauty of a beast and well trained. He'll carry you to war proudly."

"Thank you, Truslata. The wars do not seem to end these days."

He sounded a lot like Agrem. "Your leg seems...uh, better." Geth had said to change the subject, but immediately regretted it. He sucked down a mouthful of eyfra to hide the color in his cheeks.

Iyngaer reached for the skin with admirable grace, took a pull of his own. "Mmmm. Weak still, but better. We have some healers. Sythme of the Arnui could have cured it, maybe. But she is with Mereg and he is not happy with Dues."

Geth remembered the witch Sythme from his truslas, the same hag that had doubled his sentence. He wanted to spit.

"You have heard of the cowards that disturb my peace?" Iyngaer asked.

"That's why I'm here. Your fight is my fight."

"Men like us, we are shaped for war. Mmmm? But the people need peace. I have listened to every tale of the Longfathers. I have spoken with their shades, prayed at the sacred places. We live under a red moon it seems. Our fight continues."

"A red moon," Geth muttered.

But Iyngaer was in his own thoughts. "The lifetime of a man will know one war. Or two. But we were fighting under the forest long before I marched the tribes south into the Sunlands. And even after a peace was reached, the fighting has not ended."

Geth frowned. "I've been told of the rebels in Thiringia. It has to be Vongaer. Let's root him out and have done."

"It is more. Mereg and the Arnui curse us in the north. Bandits raid to the south. And of course, Vongaer and his weasels slink to the west."

Geth pulled at his mustache, mulled over those words.

The Thirings and Arnui had forged an alliance back when Othwid and the Warlock Ceter ruled those two tribes. It seemed Vongaer had managed to renew the relationship with Mereg, the new chief of the Arnus, in order to oppose Iyngaer. Or perhaps the pair of them just saw a chance to grab power. Either way, it was a tough spot for Iyngaer. Fighting a war on two fronts never did end well.

"I haven't brought many soldiers," Geth said. "But my man, Kerrel, is standing by with two hundred swords."

"Even with two thousand, victory will not come easy. I can't leave Dues undefended, march out to deal with Vongaer myself. Mereg waits for it, as surely as the forest breaths. That's when he will attack.

"And Vongaer strikes from hiding anyway. We cannot simply find him and destroy him. His numbers are not great, but they are enough to threaten anyone attempting to leave Ehken Dolae and join me. Or the other way around. They appear out of nowhere and then disappear again. By the time my warriors arrive, they're gone."

"That bastard has got to be crushed. The sooner the better."

Iyngaer hummed. "Mmmm. He will not meet in open battle. And I cannot catch him unaware. He has some friends hiding in Thiringia."

"Some?"

"More than I had hoped. His eyes are everywhere. Because of this, my wife sits stranded in Ehken Dolae. She dares not venture outside the walls even into her own lands. She longs to be here, at my side, as I wish she could. But the weasel would strike at her, in order to strike at me."

Geth didn't like what he heard. But Iyngaer's words got the wheels turning in his mind. He looked up to meet the chieftain's eye.

"I have an idea. What I'm thinking could be dangerous, but I'm going to say it anyway. If you have a mind to hear it."

Iyngaer raised his chin, undaunted.

"Your wife..."

"Gemela?"

Geth nodded. "How much do you miss her?"

CHAPTER THREE

G eth was a little ashamed of himself, using a woman as bait.

But Iyngaer didn't shrink from the idea one bit. After a night's rest, he invited Geth down to the little river running through his valley. The chieftain slid gingerly from the back of Palladine to lead Geth to one of several dug-out canoes waiting at the banks.

"Come. We paddle to the island." Iyngaer pointed.

It wasn't more than a rocky shoal, about a furlong upstream, but Geth nodded, handing his reins to one of the chieftain's escorts.

"We take our meal there," Iyngaer went on. "And talk."

The Dues ran wide but swift, pebble bottom clear through the sun-dappled water. Barid, Iyngaer's man, helped the chieftain settle in the front of the little canoe and Geth stepped over the lip and inside behind him. There was something about the fall that made even river water run blue, the skies overhead an azure firmament too, dotted with billowy white clouds. Barid gave them a shove and they were free. Geth could see why the chieftain fancied the outing.

With a paddle for each of them, Geth and Iyngaer rowed and fumbled and cursed across the river's surface. It took some effort against the current until the canoe's bottom scraped up on sand and gravel. They were both wet and a little out of breath, but they were both laughing as well.

"Your plan, it is good," Iyngaer said, before they'd even gotten out.

Geth climbed over the side first, splashed in up to his calves with a shiver and pushed the little rivercraft further aground. Wiping his hands on his pants, he came around front to help the chieftain out. "I think it can work."

"It will."

Iyngaer stretched his leg with a grimace, but clapped Geth on the back. He motioned the big warrior toward a flat space at the center of the island. Behind them, a second canoe ground to a halt and Barid and another tribesman disembarked with pelts, a basket, and two full wineskins.

"We will not let any harm come to her," Iyngaer said, lowering his huge frame down onto one of the pelts. "My Gemela will be pleased to help."

"I can't think of any better way. Still, it will be dangerous."

Iyngaer dismissed that with a wave. "He will attack us along the road. He will not miss this chance."

"We'll be strung out, vulnerable."

"Mmmm."

"Do we know how many fighters he can call up?"

"Hundreds, I think. He will muster all that he can."

"Gemela will need a healthy escort then. But not too many or we may scare him off."

"He will come." Iyngaer flicked his chin back toward the banks. Geth followed his eyes to the winding track cutting through the fields and pastures toward his great hillfort.

"Along the forest paths," the chieftain said, "she will be...vulnerable, as you say. There will never be a better time for Vongaer to strike. He knows that my hold on Thiringia depends on a union with Gemela's folk. If she were to die without a child of her blood to rule after me, many Thirings might chose to join him."

"So, his surest route to victory is killing a woman." Geth spit. "He deserves what we've got planned for him. And worse."

But taking the bastard down wasn't going to be easy. Geth squinted back across the water at that forest path again. It was the exact thing he had warned Hack about before starting north. Vongaer could employ the same hit and fly tactics they themselves had used against the tribes the previous winter.

"Men will die," Iyngaer said, reading Geth's mind. "There is no other way."

Geth nodded. "But whatever happens, we can't let him escape. The whole thing's for nothing if we don't crush the bastard right then and there."

They ate their lunch, the usual Ilar fare. Geth chewed down cold venison and cheese, hearty bread and wine, then dipped in the basket for seconds. He worked the plan over in his mind.

"If he really has hundreds," he said finally, "it won't be easy to fend him off on the road. With you and most of your fighters pinned here in Dues, we might not have the men we need. We'll need to call up more green-cloaks."

"Your men fight bravely. Bring whoever you can."

Geth thought out loud. "As long as Lady Gemela lures Vongaer into the fight, we've got a chance. She'll be in the heart of it though, no matter what."

"There is no other way."

"Maybe there is." Geth pulled at his mustache. "Maybe we can keep her away from the action, the worst of it anyway."

Iyngaer looked thoughtful. "You have something clever, Truslata?"

He did.

"Bait and switch. It's from an old tale, from Awer's book out of the Omnibus. In a battle between Atuer and the Mitheans, the Aturians sent a man, a brave hero, out in front of the battle wearing Atuer's armor. The Mitheans hated the king, so they threw everything at him, spent their best men, while the real Atuer slipped around back to rout them."

"You are saying we should dress another woman as my wife?"

"Not a woman. A man."

It would take weeks to make all the preparations. The messages flew to Towerrock and Ehken Dolae and back again. In the meantime, Geth ate and drank and talked of old times with Agrem, Barid, and the others. He was happy for the delay even if he hated himself for it. He wanted to meet his child—he missed Vriana too—but where would they stand with a baby between them now?

Vongaer and his rebels? That was familiar territory. He set his mind to dealing with them. He used the time to prepare Hack as well.

"You want me to wear a woman's clothes into a battle?" the green-cloak asked when Geth relayed the plan.

"To confuse the enemy. It'll be dangerous—"

"I'm your man."

They set things into motion. Hack was sent with a small party back south, through the Boundaries, and then north again, in secret, into Ehken Dolae to join Gemela. That eased Geth's worries.

But even with the green-cloak posing as Iyngaer's wife, he knew there were still plenty of ways things could go wrong. He stalked out in front of the hall each day, awaiting a reply to the messages he'd sent, high above his surrounds where he could really breathe.

Agrem found him there one day.

"Let me guess," the big warrior said, "you knew I would be coming this way. You *saw* it."

Agrem shrugged. "I am the Seer."

"Well?"

"Mmmm. It is *you* who want to tell *me* something."

Geth cursed. "Bloody magicks." He paced the length of the hall one last time, past those hides on their crosses, then returned to Agrem's side. "I'm worried."

"For Gemela?"

Geth paused. "Yes."

"You worry for Vriana, for the child as well."

"That's not it—"

"Mmmm."

"Alright, I'm worried about that too. A woman can die in childbirth. It happens. A child can die. It can be born sick. With a club foot, or no fingers, or..."

"You will not want the child if it has a club for a foot?"

Geth huffed a sigh. "That's not what I mean. I'm not cruel, I'd love any child. I just, I don't know."

Agrem settled himself right there on the ground, crossed his legs and looked out over the distance. "I have no sons, no daughters. Maybe it is my curse. But I know that most men fear as you do when their child is coming."

"And?" Geth looked hopefully to the Seer.

"The child will be whole and well. I have not seen it, but I *feel* it."

Geth looked away so his friend wouldn't see him. He closed his eyes, exhaled. Those were the words he'd needed to hear.

"Back to that bastard Vongaer then, eh?" he said.

Agrem eyed him from under bushy brows. "Tell me."

"He's no halfwit," Geth said, "or he wouldn't have men behind him. If we march our column into the trees, what's to stop him from picking us to pieces, bite by bite?"

"Mmmm."

"There's no point drawing him out to attack us if he gets away clean."

"Then we must catch him."

Geth gave the Seer a nod. "Exactly. Gemela may be the right bait, but only if we've set the trap just right. We need Vongaer to get close. And he'll only get close if he thinks he can strike and get away."

"You are thinking of something?"

"The thing we're doing with Hack, that's for safety, nothing more. As for the trap, that's a job for Kerrel."

Agrem just listened.

"We'll have to sneak our fighters up in wagons." Geth started pacing again. He spoke as he walked. "A few at a time, disguised as traders. Southern-style wagons, with covered tops. That way, when we set out, we'll make it look like a trade caravan. Kerrel and his green-cloaks can hide among the goods."

"And then?"

"Then once the bastard shows his face, that's when the trap gets sprung."

Leaves began falling. Birds flew south. Grey skies rolled in, carried by the blustery breath of the Hoarwinds. An icy rain fell more than once before word arrived from Ehken Dolae.

Geth's men prepared to depart. Kerrel's trade caravans had arrived in Ehken Dolae, soldiers hidden among the goods. Iyngaer didn't want to risk leaving Dues for fear of Mereg to the north, but the plan was for Geth to make the journey in his stead, escorting the chieftess back with him.

But the big warrior had another worry on his mind.

"She's had the baby by now," he told Agrem, standing out in front of the hall again. His men gathered down below near the gates, a thin drizzle, dotting shoulders, dripped down cloaks.

The Seer hummed, following Geth's eyes north and west toward Vriana's lands. "She must."

"I wanted to be there when it happened."

Agrem arched an eyebrow. "Not nervous anymore?"

"I still wanted to be there."

"Better you weren't." The Ilar sniffed. "I will tell you, it is not pretty to see it, mmmm?"

Geth rested a hand on his friend's shoulder. He knew how to make you smile, the old scratch. "You're probably right."

"I am." Agrem eyed him sideways. "Vongaer is our only worry now."

Geth clapped his back, and they started down the hill to join the men. Kerrel's mission may have called for stealth, but Geth's company didn't bother pretending. They would march in full battle gear, his original twenty-odd soldiers—minus Hack. A good hundred of Iyngaer's tribesmen lined up to join them.

The chieftain himself waited there as well. "I will see you when you return, " he said. "Sooner, perhaps."

They'd clasped hands when the big warrior arrived, but this time Iyngaer hugged him. He was nervous, Geth reckoned, but he couldn't blame the man. He must have felt powerless, afraid. Not for himself, for his wife.

Fork-bearded Barid embraced Geth as well. "Soon, Truslata."

With a wave, they rode out, crossing the little bridge over the river. Damp leaves scattered behind them. There was no bridge when they reached the North River two days later and they had to ford it, the water only waist-high at this time of year but cold as Vorda's own hell.

Geth eyed the trees on the opposite bank nervously for enemies, but they made the crossing without incident. They carried on westward. The arrangement was to meet Gemela's traveling party just outside her hillfort. Between Ilars and Umbelmen, they'd have a good two hundred warriors keeping guard over the column. And inside the wagons, Kerrel and another hundred green-cloaks would stand ready to strike.

They covered the distance in four days. Despite everything Geth had been told, they saw neither hide nor hair of any rebels. He made note of every bend in the road along the way, every dell, every uneven stretch where a company might get slowed down, make an easy target for attack. He sent scouts in threes instead of twos, found a space wide enough to circle the wagons each night, until the timber palisade and high hall of Ehken Dolae appeared ahead.

Lady Gemela met Geth at the gates, her words of welcome relayed by Agrem. "Gethe Govendi, it is good to see you. I thank you for coming."

"Thank you, my lady." Geth knuckled his brow. "My pleasure."

"Now, we suck out this—" the Seer struggled to find the word—"this grub, Vongaer, and squish him, mmmm?"

Geth looked from Agrem to the lady and smiled. Maybe Gemela was more like a certain other chieftess than he'd realized.

They paused long enough to share some berry-wine then turned their wagons right back around. It was midday—plenty of light left to travel by—and the lady seemed as eager as anyone to be underway. Geth couldn't help but think of his first exit from that hillfort, a wild scramble alongside Phelan through blinding snow, after killing the warlock Ceter's lover and riding down his gatekeeper. He chuckled just thinking of it, shook his head and sighed.

Gemela's wagon rolled up alongside Geth's mount, and, as if the mere memory of a brash moment was enough to summon the brashest of them all, Hack's face appeared sheepishly from between the flaps. He wore an identical dress as the chieftess, the same riding hood, with a tail-like braid of fake yellow hair draped down one shoulder.

"Here I am, Captain," Hack flashed a hasty salute. "Armed and ready."

Geth smiled. "And dressed for the occasion, looks like."

Hack nodded, serious as ever. "Don't you worry, Captain, I'll draw those rebel bastards like honey draws flies. And I'll stick 'em up good when they reach me too."

The green-cloak pulled back the hem of his riding hood to slap the pommel of his sword. Gemela climbed onto the bench just then and Hack retreated back inside, out of sight. The lady looked up to meet Geth's eye, plenty of mirth in her expression.

A train of well over forty wagons trailed the lady's, Kerrel and his soldiers hidden among them. Gemela changed her cloak, slid out the back of her own wagon and slipped into one of those before they'd made the first mile. If Vongaer struck, she'd be well protected.

But nothing sounded except for the groan of wagon axels, the occasional laugh of a soldier, the neigh of a horse. Miles passed. Geth hadn't really expected an attack so soon, but they circled the wagons tight that evening, pickets in twos, scouts out in threes again. Geth eyed the same bends in the road as they continued each day, the same dips and rises, the same uneven patches he'd noted on the way in.

Three days from Ehkan Dolae, as the river and the edge of Iyngaer's kingdom drew near, he began to wonder if Vongaer had sniffed out their trap.

"Nothing." Geth spit.

Agrem rode in silence beside him, but the big warrior could tell he didn't like it either. Geth opened his mouth, about to wonder aloud if they'd got it all wrong, when a commotion sounded at the front of the column.

"Is that...?"

Hack thrust his head out from the flaps behind the big warrior. "What is it, Captain?" That fake braid spilled down one shoulder, but his hood sat low over his face, just like he'd been told.

"I don't know but I'm going to find out. You just stay there and try to look womanly."

Hack snorted. "Easier for some than others, but I'll do my damnedest."

Geth spurred his mount up ahead. Across the road, a fallen tree barred the path. Agrem stood beside a huddle of green-cloaks and tribesmen eyeing the trunk and the surrounding trees in turns.

"You thinking what I'm thinking?" Geth asked the Seer. "That tree wasn't down on the way in."

The big warrior turned to scan the forest to either side once more, the hackles on his neck good and stiff now. "Shields up, men! Swords out!"

He waited, his own sword drawn, round shield lifted up under his eyes. Horses blew and snorted. Birds chirped in the trees. A squirrel rustled through the undergrowth but that was it.

A good quarter of an hour passed, all eyes trained on their surroundings. Geth looked uncertainly from Agrem to the foliage and back. A few brave men ventured out into the forest. They came back shaking their heads.

Geth sheathed his sword. "Thram's balls."

"Coward rebels!" someone jeered.

"First sign of steel and they're slinking away before the fight's even begun."

Geth had the feeling their assessment wasn't wrong. "Alright, get that log out of the way, boys! Let's get moving!"

Geth kicked his mount up close to the tree trunk blocking their path as the first green-cloaks stepped forward to haul it away. At a glance, he could tell it hadn't been felled, but scores through the moss and leaves of the forest floor betrayed the path along which it had been dragged from its original resting place.

"Mmmm," Agrem hummed.

Geth couldn't agree more. "You think maybe we got it wrong? Did we bring too many men? Did someone spy out Kerrel and his boys? Or is this scratch Vongaer less concerned with Iyngaer's woman than we thought?"

The Seer frowned. "He will come."

Geth's steed snorted and stamped. "But when?"

CHAPTER FOUR

The company was moving again within a few minutes. They expected to reach the North River later that afternoon at the same crossing point Geth had used a few days earlier. He didn't anticipate much difficulty in fording it, especially with so many soldiers to lend a hand.

They came over the top of a low bluff, their path winding downwards. The green ribbon of Vorus appeared ahead, catching the sun in places, rippling lazily on its inexorable journey to the sea. Geth scanned the far bank, up and down the water as far as he could, but his confidence in their plan, that Vongaer would show himself, had evaporated.

"Spread out, boys," he said. "Set a perimeter, scouts out in twos."

Soldiers saluted or simply nodded, the Ilar way. The first wagons were hauled into the water, dragged by horses and guided across by green-cloaks and tribesmen. Footing was tricky, as always, but one by one, the first group made the far bank. Geth's mind wandered to Vriana and their child.

How was she? How was the baby? What did he look like? All pink and wrinkly, more than likely. But still his child. His apprehension wasn't gone—not in the slightest—and yet it was funny how the prospect of a longer delay in Dues suddenly made him want what he couldn't have.

"Bloody fool," he cursed himself.

From his horse's back, on the muddy track at the water's edge, he waved wagons forward until Gemela's—Hack's, in truth—came up next. The green-cloak sat the bench, peeking out from under his hood with uncertain eyes. Geth heaved a sigh, motioned the driver beside him forward.

"Damn you, Vongaer."

On the far bank, men gathered around wagons, chatting, shaking water from their cloaks. Geth turned his mount, started muttering another choice one, then squinted down the track.

"What the hell?"

There was movement in the brush, soldiers nearby laughing as a green-cloak came staggering into view. Someone cursed him. Another started in his direction, but froze halfway. The man teetered where stood, fell sideways, and the first cry pierced the air.

Then came the arrows.

As always, the bolts were most deadly at first, when no one knew where they were coming from. Few of Geth's soldiers had their shield to hand either. They cried out, ran for those shields or slid under the nearest wagon. The arrows seemed to be coming from everywhere.

Men went down in that first panicked moment, but Geth couldn't do anything about it. He looked back; Gemela's wagon was already well into the water. He kicked his horse in that direction, splashing out to join them as the first warning cries and fingers pointed north.

'Boats! Boats!"

Frigid water sprayed Geth, obstructed his view as his mount charged toward the wagon. He left Kerrel to the defenses behind him—he had no choice. Hack had ducked inside the canvas, but that wasn't about to stop anything. At least he had the sense to keep the ruse up, keep the enemy focused on him, the poor brave sonofabitch.

"The lady!" Geth yelled, "The lady!"

An arrow whistled past. He could only hope someone was tending to the actual lady, back behind him. He was out in front of Hack's wagon by then, deep in the current. Squinting upriver, he finally saw what everyone had been pointing at; yards away still but coming down fast, a goddamn flotilla of canoe boats was headed straight for him.

"Thram's bloody cock."

But this was where he had to be, where Vongaer would end up himself, if he was worth his salt. The soldiers that had been guiding the wagon across readied weapons and fell in beside Geth. They knew their part, gods bless them. They formed up like the Queen of Mithea was in that wagon behind them, shouting defiance, in Aturian and the Ilar tongue alike.

Kerrel's boys must've been doing their job. The arrow barrage had lessened, from where Geth was standing at least. His mount neighed and bucked in protest, wanting to go sideways and out of the water, but in mere seconds the first boats were on them, Thirings with swords and spears, jumping out of canoes or slashing as they passed.

"Arggghhh!

"Ahhh!"

Men yelled. Others shrieked and fell. The clamor of battled shook that peaceful river valley.

A canoe whizzed past Geth's left, the front man steering, a second jumping over the other side, and a third jabbing his spear like a lance in passing. Geth took the blow on his shield, and the boat was gone. But the man that had leapt in the river was coming at him from behind, sword upraised. Geth struggled to get his mount turned.

It was a cumbersome business, fighting against the current. The Ilar had Geth flanked well and good. His sword should've struck right between the big warrior's shoulder blades, but the water slowed him too. Once he'd gotten himself behind Geth—and downstream a few yards—he had to thrash his way back towards him. Geth had just enough time to slide from the saddle, his mount in between him and his enemy.

The savage bastard didn't care who he killed. He chopped down viciously at the animal. Geth reached over the horse's back to parry, the force of the blow driving both blades down into the poor beast's shoulder. The swing lost plenty of force, but it still cut. The animal screamed, bucked, and by some luck turned back toward the Ilar, trampling him down on his was way toward dry land.

A few yards down, the Thiring resurfaced with a gasp. More tribesmen had disembarked downriver as well, a good dozen of them splashing their way upstream toward Hack's wagon. Geth spared a glance up the river for Vongaer's silver head but saw nothing. Except for more and more rebels, cutting through his men as they slipped past, lancing them, loosing arrows, or jumping into the water to fight sword to sword.

His green-cloaks were taking the worst of it. "Damn you, Awer!"

Few of the Ilars wore anything heavier than boiled leather or scale-mail, but most of the Umbelmen had an iron ring shirt at least. If a man's foot slipped, the current did the rest. To lose balance was to drown, swept down, under, and into the realm of the dead.

"Duesmen!" Geth cried.

Iyngaer's men heard. They saw as well, rushing best they could to pull Umbelman free and out where they could, stepping in for them in the thicket of wood and iron and steel that had formed around Hack's wagon.

But they were sorely outnumbered. And that's when Vongaer's silver head appeared, spear held over head like a javelin as he balanced precariously in the back of a canoe. This one had outriggers, an archer loosing bolts from in front of the rebel leader as well. Vongaer growled as his eyes landed on Geth, heaved that spear with impressive aim, and stripped the shield right off Geth's arm with the force of his throw.

The blow knocked him to one knee, water rushing up around his face. His own ring shirt dragged at him as his standing foot started slipping on smooth wet stones.

"Agghhhh!"

Water filled Geth's mouth and he closed it, spit, held his breath. His foot slid loose of its purchase, and he went under, scrambling for handholds first, toes curled in his boots, trying to find a hold. No one could have heard him even if he screamed.

In desperation, he turned his sword point down, jammed the blade into the river bottom. It struck deep, tilted, but held. His feet windmilled behind him, until they finally found some grip, and his head came up out of the water to suck in air like he'd never breathed before.

"Ahhh!"

A Thiring was on him before he could pull his sword free. Leaving it stuck, Geth lifted his feet slightly, let the current move him faster than his enemy could react, downstream, and away. He looked up, for a weapon, and for a look at the battle. He was a good ten yards from Hack's wagon. He could only hope the green-cloak was still alive.

For the present, he had to worry about himself. That Ilar hadn't forgotten about him. Learning from Geth himself, he used the river's flow to propel his next attack. But he lost control, slipping as he came, landing right in the big warrior's clutches.

"Die, you filthy rebel bastard!"

Geth had the tribesman's sword arm trapped up high, both hands wrapped in a bear hug around his body. He heaved and squeezed, heard the man moan as he lost his breath, then whirled, shoved him into the current. The water took him out of reach, downstream. It sucked him under and didn't give him back.

But Vongaer had that one big canoe leaned up against Hack's wagon by the time Geth turned. The gods only knew how the whole thing hadn't started floating off. The Ilar bowman climbed onto the bench with a hoot, disappeared through the flap, only to reappear a half-second later, hand against a wound in his side.

Hack leapt through the opening right after him. He howled for joy, red sword in hand, blond wig sideways on his head. It would have been funny if there hadn't been more Ilars waiting for him. Vongaer produced a second spear from the hollow of the canoe while his paddle-man rose to trade sword blows with the green-cloak. The rebel leader could damn well see it wasn't Gemela in the wagon, but by the look in his eyes, that only infuriated him more. He turned his spear to grip it like a staff, lining up a strike to send Hack off his perch and into the current.

Occupied by the paddle-man, Hack was defenseless. Geth thrashed towards them, but wasn't going to make it.

"Look out!"

It was too late. Vongaer aimed a wide arc, over the head of his paddle-man, directly at the green-cloak's temple. Hack saw it last second, jerked back to dodge, but the motion took him off balance. Arms flailing, he went over backward, hit the wagon's bench, and tumbled into the water.

"Hack!"

Geth splashed sideways, toward the green-cloak's drifting path. He caught hold of that riding cloak—barely— drew him in, raised his head up out of the water.

"Talk to me, Hack! Breathe, damn you!"

He smacked the Umbelman across the face, squeezed his cheeks to force his mouth open. Hack gasped, pulled weakly at Geth's grip and swore.

"Bloody tits...you didn't have to hit me so hard!"

Geth didn't spare time for a reply. He looked up, but Vongaer hadn't tried to advance. The sound of splashing behind the big warrior turned him in time to see why.

"Kerrel!"

Stripped to the waist, the young captain and another dozen shirtless green-cloaks had crashed out into the river in support. Unable to glide down past them, Vongaer and his Thirings waded or steered their canoes for the eastern bank instead. At the water's edge, scrabbling onto the banks, the silver-haired bastard turned to mouth curses before regrouping his men and sprinting away.

"After them!" Geth shouted. "Go! Go! Don't let them escape!"

One arm around Hack still, he had no choice except to leave it to Kerrel and the boys. Geth reached the muddy ground only a few seconds behind them, but they were already cursing, standing in a knot a few yards down the road.

"He's gone," Kerrel called back "We—"

The noise of heavy hoof-beats turned all eyes to the road again, and Geth felt his heart drop. He snatched a sword from one of the men and hopped up beside Kerrel, a hasty line forming across the road. Hack held a broken arrow tip in one hand, nothing more. They braced for the worst.

But it was a familiar grey horse that appeared around the bend ahead, carrying a familiar rider.

"Iyngaer?"

Barid with that forked beard came right behind him, along with a host of Duesmen. The chieftain howled, seeing Geth. "Haha!"

Iyngaer raised his fist and a cheer sounded from the shirtless fighters to Geth's left and right.

"I reckon we did it."

Hack saluted, serious as ever, then turned his eyes back toward the tall chieftain. In one raised hand, held out for all to see, hung the head of Vongaer, gripped by that silver hair.

CHAPTER FIVE

I yngaer celebrated the victory with his wife that night. Three huge bonfires had been lit beside the river, and Hack—hero of the day—celebrated with all the men. Drink flowed like the North River's current as Umbelmen and Ilars alike cavorted around the flames. But Geth wandered off first chance he got.

He sat on a log a ways into the woods, just a blanket and a skin of forest fire for company. Regret hung heavy on him, even if he couldn't say why. They'd won, hadn't they? He sipped from his liquor, good and drunk already, and muttered curses into the dark.

Agrem found him there.

"Bloody magicks," Geth muttered.

The man just stood there, eyeing him from under his brows. "Mmmm."

"What? I'm resting." The big warrior took another hearty swig of eyfra. It burned, but gods all be damned if it wasn't just what he needed.

"Resting." Agrem stepped up, settled himself a couple feet over on the log with a sigh. "I will rest too."

A few more curses came to mind, but Geth held his tongue. He didn't offer the skin though. They sat in silence until he couldn't take it any longer.

"Look, we lost a lot of men," he said. "Two dozen, not to mention the wounded. Some of those won't make it. Others won't fight again."

"Mmmm."

"Was it worth it, for peace?" Geth shrugged. "I reckon it was."

Agrem eyed him sideways, waited.

"I said it was worth it."

"For peace. But you are not worried about peace. And not about men who died."

Geth glared at his friend down the length of the log.

"You are worried about men who *almost* died."

"Bloody magicks."

Agrem reached for the skin. Geth didn't try to stop him. The Ilar took a drink, winced, swallowed it down. He looked at Geth, waited some more.

"Alright, fine. You're right. I was just thinking about, well..." He huffed a sigh. "Sweet Selel, I don't even know my boy's name."

"And?"

"Well, things could have gone real bad, that's all. One stone slides under my foot, and that baby grows up without a father. I'm not saying I'm much, but I'm better than nothing."

"You are the truslata."

"And what does that mean? If my boot slipped another inch, I'm just a memory. It's like a weight on my shoulders, 'Grem. How can I fight now that I'm...*afraid?*"

Agrem reached out, gripped Geth's shoulder, squeezed. "You have always been afraid. But fear is the river. You have to swim, mmmm?"

It took a minute to work out what the Seer meant, but after a moment Geth nodded. "You're right." He wanted to curse. He snorted a laugh instead. "You always are, aren't you?"

Agrem didn't argue.

"Maybe it's the eyfra, but I feel a little better now." Geth pushed up from the log, gathered his blanket. "Better go congratulate Iyngaer, ask him how he did it, if Vongaer begged in the end, the filthy traitor."

"Mmmm."

"You know, Iyngaer said he'd see me sooner than later." Geth touched a temple. "Always thinking, the chief. Looked damn good on that horse I gave him too."

The wagons were loaded, tents and bedrolls packed. Men tightened cinches on their mounts and shields were thrown over shoulders. The company would ride on to Dues, all except Geth and his original traveling party.

He made his goodbyes with Iyngaer and they started off, northwards. Kerrel and his wagons creaked eastward with everyone else. And they wouldn't return to Towerrock until those wagon beds were full of stores. What would Willa have to say about that? Geth smiled as he watched them disappear around the first bend.

The roads were starting to become familiar, and they made good time. The world was a crazy place, he mused. He frowned at the back of the green-cloak ahead of him, his horse's hooves clopping rhythmically over leaf-strewn paths. He'd been so impatient for his child to come, then afraid when the summons arrived. Now he'd come full circle, all excitement, fear of fatherhood gone, even if it was replaced by a new kind of fear that had nothing to do with the child.

But he had no one to talk to about it. Agrem's duty was to Iyngaer; he'd gone back to Dues with everyone else. Vriana herself waited ahead, while Mother, Melagus, Ratcher and the rest were behind him. That left only Hack, and gods bless him, but he wasn't the deepest well, if Geth had any right to say it.

"I miss Phelan," he muttered aloud.

Hack must have heard him. His voice floated over the big warrior's shoulder. "We all do, Captain."

"I wonder if he misses us? He's probably pouring himself an ale right now. Or fleecing his patrons at dice."

"Or bouncing a barmaid on one knee."

"Or getting bounced on his head by Eora. Ha! I can see it now."

"But what about the chieftain?" Hack asked.

"What do you mean?"

Hack had spurred up alongside, but he looked down at his horse's neck, face screwed up, then back at Geth. "Well, gotta say, I've taken a liking to the man. To all of them, really. They saved our hides, the Duesmen. I hope they can manage without us."

Geth nodded. "Iyngaer? He'll be alright. Still got Mereg and the Arnus tribe to deal with. But he looked damn fearsome on that horse, didn't he?"

"Fearsome." Hack agreed. "It was a good gift. You always think of the right thing, Captain."

That reminded Geth of the knife he'd brought for Vriana, the little sword for his child. A hand strayed to his saddlebags where he'd stowed them, a foolish grin across his face.

The miles couldn't pass quick enough, but Geth tried to be at peace, take in the beauty of the road. It was all around him, the falling leaves, each little stream they crossed, the occasional fox, or rabbit, or deer that crossed their path.

Then again, he wasn't built for peace. He thought of Iyngaer and the looming possibility of war with Mereg's Arnui. The cold deepened the farther north they went, but Geth didn't mind it. He wondered if he'd ever really breathed anything like the crisp air of Ilia. Perhaps there would be war. And a reason for an ally like him to stick around.

Many an hour was spent on indulgent imaginings of battles against Mereg's lot until the valley of Laer opened ahead. It wasn't so different from Dues; a wide vale, a little river, a town and fort on the hill. Except that his child waited for him up there. Geth straightened his cloak, smoothed the short locks on his head. He kicked his mount to a canter and the rest of the company followed suit.

The gates stood open and shouts of welcome rang down from the timber palisades. A familiar horse-faced warrior waved as Geth rode under the gates. He escorted the big warrior up the gravel path toward Vriana'a hall. Geth's palms sweated, but by the time he reached the summit, Vriana stood on the threshold, a fur-wrapped bundle in her arms.

Geth's heart thumped in his chest. Gods all be damned but had there ever been a more beautiful woman? And she wasn't even smiling, that wasn't her way. Ehken Laer had the same hide banners on crosses as Dues, but they hung still. Even the wind seemed to be holding its breath.

He remembered the knife he'd brought her. "A gift," he said, offering the weapon in its ornate sheath. He crossed the distance to the chieftess. Every eye was on him, but he didn't care. Vriana shifted the bundle in her arms, reached out to take the knife. She looked down at the green gem on the hilt and a hint of a smile touched her lips.

The whole fortress could have been on fire for all Geth cared. She looked up at him. He grinned, met those honey-brown eyes. She tilted the bundle in her arms—their child—so that a little white face appeared, eyes closed, lips parted in deep sleep.

"This is your gift." Vriana turned her eyes down at that little face, her cheeks a touch pink, eyes aglow. "And I am grateful for him. Together we will name him."

Geth stepped closer, peeled back the edge of the furs to get a better look. Such a tiny thing. He flicked a glance up at Vriana, she held their son so fiercely the love came off her in waves, Geth would have sworn it. He thought of his own mother, wondered if she'd looked down at him like that, once upon a time. The thought dredged up all kinds of emotions.

But none of it mattered. This boy was the child of a queen, not a pauper. And he had a father as well.

"He'll be a bastard unless we marry," Geth said.

His clamped his mouth shut even as he said, cheeks gone hot. The words had just come out, all by themselves. *Damn it all!*

Vriana just laughed though, gripped his arm with one hand, eyes shining. "We do not have this custom. If you claim him, he is yours, and no bastard. Do you claim him?"

Geth couldn't help but laugh. "I claim him. By all the gods." He turned to face Hack and his men, emotions rushing through him that he'd never felt before. Tears welled in his eyes, but he grinned like that she-devil Vorda herself. "I have a son!"

A cheer went up, and all as one the men mobbed him, slapping his back, hugging him, proclaiming how handsome the child was, how beautiful his mother. Ilars shouted and clapped as well. The entire group went inside the hall. The wineskins and forest fire and meats went around. Vriana called for musicians, and they feasted.

"Amazing thing, a baby," Geth said, sitting cross-legged on a fur pelt beside Vriana's central fire, cradling his son against him. "Warm, like a fresh-baked loaf of bread. And about the same size."

The boy stirred, opened his dark eyes for a moment, lips parting like he wanted to speak. Or cry at least. He wore that confused look again and Geth rocked him gently as he'd seen Vriana do, hummed from deep in his chest.

"He is hungry," the chieftess said. "Give him to me."

Geth handed the baby over with a sigh. The fire crackled, throwing off its heat, casting shadows across sleeping warriors around the high-ceilinged hall. Vriana rose with their son in hand, motioned Geth to follow, and started toward the hide screens at the back of the chamber.

She settled down again among a nest of furs in her quarters, a single candle lighting the space. Pulling up her shirt, she bared one pink nipple, slipped it in the child's mouth, grimaced and sighed. Geth's mouth had dropped open, but he managed to close it again before she looked up.

"He bites hard," Vriana said. "He will be a healthy eater, like his father."

"Of course he will." Geth smiled. He eased down onto the pelts across from her. "Have you decided what we should name him."

Vriana looked down into the child's face as he suckled, her brow pinched. "My father was called Vather, but he doesn't favor him. What was your father's name?"

"Uh..."

"No matter. He should have a name of his own, mmmm?"

"Yes."

The sat there in silence, the only sound their own breathing, the occasional mewling of their son. Geth tried to think of something clever—something grand like Paelleus or Atuer, or poetic like Jewel or Stream. But common sense told him everyone would be better off if he left it up to Vriana.

"How about...Ethen?" She looked to Geth.

He mouthed the name once and nodded. "Ethen."

Vriana turned her eyes back to the child, still suckling at that beautiful breast. She whispered, just loud enough for Geth to hear. "Ethen, mmmm?"

The boy opened his eyes, stopped eating, and gazed up at her for moment. He blinked, closed his eyes again and went right on sucking again.

"So it is." Vriana looked up, a pleased expression on her face. Ethen ate for a few more minutes, then she pulled the nipple from his mouth, set him against her shoulder to pat his back until a loud burp sounded.

"Gods all be damned, he *does* eat like me." Geth started to reach for the child, but Vriana pulled some sort of wooden box closer, set Ethen inside, and knelt to one side to rock it gently. A crib, Geth realized, but built low and sitting on a curved bottom like a rocking chair. The crying stopped before it started and Vriana looked to Geth, a triumphant smile on her lips.

"He is a good boy. He doesn't complain."

Geth nodded. But a thought occurred to him. "How old is he now?"

"Six weeks."

"Six weeks." Geth did the math in his head. "You waited some time before sending the pigeon to Towerrock."

Vriana frowned. "Not because I didn't want you to come. I needed to rest. It is no small thing to birth a child. I give respect to all women who have survived it."

"You needed rest before you could see me?" Geth asked.

Vriana must have heard the hurt in his voice, but she didn't look up. Her eyes were on Ethen, her hand still rocking his little box-crib. She eased it to a stop and carefully took her hand away, reached out to take Geth's in her own.

"I needed rest before I saw you. So, I could do this."

She pulled him closer, leaned forward at the same time to kiss him on the mouth. Her hand moved up to the back of his neck to pull even harder. Her tongue found his and she shuffled forward on her knees until her body was up against his. Geth gasped, his breath stolen in the most delicious way.

"Oh—"

Vriana pressed a finger against his lips and laughed. "Shush. We don't want to wake him."

Geth spent all his hours with Vriana and Ethen. They slept together and ate together. He grew comfortable carrying the child and started taking him on walks around the outside of the hall, up high so he could breathe the fresh air.

He told him tales of battles—his own and others, from the Omnibus, from history—leaving out the bloody bits, best he could. Even he knew it was a little much, but he reckoned the boy would forget it all anyway.

"He likes me, the little pup," Geth told Hack, turning Ethen in his arms to show him off for the Umbelman.

Hack cocked an eyebrow. "That's a prince there, Captain, the way I see it."

Geth just cooed at the baby. It really was colder in Laer than in Dues, and he made sure to keep Ethen's little pale arms wrapped in warm fur. The boy seemed to like the heights and the fresh air as much as Geth did. Peace? It was growing on him.

But from up there beside the wind-shaken banners on their crosses, Geth was first to see the pigeons when they came. One and then another and another. He went back inside the hall, found Vriana behind the screens with her birdkeep, their eyes wide.

"What is it?"

Vriana reached forward, took Ethen, pressed him against her bosom. Her brow was pinched as she looked from Geth to the little messages in the birdkeeper's hands and back.

"Bad news, from Towerrock."

Geth swallowed, licked his lips. "From Towerrock? What about the other two messages?"

Vriana shook her head. "They sent the same message three times, to make sure you got it, mmmm?"

Geth's hand had gone to his hilt, white knuckled already. "And?" he growled.

"Someone has tried to kill your mother."

CHAPTER SIX

A dozen thoughts collided in Geth's mind, only half of them rational. What the hell happened? Was Mother alright? And *why*, by all the gods?

The answer to that last question, at least, was obvious. *To get back at me.*

"Thram and bloody Awer." He stalked out the doors to Vriana's hall, paced the length, hoping a brusque wind might bring some clarity, help make sense of the news. He pulled at his mustache, swore, and kicked over one of those banners on its cross.

Vriana came outside, Ethen in her arms, just as he bent to right the thing. He stood there holding it and cursed some more. He'd kicked the stave in two.

"Mmmm," Vriana said. But there was no judgement in her voice. Her eyes smoldered, like she might kick one of those crosses down herself.

"You sound like 'Grem." Geth said.

"Good. He is wise. But I do not think he knows more about this thing than you or me."

Geth didn't suppose they needed the Seer's wisdom this time anyway. That someone might use his mother to get to him was the only thing that made sense. He thought of all the enemies he'd made. The list was long, but only a few of those could have been involved.

"It had to be one of Towdric's people." He set the broken banner and stave down, blew out a sigh and stalked to the edge of the hall and back to the chieftess, thinking out loud. "There's plenty of sonsabitches out there with a score to settle, but none of them are in Umbel."

"It could be a tribesman. Or woman," Vriana offered.

She wasn't wrong. But who among the tribes even knew about his mother? And an underhanded move like that just didn't *feel* like something an Ilar would try.

"What else did the message say?" Geth asked.

Vriana passed all three of the tiny notes over. They were all the same, offering little more than what he already knew.

"She was attacked, but she's alive," Geth said. "The bastard got away. Nothing more."

Vriana reached out, gripped Geth's arm tight enough to make him look up. "That is good, mmmm? She is alive."

"For now."

"You are right. You must go."

Geth heaved a sigh, looked from Vriana down to Ethen—asleep in her arms—and back up. There was anger in her eyes to match his own. But it was a cold, cunning emotion, not raw and heedless.

"I'm glad I have you. I don't want to leave."

"Do what you feel. But you will not be at peace until you know she is safe. Mmmm?"

The cold of Ilia had turned bitter. Or so it seemed to Geth. Vriana and his child were behind him, enemies ahead. He longed to be with his woman and his child—his family—but he had other family too. And they needed him.

The same paths he'd thought beautiful on the way north seemed sinister now. Trees like that, hills and caves, they could hide a lot of nasty things. Nasty men. The kind that went after innocent women instead of bloodletting bastards that deserved it.

"Who would even do such a thing?" he wondered aloud.

Hack heard him, but Geth's dark mood was no secret and the green-cloak let him be. No doubt Hack was thinking along the same lines: it had to be one of Towdric's vengeful lackeys.

Who else would try? Towdric himself would have done it without reservation, but he was dead. Hadean, ever merciful, had pardoned all his men though. The measure had gone far toward healing the realm. Or so they'd all thought.

"One more reason to ride south." Geth spit. An enemy to him could be an enemy to Hadean as well. If rebels were to sprout up in Umbel—as they had in Ilia—the king would need him.

"Melagus will know something," Geth told himself. "Ratcher too."

Between the counselor's network of contacts and the assassin's years of experience, there would be answers. A few at least. He tucked his hands under his arms and out of the wind and focused his eyes on the road.

Mother was fine. They would have said so if she wasn't. And young Orie, Melagus, and everyone else. He'd get there, root out the sonsabitches, and ride back for Ilia. Iyngaer could still need him if this business with Mereg turned worse. And Vriana, it turned out, didn't seem to mind his company after all.

Agrem's voice woke Geth in the middle of the night, sat him up straight in his bedroll.

Go back!

There was no Eko this time, no image at all, but the urgency—the *command*—in the Seer's voice had Geth looking around the low-burning fire in vain for his friend.

Trees swayed in the wind, smoke drifted up and away. The night sky spread purple and star-smeared above him. "Go back where?"

Geth cursed out loud. But he knew.

Hack, sat up, scrambling for his sword until he saw Geth sitting there.

The big warrior rubbed his face with both hands, pulled at his beard. "Gods all be damned."

"Alright, Captain? Bad dream?"

"The worst. A message from Agrem."

Hack frowned. "Magicks?"

Geth nodded. "We have to go back to Laer."

They broke camp immediately, started back the way they'd come. Geth's green-cloaks rode with hand on hilts, bows strung. They followed without question. Geth couldn't have told them much anyway.

If the news of his mother had been bad, at least it had told him *something*. Not knowing what Agrem's message meant was far, far worse.

"Why, 'Grem?" He tried thinking of the Seer, to *will* him into some kind of waking dream-speak. That only made his head hurt. What had happened, what could warrant that command? He had no way of knowing.

That night, he tried again to summon his friend. His dreams were of war and fire instead. And a cold, insidious fear.

He rode for Ehken Laer. That had to be what the Seer had meant. As they drew near, it seemed like fear was on the wind itself. Geth wasn't the only person who felt it, he saw it on the face of Hack and the others.

Things only got worse.

"Is that..." Hack breathed deeply, nose lifted. He turned a worried eye toward Geth.

The big warrior smelled it too, the thin but acrid scent of smoke. "Ride!"

Geth kicked his mount to a full gallop. Rounding one final bend, plunging out of the trees, the valley and hill of Ehken Laer came into view. Recognizing Geth, fighters on the walls opened the gates. Their faces look shocked, panicked.

Horse-face met Geth on a horse of his own. He waved him up the hill. "Come, Truslata. Fast. Vriana..." He turned, spurred his mount, not waiting to see if the big warrior followed.

A great black pile of ash smoldered beside Vriana's hall, the source of that smell. It was the remains of a pyre, and a big one. As Geth drew near, he picked out blackened bones resting among the cinders. He slid from the saddle without a care for where his horse went.

"Dear gods." His heart leapt up into his throat. "Where's Vriana? Where's the baby?"

"Inside."

Geth crashed through the high doors, sprinted down the hall, around the screens. The chieftess lay still on her furs, an old woman wiping her brow with a rag. Gods, but Vriana looked pale. Their son's little crib was empty.

"Where is my son?"

The old woman blinked. She didn't speak Aturian. Geth swore, kneeled down beside Vriana, took her hand. "Vriana! Vriana, I'm here!" He squeezed it, desperate for some reaction.

She gave none. The old woman said something in the Ilar tongue, a negative, Geth thought. It was a moment before Horse-face caught up to him, arrived around the edge of the screens to translate.

"She is hurt," the tribesman said. "She cannot speak."

"Hurt?" Geth didn't see any bandages or blood.

Horse-face must have read his mind. He shook his head. "Not that way. He used his fear."

Geth's mouth opened. His breath went in and out but he couldn't speak. That feeling that had hung on them as they approached Ehken Laer, it all fell into place. "It was Ceter."

Geth rose, fist white-knuckled on the hilt of his sword. Horse-face took a step back and the old healer woman's eyes widened. Geth forced his grip to let loose, breathed in hard and deep. He knelt down beside Vriana again.

"How many times do I have to kill that bastard?" His eyes fell on his son's little box, his crib, and a new panic rose in him. "Where's baby Ethen? Tell me, damn it! Where is my son?"

Horse-face hurried to answer. "He is not among the ash."

Geth went a little lightheaded, but he closed his eyes, steadied himself. "Well then—"

"He is gone."

"Gone?"

The old woman at Vriana's side rushed to say something in the Ilar tongue. Horse-face replied, words flying back and forth in urgent tones until the warrior finally nodded, turned back to Geth.

"He is alive."

"Ceter took him?"

"Yes."

Geth rose again, paced the little space once, cursing all the while. A hundred possibilities flew through his mind. He came back to stand in front of Horse-face. "You said he's alive. How can you know?"

"They took him, Truslata. But they brought a woman with them."

"A woman? A witch?"

"Not a witch." Horse-face looked to the old woman, frowned, looked back at Geth. "A special woman."

He cupped both hands in front of him, a gesture that couldn't mean what Geth thought it meant. The big warrior pulled at his mustache, cursed some more, until he realized what Horse-face was trying to tell him.

"A wet-nurse!" He copied the cupped-hands gesture. "Milk, for the baby?"

"Yes! Yes, Govendi!" Horse-face and the woman both nodded vigorously. "Why bring this woman unless they want the child to live."

Geth didn't say anything. Exhaustion caught up with him and he sank to the floor beside Vriana. He took her hand in his again, blinked away the frustration.

"They've taken him," he told her silent form. "They've taken our son because of me. But I swear by the seven gods, I won't stop until I have him back."

CHAPTER SEVEN

Oaths weren't going to get Ethen back. And with Vriana on the brink of death, Geth had a more immediate concern. There was nothing he could do for little Ethen. He had to trust that Ceter did, indeed, want his child alive. At least for now.

He didn't know where the sonofabitch had gone anyway. The bodies in the pyre belonged to the men that had gone after Ceter, he was told. They'd been found in the forest, to the east. The direction in which Ceter had fled was all they knew.

Gods all be praised, Agrem arrived the next day. "I rode quickly. I *saw* him."

Geth smothered the man in an embrace, felt tears try to mist his eyes, forced them away with savage, vengeful thoughts. "How is he even alive?"

"Mmmm."

"They took my boy, 'Grem. We have to find him. And Vriana...."

He couldn't find words, but the Seer didn't need them. He hustled toward the back of Vriana's hall, went straight to work. He crouched down, touched the chieftess's forehead, spoke to the old healer woman. He hummed over her, eyes closed, swayed in place. He looked tired when he stood—tired and worried—but he started asking questions of each and every person that had been with Vriana and Ethen straight away.

The fear had struck them, Ceter had stolen in, taken the child, and left.

Geth had heard it already, but he followed Agrem to see if he could learn more. That head of spikey hair swung this way and that as he wandered around the hall, sniffing like an animal, even tasting the ash of the pyre. He walked the perimeter of the fortress, zig-zagged down the hill, Geth right behind him until he went outside the walls and out into the woods. The big warrior waited at the gates. Agrem didn't come back for several hours.

He looked exhausted when he did. Geth called for wine and bread, slipped an arm around the man and helped him into the gatehouse. Breaking a loaf, he made sure his friend ate. He swallowed his own share almost without chewing, washed it down with berry wine, though he didn't taste a thing.

"Well?"

"He came at night," Agrem said. "Ceter. He is not dead."

Geth stifled a curse. "I already knew that."

The Seer raised a finger. "Ceter is not the only creature that throws the fear. I had to be sure. But it was him, truly. He did not die."

"It must have been him that went after Mother too. They stopped him though, somehow, far as I know."

"Mmmm." Agrem frowned. "Ceter was here, not in your sunlands. He fears you."

Agrem gave the big warrior a significant look, waited. It took a moment before Geth understood.

"Sonofabitch. They attacked Mother just to draw me away. They used her to draw me out, the same way we used Gemela to draw Vongaer out."

"He fears you," Agrem said again. "His spell does not hold you like it holds other men."

Geth felt his hand grip his hilt, pulled it away, forced it to down at his side. "But why take the baby?"

Agrem looked at Geth from under those brows.

"It's another ploy, isn't it? He wants to draw me to him, somewhere where he thinks he can get the better of me."

"Mmmm. This is his only way. He didn't bring an army. He has none."

"And even if he did, he'd have to wage war against the whole of the Laeri to get to me." Geth thought that through. "But he's not without a few friends, I reckon. Where would he get the wet nurse from otherwise? And you said he was headed east, toward Arnus, no doubt. Mereg might not have given him men to storm Ehken Laer, but he's given him sanctuary."

Agrem loosed a sigh. "He is gone. Vriana Govendis is here. She needs us."

She did. Geth had spent the night holding her hand, whispering to her, patting that stupid cloth against her brow. He didn't sleep a wink, just sat there, listening to her breath, to the terrifying, long pause between each one.

"What did he do to her?"

Agrem shook his head wearily. "The fear took her. She fought. He used all his strength."

"Is she..." Geth swallowed hard but couldn't continue.

The Seer lifted his chin. "But he could not kill her. She was too strong. Even if it broke her heart."

"Her heart?"

"Her heart, mmmm. I am not a strong enough healer. I must have help."

Geth took him by the shoulders. "Amalia, Pythelle; they can help! Like when you healed me of Weeping Willow's poisons!"

Agrem shook his head. "Too far away. They will not make it in time."

"Too far away? No, there has to be someone else!"

"There is."

Geth looked up. "Who?"

Agrem's mouth twisted like it was full of something foul. "Sythme, of the Arnui."

The gods, oh how they toyed! Geth paced a little circle, cursed them all. "Damn you to Ord's hairy asshole! All seven of you!"

He stamped back up the hill, Agrem in tow. It was several days ride to the lands of the Arnus, and several days ride back. Did Vriana have that long?

And how the hell were they going to talk Sythme into helping the chieftess when her master was in on the plot?

"Tell me something good, 'Grem. Tell me anything."

"Mmmm."

"Thram's crooked cock."

Geth stopped himself from pacing. He must have picked up the habit from Hadean, but for himself at least, it only made him more anxious. He exhaled a long breath, tried to think. It could be done. They could get Sythme. It would take a lot of bloodshed though.

There was always the chance Ceter would be there as well, with Ethen.

"We have plenty of swords here," he told Agrem. "We raise an army, march east. Iyngaer and the Duei will march north to meet us. Together, we'll get Sythme, scour the land of Mereg, and get my son back."

The Seer frowned. He said only one word. "Time."

"How long have we got?"

"Two days."

Geth felt his heart drop.

"Maybe longer."

"We can't get to Arnus, snatch that witch, and get back in two days."

"But we can get Vriana to Isa Vlen."

"The cave with all the paintings?"

"It is more than a cave. It is a..." Agrem searched for the word. "It is a special place. It could be enough. It's on our path."

Geth didn't ask questions. They readied a wagon and a company of escorts and rode out within the hour. He watched the wind play through the trees as they traveled, watched the sun dip in and out of the clouds like he'd never seen such things before, like he might never see them again. The Seer was right; Vriana looked even weaker than she had just hours before. There would never have been time to raise an army and march to war, even if every shred of his soul screamed for retribution.

It was night by the time they reached the craggy ridgeline, the rough-cut stairs leading up to the yawning mouth of Isa Vlen. Geth carried Vriana himself. They crossed under the archway, through the low anteroom and into the cave's great belly. He remembered thinking it was a devil pit the first time he came, watching torchlight breathe life into the figures painted on the walls. He hoped he'd been wrong.

"Lay her down." Agrem said. He spread several layers of fur down on the stone floor and a fire was lit beside it. Geth kneeled carefully, settled Vriana on her back with another rolled pelt under her head. He muttered a prayer to Neyna. And a warning to Vorda too: if there was a way to kill a goddess, he'd find it.

"Her heart labors," The Seer said. "It will tire and stop. Unless we slow it, make it rest, mmmm?"

"And that will buy us time?"

Agrem nodded.

"Isn't it dangerous though? It's almost like she's not breathing already."

"It is dangerous. She will be more dead than alive. And it will need strong magicks, as you call them, when it is time to bring her back."

"How strong?"

"With Sythme, we can do it."

Geth looked down at Vriana's face. The firelight, at least, gave it some color. "Are we doing the right thing, Agrem?"

"Mmmm. Unless we don't get back in time."

Agrem did the hum and sway thing again. Afterward, he looked positively ill. But he looked pleased as well.

"It worked."

Geth knelt down beside the chieftess. She lay there, still as a corpse. "She looks..." He couldn't make himself say it.

"She is alive. But we must get to Sythme."

Geth blew out a sigh. The easy part was done. Now they just had to march into hostile lands, steal a witch from under the nose of their enemies, and force her to heal a woman she despised.

"We need a distraction," Geth mused aloud. He led Agrem out in front of the entrance to Isa Vlen, night sky purple-grey, thick with clouds above them.

"Iyngaer," said Agrem.

Hack appeared from down beside the horses and wagons. He nodded his agreement, brow furrowed, face as serious as ever. "He's the one. If he can't stick it to Mereg, no one can."

"And he's supposed to march his army against the Arnui just for me?"

"You don't think he would?" Hack asked. "He never liked those bastards. And they've been eyeing him sideways for weeks already. Give him a reason."

"Mmmm," Agrem agreed.

"But how do we get a message to him in time?" Geth asked.

The Seer just snorted.

Agrem worked his magicks while Geth and everyone else slept. The big warrior curled up beside Vriana. She never stirred, not a hair. In the morning, the Seer entered the cave, woke Geth, told him it was done.

"So, Mereg's attention will be pointed south?" Geth said, "at Iyngaer? Thank the gods for our friends."

Agrem hummed.

"How long will it take to get in and out you reckon?"

"No horses, we must walk. We follow the paths of the wild things, but this way they will not catch us on the road."

Geth nodded. "Then we go alone, just you and—"

"Not a chance." Hack stood in the mouth of the cave, hands on hips lit from behind by the dawn. Geth had to admit, he looked formidable. He thought it through; a loyal sword to watch his back might be just the thing he needed, especially if it turned out Ethen was, indeed, there.

"Alright, the three of us," Geth said.

Hack nodded, expression as serious as ever.

They gathered supplies and threw packs over their shoulders. At Geth's insistence, Hack brought along a bow as well. The green-cloak didn't claim to be a great marksman, but Geth reckoned anyone was better than himself.

Agrem frowned though, first up at the sun, then back at the mouth of the cave.

"What is it?" Geth asked. "That's right, we're losing valuable daylight. We don't have time."

Agrem shook his head. "You are right, Gethe. We don't. Not enough."

It was the big warrior's turn to frown. "Are you saying what I think you're saying?"

Agrem just muttered a curse for an answer.

"You slowed her heart. You said that would buy us enough time."

"But what if we can't find Sythme, mmmm? What if we are wrong?"

"Thram's balls!"

Agrem paused him with a raised finger, turning to look thoughtfully back at the cave. He stalked back up the rough stairs and under the opening without explanation. After a moment he poked his head back out, waved Geth and Hack inside.

"You've got an idea?" Geth said. "Out with it."

The Seer motioned them to sit a few paces from Vriana and her minders. He settled down beside them, reached out took Geth's hand with his right, Hack's with his left. He frowned at the pair until they closed the circle by taking each other's hand. Then he closed his eyes.

A good long moment passed. Minutes? Half an hour? It was hard to say. A huddle of Ilars around the chieftess looked on until eventually Agrem opened his eyes. He nodded once. "I have *seen*."

"The future? Can we do it? Gods all be damned, 'Grem, tell me something."

"Wait."

The Seer hurried back outside. Hack offered the big warrior a determined nod. Geth was glad for it. Another half hour passed, and he started to fret until Agrem burst back through the cave entrance, grinning.

"Drink," he said. He offered a steaming cup of...*something*. Geth smelled it, felt tears spring instantly from his eyes, but Agrem just kept smiling.

"What the hell is that? Dear gods, it's like my nose just opened up but my eyes want to close down."

Agrem pushed the cup to the big warrior's lips and Geth drank. It tingled down his throat, but it actually wasn't so bad. Hack drank next. Within moments, the pair of them were grinning right alongside the Seer.

Geth slapped the Seer on the shoulder. "That's some brew."

Hack just giggled.

"Mmmm," Agrem agreed. "The Govendis gave me the idea. We slowed her heart for time. With this tsook, this brew, we make our hearts go faster."

"So, we can travel faster?"

"Faster. Farther. Without rest. But we will tire after. We will tire like the dead."

"I'm willing to risk it," Hack said. He smacked a fist into his palm.

Geth shook his head to clear it. Agrem's brew, it was like being drunk, but without the dizziness, the fog, the dulled senses. He wondered why the Ilars didn't use this *tsook* more often. *Gods be damned, but I feel great!* A little voice told him he'd know the answer when they tired out, as Agrem predicted. But for now he was all smiles, just like the others.

He skipped to Vriana's side, his feet moving like they wanted to dance. He knelt, kissed her harder than he'd intended, then straightened the blankets around her, clutched Horse-face on the shoulder, nodded vigorously, and started straight out the cave. He didn't even know which direction they were going.

Agrem led the way, trotting like a man decades-younger. Geth and Hack followed right behind. They covered miles without halt, arriving at Vorus's bank before sundown. No one spoke, they just plunged right in, swam with hoots and laughs across the water, came up shivering but still grinning in the lands of the Arnui.

"Shhhh," Agrem warned them. The sun had begun to dip, and Geth felt the first hint of discomfort as the wind blew across his dripping clothes. Hack stood there blinking, looking confused, but the Seer came around with a skin and another drink of tsook solved all their problems.

"Very little," Agrem warned. "We do not have much. We must get Sythme and return before we run out. Or we will drop in the road and Vriana will die."

"She's not going to die," Geth said. "I have *seen* it."

Hack giggled, slapped Geth on the back. That little voice told Geth the Ilar tsook had gone straight to his head. He rubbed his face and tried to wipe the grin from his mouth, but it wasn't easy.

It wasn't easy to stand still either. Agrem got them moving again and they took off at a jog, following game trails in lieu of proper roads now that they were on enemy soil. Night fell, slowing their progress, but a bright moon peaked out through the clouds to light the way. For Geth at least, the cold was nothing. Agrem forced them to eat, washing the meals down with water and another swallow of tsook. Tree-covered ridges, valleys, and streams passed under foot until the sun began creeping up over the pines to the east.

"We are almost there," the Seer announced, motioning them to a halt. "Over that hill, Mereg's army prepares for war."

"With Iyngaer?" Geth asked.

Agrem hummed. "I must speak with him. It is time."

He said nothing more, but sat up against a tree, tilted his head back and closed his eyes. Geth just watched, wondering how the hell the man could sleep after drinking his magick brew. "Maybe he isn't really asleep?" he wondered aloud.

"Sleep?' Hack said. "Ha!"

Whatever the case, it wasn't long before the Seer stirred. "All is ready. Iyngaer will draw Mereg's eyes. And Sythme's too."

"Where will she be?" Geth asked.

Agrem stood up, waved him to follow, and started up the hill. They reached the summit, and Geth's jaw dropped. He retreated behind a tree bole, motioned for Hack to do the same. Down below them in a wide valley, a camped army awaited.

CHAPTER EIGHT

"Dear gods," Geth breathed, sobered by the sheer number of tents and campfires below.

"Iyngaer and the Duei are coming," said Agrem.

"But where will we find Sythme?"

The Seer made a face. "Far from the fighting."

"And Ceter? My son?"

"Mmmm."

"Maybe he's here. Maybe—"

"Ceter is not here. If he is, if I am wrong, we will *feel* it. He will use his magicks, as you call them, to help Mereg. But I am not wrong, mmmm? We are here to take Sythme."

As much as Geth wanted to sneak down and see for himself, he knew Agrem was right. At the Seer's insistence, they sat, ate some more. Geth wasn't hungry at all, but the dried venison Agrem offered tasted like a fine cutlet once he did, reluctantly, bite off a mouthful. The miles had started to catch up to them and Geth felt a dizzying exhaustion creeping in.

But Agrem passed his skin around once more, this time with a stern warning. "Just a sip. Small!" He directed an especially stern look toward Hack. "Need your wits, mmmm?"

Horns sounded somewhere in the distance. Geth stood, moved back up to the crest of the hill to peer down into the valley. Tribesmen scrambled in every direction, their shouts carried on the wind to Geth's ears. It wasn't long before another army appeared at the far end of the vale.

"Thram and Awer but I wish I was down there," Geth muttered.

"Me too, Captain. Me too."

Agrem motioned them on with the flick of his head, toward what appeared to be a deer-run, and they started down the hill. They couldn't help but jog, like animals themselves, tsook coursing through their veins. Geth shook his head, told himself to stay focused, thanked the gods Agrem had only let him take a sip this time.

Down in the valley, the horn blasts and shouts of the two opposing armies grew louder, rising until the noise seemed to thunder up from the ground itself. Iyngaer had wasted no time. Geth thanked the gods for his friends. The din of war rumbled through the air as opposing armies clashed. Geth kept his eyes on Agrem's back, tried not to let any foolish, brew-born notion steer him toward the battle instead of the witch they were after.

The Seer pulled them to a stop beside a stand of trees. "Wait here."

Geth strained his eyes. But it was a few furlongs to the first wagons and tents at the rear of the Arnus war camp, too far to make out any individual person clearly. "Where is she?"

Agrem just grunted. He motioned Geth and Hack to sit. "I will call to her."

He started toward the camp, walking at an easy pace, then crouched down in the tall grass a few dozen yards from their hiding spot in the trees. Hack frowned at the Seer's back. Geth just watched. He didn't know what Agrem had in mind, but he knew he was capable of a lot more than mixing heady drinks.

At first Geth thought he was imagining it, but after a moment, he was sure. Someone was coming. Hack fumbled for his bow.

Geth raised a hand. "Wait!" he hissed. "It's her."

"How..."

Magicks.

Geth didn't know if Agrem had spoken into the witch's dreams or something, but as the figure drew nearer, he saw that it was, indeed, Sythme. He remembered her from his truslas; grey hair, deeply lined face. Her eyes darted this way and that, and Geth crouched lower beside the trunk of a tree until the woman was nearly on top of Agrem. Without warning, the warlock stood up. Sythme screamed and ran.

"Thram's balls!" Geth cursed the old Seer for not giving him any warning and sprinted after the witch. Thin, high grass parted as he ran, a wolf running down its prey.

Sythme didn't make it far either. She moved like a lame deer, old as she was. He had a hold of her before she'd made it ten yards.

Agrem arrived laughing behind Geth. Sythme sagged in the big warrior's arms, but managed a choice curse in the Ilar tongue when the Seer came around to face her.

"How'd you do that?" Geth asked.

"You know, mmmm?"

Hack trotted up, mouth agape. He shook his head, then helped Geth tie the woman's wrists, wrap a gag in place over her mouth. Sythme hardly struggled.

"How did you know she would be back here?" Geth asked,

"She is a coward." Agrem moved to stand even closer to the witch, hands on hips. He said something in their tongue. By the way the woman flinched, Geth reckoned he'd repeated the accusation to her face.

She looked defeated already. Her thin grey hair, twisted up in a single braid, had come partially undone. For an esteemed witch, there wasn't more than a few dull beads to adorn her leathers, mark her station. To Geth at least, she had seemed a cunning old hag at the truslas, someone to be reckoned with. But perhaps that's because he'd been the captive then, not the other way around.

"Come," Agem said. He dusted off his hands and started back toward the hill. Hack took the witch by the arm and fell in stride. Geth glanced over one shoulder. No one was close enough to see or hear them, best he could tell. They were about to get away clean.

Geth didn't speak until a good mile lay behind them. "That was incredible," he said. "She just came right to you."

Agrem didn't try very hard to look humble. He passed around his brew for another swallow each. He made sure the witch got a mouthful as well. They picked the pace up to a jog.

Sythme grinned behind the gag they'd tied over her mouth. At least it looked like she grinned. A few miles farther down their game trails, the Seer stripped the rag from her with a stern word in the Ilar language. The witch licked her lips, said nothing, but jogged as fast as any of them despite her age. Geth had plenty of reason to grin himself; best he could tell, they'd be back at Isa Vlen by nightfall of the next day.

He thought of Vriana, how she'd reacted the last time he'd saved her life. Lustful imaginings playing through his mind, another side-effect of the tsook, perhaps. He didn't let it slow him. They kept right on—stone, moss, and leaf passing in a blur underfoot.

Eventually, Sythme pulled them up with a moan.

"What's wrong with her?" Hack asked.

Agrem shook his head. He produced his concoction in answer. With a warning in Ilar, he started to press it to the woman's lips, but the old hag raised bound hands to tilt it high, sucking hungrily from the skin.

"Ah!" The Seer hissed in alarm, too late. He pulled the tsook away, spat a few of the Ilar words Geth knew to curse Sythme roundly.

Muttering another curse, Agrem turned to his friends. "Eat." He tucked the skin in his pack, handed out more dried meat.

Geth gnawed at it, nodding approval, but he could see Agrem was upset. "What is it?"

The Seer just shook his head.

Geth let it be. They ate and moved on, jogging as they had before. A cold night fell, but Geth didn't feel it. Not at first. They kept on moving.

Dawn was only a few hours off when the effects of the tsook began to wear off. Sythme didn't slow, but Hack huffed as he ran. Agrem's nimble steps turned into a hobble. Geth frowned each time the wind found its way under his collar.

The Seer finally reined them in for a rest. He looked from one man to the other, eyes narrowed. That stare landed on Sythme last, accompanied by another string of curses. Pulling out his skin of tsook, he paused to heft it weight. He cursed Sythme again. The old woman cackled.

"What...?" Hack just looked from witch to warlock and back, face slack. Sythme hadn't stopped laughing. There was more to it than that meaningless tsook-giggle too.

Geth's eyes went wide. "Aw hell."

He would have reached over and strangled the woman if she stood a foot closer. He sank down to the seat of his pants instead, back against a tree. "She drank up all the brew."

Agrem didn't confirm it, but he didn't deny it either. He still stood there, holding that skin, grimace stretched across his face.

"How much have we got?"

"Not enough, mmmm?"

"Enough for one man to get her back to Isa Vlen?"

The Seer made a face. "One man cannot bring her back."

"But—"

"If we leave someone behind, they will die."

"From the tsook?" Geth asked.

Agrem nodded. "When it is all spent, we will fall. And we will sleep. The sleep will grow deeper and deeper unless we drink the ata-tsook."

"The antidote?" Geth rubbed his face with both hands, his mind trying to go foggy already. They had to save Vriana, but there was no chance he was leaving anyone behind either.

"The witch already drank her share," he said after some thought. "You're no spring chicken and we need you to prepare the antidote when we get back anyway. So, you have to drink a share."

Agrem couldn't argue with that. He nodded.

Geth opened his mouth to continue, but Hack beat him to it. "You take what's left, Captain." He thumped his chest. "I'll meet you back at Isa Vlen. It'll take more than a hangover to stop the likes of me."

Geth didn't know whether to laugh, or cry, or both. "You don't even know the way, Hack."

"Well—"

"I've got a bigger job for you anyway." Geth pushed up to his feet. "You're going to take what's left of the tsook. You and 'Grem. But if I get tired, your job will be to carry me."

Any sane man would have cursed. Hack just saluted, fist to heart, chest puffed as far as it would go. "I'll carry you, Captain. Yessir. All the way to the Mouth of Hell if I have to."

Agrem and Hack drank. Hack insisted that Geth drink the last tiny sip, to perk him up, and truth be told, the big warrior knew he needed it. After that, the Seer used a knife to cut the skin open, instructing him to lick the inside, make use of every last drop.

It worked. Geth felt a new man. *Two* new men.

"Gods but this stuff is dangerous," he muttered. That stupid grin was already spreading across his face. And he didn't want to think about the reckoning that would come afterward, when the effects wore off. Behind him, Sythme snickered.

"Old bitch." Geth took one step towards her and the witch cowered down, almost to all fours. "You're right, 'Grem. She *is* a coward."

They ran as they had before, fording the river and coming up on the Laeri side well before midday. Clouds had rolled in overhead, and it wasn't long before Geth began to feel the chill. The wind cut like a knife, searched like icy fingers through his clothes, numbed bare skin wherever it could be found.

The others kept on running and Geth didn't dare stop. If he did, he wasn't sure he'd be able to start up again. Agrem's brew was gone. They had a good eight hours of running ahead of them still.

Geth looked up at the sun as it crawled from east to west across the sky. "Gotta be past midday by now," he said.

Agrem cast a worried glance back at him. Sythme cackled. Hack slowed a hair to jog at his side.

"That's right, Captain, almost there." He spoke as he ran, like it was nothing. "We've done it. The chieftess will be saved and the whole place will celebrate. We'll be heroes, Captain!"

Geth just grunted. He didn't miss the meaningful look that Agrem directed at Hack.

"Almost there," the green-cloak said again. "A few hours, that's all."

A few hours sounded like an eternity, but Geth clamped his mouth shut, focused on putting one foot in front of the other. *This isn't your first day in the sword-yard,* he told himself. He kept his eyes on the trail ahead, the crest of the next hill, the next curve in the road.

Maybe the miles passed, the hours too, but it sure as hell didn't feel like it. They'd slowed the pace, he was sure, but a lazy jog was all he could manage. At Agrem's insistence, Geth discarded his pack. Hack took his sword-belt so he didn't have to carry that either.

"Almost there," Hack said for a third time. "Over the next hill, then it's all down. Pretty sure I remember that."

"Thram's...balls."

Geth barely had the wind to curse properly. Let alone run for another half a day. He flicked a glance at Hack, wanted to tell him he was done, that they should go on without him.

But the green-cloak spoke before he did. "Gotta make it back for Ethen, Captain. Gotta save the chiefess, but we gotta find the baby too. Still got some work to do."

"Ethen..."

"After the celebration, I mean," A smile split Hack's ever-dauntless expression. "We'll be heroes when we get back, remember? The chieftess, she's gonna be awful happy about how we saved her. About how *you* saved her."

"I'm...tired...Hack."

"Just keep your feet moving. You know that's the first thing you ever said to me? In the sword-yard, back when that traitor Wayan was kicking my ass every day. Sure taught me a lot about swordplay, you did, Captain."

"Remember that time you whipped him? Wayan that is, in the sword-yard? Eldric saved his hide. Another treacherous bastard, the lord, but who knew? I was there that day, you know that?"

Hack just kept on talking. They weren't running any more, or jogging either, but at least they were still moving. Geth thanked the gods he had the man along. Agrem couldn't have done it, he just wasn't a man of many words. He did take Sythme from the Umbelman though, making it even easier for Hack to continue with the chatter.

"...that time you fought that big blond bastard out in front of the ranks.," he was saying. "That was something. But I already knew after Point-fort that I'd follow you to Vorda's cold hall if I had to. You were the best man I'd ever met. The bravest and the strongest. And the kindest too."

Geth didn't know about that last, but Hack's accolades did seem to help. He pushed the pain in his knees, in his lower back, to one side, and relived each and every dust-up as the green-cloak spoke. It didn't hurt to be reminded how strong he'd been, how strong he could be, for his men, for Vriana, and for little Ethen.

Hack didn't run out of words, but their effect couldn't last forever. Geth wasn't sure what had become of Agrem. The Seer was no longer ahead of them. A stumbling glance over the shoulder didn't reveal him on the trail behind either. He must have taken the witch and gone ahead, Geth reckoned.

At least he'll get her to Vriana, he thought. His vision blurred and his knees shook. With a groan like old wood cracking, his eyes rolled up into his head and he tumbled face-first into the dirt.

CHAPTER NINE

"C'mon, Captain," Hack's voice parted the mist. "We're almost there. It's just over that hill. We made it!"

Geth's eyes opened. He felt the green-cloak tugging at his arms. With a curse and heave, Hack had him sitting up. Some more coaxing, grunting, and swearing got the big warrior all the way to his feet.

"I can't...Hack. I—"

"I got you!" Hack thumped his chest. "And we're almost there. You'll be the hero again, mark my words."

"You're...the hero, Hack."

The Umbelman started talking about the feast they'd lay out for 'the heroes.' One step at a time, he got Geth moving again. It didn't seem like they were making much ground, but Geth decided he'd rather die like this anyway, on his feet, than face down in the mud.

They walked, Hack talking all the while. Eventually they reached the top of that hill. Geth lifted his head, but no little river, no valley, and no timber hill-fort met his eyes. Just another rolling hill, another unending, leaf-strewn path.

He collapsed into Hack's side.

"I gotcha, Captain! I gotcha, we're almost there."

But Geth went limp, let the green-cloak ease him down onto his back. "I'm cold, Hack. And...it hurts."

Hack rubbed his hands together. "I'm a little cold too, truth be told."

"Did they...make it?" Geth asked.

Hack frowned. "Agrem and the witch? He's probably healed the chieftess already." He reached out, took Geth's hands in his own. Gods be praised, they were warm.

"That's better, isn't it?"

Geth didn't hear him. He closed his eyes. He didn't know if he was about to sleep or if he was going to die, but before he could do either, a thumping noise reached his ear. His lids flitted open.

"Wha...?"

Hack sat smiling over him, still holding his hands. "Huh. Guess they managed it quicker than I thought."

"Who?"

"Agrem," said the green-cloak. "Here he comes now, Captain. And he's got a wagon and some horses for us two heroes."

Magicks. Geth shivered just thinking of it. With one brew, Agrem had stilled Vriana's flesh to within an inch of death. With another, he'd spurred Geth to run clear across the forest. A with a third, best he could tell, the Seer had snatched him back from the bosom of Vorda herself, lips all puckered to suckle at death's tit.

Geth would have hugged the old warlock if he wasn't too weak to stand up.

"Rest, Captain."

From beside him, Hack lifted a waterskin to let Geth slurp down a mouthful. He muttered his thanks and settled back beside him among the furs. He was behind the screens in Vriana's hall, he realized. The Umbelman never left his side.

"I think I might've shit myself," Geth said.

Hack just laughed.

"I'm serious. And I'm sweating all over. Maybe I just need a sip of that tsook to get me right. Do you think—"

"That's what you *don't* need." Hack frowned. "I wanted it too, it's like that, Agrem says. But you gotta sweat through it. For Vriana. For Ethen."

For my family.

It wasn't so hard, when he put it in those terms. The ata-tsook helped too. "Thanks, Hack."

"For what, Captain?"

"You saved my life out there. Vriana's too. We couldn't have done it without you."

Hack puffed up. "Bah! That was nothing."

The Umbelman nodded for emphasis, serious as ever. Gods the man was crazy. He was a real blessing too.

Geth wasn't sure how long they'd been back at Ehken Laer, but it was only another day before he was able to stand and walk. As soon as he could, he moved over to settle himself beside Vriana's silent form. He held her hand, prayed.

"She will be well, mmmm?"

Geth turned to find Agrem standing at the edge of the screen. "But what happens when she wakes? What happens when she finds out they have our son?"

Agrem bent with a groan to sit beside the big warrior. He folded his hands in his lap. His eyes were on the chieftess though. He muttered to himself in the Ilar tongue before turning back to Geth.

"Sythme has spoken. She says Ceter did not come to Mereg, that she did not know about your son. Or the plan to steal him, mmmm?"

"She lies."

Agrem shrugged. "Ceter was not there."

"Are you sure?"

"I have searched for him—" the Seer touched the side of his head—"*here*. He has gone from the forests."

"And taken my son."

"Mmmm."

"But where?"

—|———

Geth's strength had returned by the next day. Vriana, however, did little more than frown and mutter in her sleep. Agrem assured the big warrior she was on the mend, that she would make a full recovery. In the meantime, there was nothing he could do but pace out in front of the hall, wind stinging his eyes.

"Bloody Ceter."

In one way it all made sense, the puppet-master pulling the strings in Ilia again. Perhaps it was Ceter that had set Vongaer to dancing? And Mereg as well. No doubt, he missed the influence he'd once had—the power. The power to deliver his revenge.

But there was more to it all, Geth could feel it. How had an outlander like Ceter managed to orchestrate the attack on Mother, leagues away in Umbel? And where outside of Ilia could Ceter have taken his son? He wasn't from the forests, that much Geth knew, if he knew little else. Perhaps Ceter was a puppet himself.

Resisting the urge to kick one of Vriana's hide crosses again, Geth headed back inside. He strode the length of the hall, ignoring the hails of Horse-face and other familiar tribesmen to circle behind the screens and check on the chieftess. Her breath came even and deep. She muttered something, pursed her lips and sighed.

"Thram and bloody Awer." She'd be awake soon, Geth reckoned, and their son would still be gone. And he would be sitting there, having done nothing.

A commotion in the hall turned Geth before he could dwell on it further. Voices speaking Aturian floated over the screens.

The big warrior jumped to his feet and made toward the central fire.

"Ratcher? Neary?" Gods but it was good to hear some old friends. "Is that you Amalia?"

The Paellian and the Umbelman caught sight of him, grinned in reply. But the witch ignored Geth, hurrying around the screens to kneel down beside Vriana. Everyone followed. The sturdy hands of Geth's friends came to rest on each of his shoulders as they gathered over the chieftess, watching.

Amalia closed her eyes and swayed over Vriana. Geth reached out to either side, wrapping an arm around his friends. An age passed, maybe more.

"She is well." Amalia said finally. She put out a hand and Neary hurried to take it, helped her to her feet. She dusted off her skirts and straightened that great beehive on her head.

"Agrem was wise to enlist Sythme," she went on. "The sneaking rodent saved her life, even if she did little more."

Geth followed her eyes back to the chieftess. Was he imagining it, or had Vriana's cheeks gained some color? As he watched, she lifted a hand, rubbed the tip of her nose and rolled to curl up on her side.

"Amalia!" Geth said.

The witch nodded, hands on hips. "She won't be fencing in the sword-yard for a while, but she'll be up and about before long."

Ratcher patted Geth's back. "You hear that?"

As a group, they circled around toward the fire for food and drink. For the moment, they pretended nothing was wrong, or that all would be well. Of course it would.

Agrem arrived through the big doors as the plates were taken away, spikey hair waving as he hurried to meet them. Ignoring the others, he addressed Amalia in the Ilar tongue. Geth blinked as the witch replied just as fluently, going so far as to hum in the fashion of the tribes.

"We're going to speak with Sythme," she explained, turning to Geth. "Maybe together we can wring something out of her."

Geth watched the pair exit the hall. Neary made small talk, the usual sort. But Ratcher sat silent, licking his lips and frowning like he'd just tasted a toad's piss.

"Thram and Awer," Geth told the assassin. "If you know something, spit it out."

Ratcher frowned. "It's just that I didn't want to unload too much on you all at once." He flicked a glance at Neary.

The oldster encouraged him with a nod.

"Your mother—"

Geth felt his heartbeat quicken. "The letter said she was fine."

"And she is!" Ratcher spared another glance at the old green-cloak, received another nod in return. "They didn't get to her. Came damn close, but Melagus sniffed out the danger just in time. Truth be told, the way it all happened, I don't think they really thought they could get to her when they finally tried. But they wanted to send a message."

Geth's stomach tightened up. "What are you trying to tell me, Ratcher? Just say it."

"It was Snake Eyes."

The big warrior blinked.

"The twins, from Pellon. The same—"

"I know bloody well who Snakes Eyes is. Bastards got me with a slingstone and dragged me blindfolded all the way to the Tower of the Moon. But back then, they were working for..."

Palladine.

Geth's mouth opened and closed. The last piece of the puzzle fell into place, what he should have suspected from the first moment. He felt a fool.

"Are you sure?" he asked, voice gone quiet.

"Sure as I can be. Your mother saw someone. He fit the description. How they got in the sword-yard, I'll never know. But by all accounts, there was a second man creating a distraction, that one was described the same way. A team of two, operating up close with knives...it had to be them."

Geth didn't ask about the knives. Or how Melagus had saved Mother. They'd both survived, that's what was important.

Along with the obvious implication of an attack by Snake Eyes. "It was all Palladine's doing."

Agrem and Amalia rejoined the trio before long. The Seer un-stoppered a skin of eyfra, sucked down a few swallows with a grimace. Amalia sat heavily on the pelts.

"Nothing?" Geth asked.

The witch shook her head. "She doesn't know anything. The only question is, what do we do with her now?"

"Mmmm." Agrem frowned. "Send her back."

Amalia met his eye, expression thoughtful. She nodded. "You're right. Iyngaer may need to be in contact with Mereg. There's no faster way than through her."

"Bloody Iyngaer." Geth shook his head, muttered a curse. "After all he's done for me, I haven't even thought of the man. What happened at the battle? I reckon it didn't decide anything, otherwise I would have heard."

"No," said Agrem.

"I don't like that tone, 'Grem. What happened?"

Amalia answered for him. "They took losses. It was a hasty plan they threw together, and Mereg was ready for them. He'll call it a victory."

"Damn." Geth ran a hand through that short hair. "Men died, a battle lost, and here I am, no closer to getting my son. The gods hate me."

"There is one piece of good news." Amalia raised a finger. "Sythme may not have known anything, but I can tell you this: Ceter's path took him by boat, downriver."

"Why didn't you tell me sooner? He has my son!"

"All things in due course. Vriana needed me. Sythme's touch was never going to be enough to heal her."

Geth rose from his seat on a pelt to pace. He felt Ratcher and Neary's eyes on him, but he turned back to the witch. "Alright, Ceter went south, not east, to Mereg, like we thought. How is that good news?"

Amalia nodded, that great beehive shaking. "It's not the direction that is good news, but the manner in which he left. He could have covered his trail. He didn't. Wherever he's headed, it's somewhere to the south. And he wants us to know it."

Ratcher looked to the big warrior, eyes bright. "It means the child is safe, Geth! Ceter wanted us to know which way he's gone so you'd follow."

"You didn't tell them, did you?" Geth said.

"I thought you should hear it first," Ratcher turned to the witch. "Melagus thinks the attack on Geth's mother was carried out by a pair of assassins known as Snake Eyes. The last person to hire them was a Paellian Captain by the name of Palladine."

Looks passed between the Seer and the witch. Neither spoke. If Ceter had taken Ethen down the North River, toward the sea, the implication was obvious, to Geth at least.

"He's taking my son back to Pellon."

CHAPTER TEN

P alladine and Ceter, Ilia and Pellon. Geth muttered curses, tried to make sense of it all. He left his friends to walk circles around Vriana's hall again, up at the highest point of the hillfort. The wind whipped his cloak, but neither the air nor the view led to any breakthrough.

"Think," he muttered out loud. "What does it all mean? What the hell do they want?"

"They want revenge," he answered himself. "You said it yourself."

"And the attack on Mother? Just a distraction to get me away from Vriana? Or another attempt to get back at me?"

"Both. That bastard Palladine said he'd hurt anyone close. Practically the last thing that came out of his mouth before they dragged him off."

"He didn't appreciate how that all went. Towdric jailed, my head still attached to my neck. He had to crawl back to the Golden City, the evil bastard, with nothing to show for it but a string of failures."

"So this time he wants to draw me back to Pellon, where he can get even."

"But what's next?"

Geth looked up to find an Ilar woman with a basket under one arm watching him talk to himself like she'd just come upon a stray dog, the kind that might bite. The big warrior clamped his mouth shut, question still out there, on the air. Daylight didn't last so long that far north, anyway. The chill drove him back inside toward the central hearth.

His friends had all retired to their various longhouses by then, all except Ratcher. The assassin-turned-green-cloak sat hunched on a sawed tree ring. He watched Geth's approach, passed over a skin of eyfra without a word.

Geth sat directly on the pelts, swallowed a burning mouthful. "Gotta remember to bring some of this to Phelan."

Ratcher shook his head. "Don't do it."

"Do what?"

"You know what."

Geth snorted. "Tell me."

"You just said it, go back to the Golden City."

Geth clamped his mouth shut. The fire crackled, throwing yellow light and dancing shadows across Ratcher's face. The silence hung there for a good minute. It took Geth that long to realize the man was right.

He took another long pull at the forest fire, grimaced, squeezed the skin like it was someone's neck. "He had to come back for more, just couldn't let things lie. Damn you, Palladine!"

"How could he? It's not his way. Hers either."

Geth frowned. "The queen?"

"Who else?"

"No way she—"

"Did you ever know a woman to forget a slight? What you did to her lapdog Palladine, and how you used her son against her...there's no way she'll forget about that."

Geth's eyes went from his friend to the fire in the great hearth. He watched the flames, the logs burning, crumbling to dust. He'd only ever wanted to help—to help his friends, to help a rightful king. But his enemies, they couldn't leave him be. They wanted him hurt, or dead. In most cases, both.

"I know what you're thinking, Wolf." Ratcher's eyes shone bright. "You want to follow them east, separate a few heads from shoulders. Don't do it! It's what they want."

"I have to, Ratcher. He's my son."

"It's a trap, Geth. You hear me? That's all this is."

"You don't think I know that? They can't get to me here—they tried. They threw everything they had at it; an army and an insurrection and the best of the best assassins, some scratch called Blacksheep."

Geth met his friend's eye, offered a smile, but Ratcher didn't match it. He leaned forward, almost off the edge of his seat. "But now you want to make it easy for them?" he said. "Stretch your neck across the block of their choosing? Don't do it, man!"

"What am I supposed to do then?"

A log broke, as if in emphasis, sending a cloud of angry red embers up toward the smoke hole above. Ratcher blew out a sigh, ran a hand over his hair. "I don't know."

Geth lifted the skin, swallowed another mouthful of eyfra. He tossed it back to his friend, started to rise.

But Ratcher lifted a finger, paused him there. "I do know one thing."

"What's that?"

"There's going to be a note."

"A note?"

"A message of some kind. There always is. You don't ransom somebody and then forget to tell his friends how to pay you."

"If only they wanted gold..." Geth muttered.

Ratcher nodded. "Ceter left a trail, but he'll leave more than that. Or Palladine will. If they wanted to kill your child, they would have done it here, in Ilia. No, they want to lure you out, that's what they want. To the killing ground of their choosing."

Geth laid down beside Vriana that night, as had each night before. She snuggled into him and he held her tight, but she still didn't wake. She shook and murmured in her sleep, brow creased. She knew, even in slumber, that their son was gone.

Geth stared at the ceiling high overhead. Message or not, he had to do something. He thought of his mother, of Phelan, of

Hadean. Who would Palladine go after next? He had to act. He had to catch Palladine's eye before he hurt anyone else.

He rose before the sun was up and packed his things. A sword and a horse was all he really needed. He kissed Vriana's brow, whispered his oaths, and crept around the screens.

"You just don't listen."

Geth froze, one foot still raised. "Damn it, Ratcher."

"You really want to do this?"

"I have to."

Ratcher materialized from the shadows to plant himself in front of the big warrior, hands on hips. "What the hell is it gonna' accomplish, marching all the way to Pellon?"

"Everyone will be safer, for starters. It's me Palladine wants. And Ceter, and Lyanne. If attacking my mother and my woman, and stealing our son doesn't work, what will they try next?"

"You do make a fair point," Ratcher admitted.

"Now, you gonna' stand there in my way, or you gonna' let me save my son?"

Ratcher snorted. "Fine. I got the horses saddled already."

"Horses?"

"C'mon, Geth. You can't do this alone. You need me."

"I—"

"Listen, the way I figure it, I owe you one. Last time we were in Pellon, I had a pack of assassins after me. But I also had one ferocious sonofabitch to watch my back."

"Doesn't mean I need help now."

"Let me return the favor, Geth! And yes, you do. Truth be told you could use a lot more than just me. When we get to the Tooth—"

"Not a chance. The last thing King Hadean needs is for me to make matters even worse by marching a gang of green-cloaks into Pellon. Elius and Lyanne are just the kind to throw away eight-hundred years of friendship over something like this."

"Fine. Just me then. Like I said, I've got the horses saddled."

Geth swore. "How the hell did you even know I was leaving?"

"He didn't, mmmm?"

Agrem's voice turned Geth towards the shadows to one side. The Seer stepped into the light of the central fire, spikey hair gleaming orange and red.

"'Bloody magicks."

"Vriana will be waking now. Go to her."

Geth forgot all about Ratcher, hearing that. He hurried back around the screens to kneel at the chieftess's side. He stroked her forehead. Just like Agrem said, her eyes flitted open.

"Vriana!"

"Mmmm." She took his hand, squeezed weakly.

"Don't worry, I'm going to get our son back. I'm going to get Ethen—"

"Gethe," Her voice was barely a whisper, but her brow was pinched fiercely. "Wait for me. I will come too."

Geth shook his head. "No, no, you have to rest, Vriana. Rest, my love! Get strong. I can't wait. Gods all be damned but I wish I could."

"Gethe..."

Her eyes closed, even if her lips still moved. Geth could make nothing of it anyway. He kissed her again and rose.

"The horses are ready," Ratcher said.

Geth didn't argue with him this time. Beside the assassin, Agrem took something out from under his cloak, passed it over.

"Take this. Keep it, always."

Geth looked down into his hands. It was the little wooden sword he'd carved for Ethen. He'd forgotten how small it was.

Ratcher's horses carried them only so far as the river. A proper boat from Greenfell stood waiting. With Iyngaer holding both banks to the south, their only care was the Arnui, due east. But Mereg's eyes would be on the tall chieftain, not Vriana. Geth suspected he knew full well the predicament she was in.

The pines slid past to either side as their boat glided downriver. "We'll reach Umbel City in a couple days," Ratcher said. "We'll attract less notice this way as well. You said that's what you wanted."

"I don't feel good about it." Geth frowned at the fields and treeline like his son might be hidden there. "But Kerrel and the rest, they'll want to help. I just can't touch off a war between Umbel and Pellon. That could be the very thing Lyanne wants."

Ratcher nodded.

"And Hack..." Geth trailed off. "He's probably furious. Or hurt at least. But there's no way he would have let me leave him behind, not after all he did to help snatch Sythme."

"Ah, Hack." Ratcher grinned. "You owe me one where he's concerned. I left a note, on your behalf. He's been trusted with protecting the chieftess in your absence. That's some responsibility I'd say."

Geth blinked. A smile touched his lips. "That's perfect. He probably won't leave her side long enough to let her piss. Thanks, Ratch."

Before long they were gliding past Towerrock. Geth had responsibilities there, duties he'd be neglecting as long as he was gone. But he'd already left Kerrel and Willa to run the fortress. And with an ally like Brant to the south, not to mention Iyngaer to the north, he didn't worry overmuch for the young captain and the stewardess.

After the Tooth, it was Waterset sliding past, towns and villages one after another until the great hill of Umbel City appeared ahead. Erehan Keep caught the sun, gleaming white-walled in the distance.

Geth sighed. King Hadean, Mother, and Melagus would all be back, but he didn't dare share the news of Palladine's attack. That could only lead to disaster, even if they only meant to help.

Lyanne and Elius had already made plain their disregard for the bonds of the Sworn Realms, and an army of green-cloaks on Paellian soil would more than provide the excuse they needed to employ force. No doubt, they'd be happy to remove the nuisance of King Hadean and replace him with their own choice.

"I'll go," Ratcher said, reading Geth's mind. He motioned the boatman toward the marina of Rivertown, but Geth clutched his arm.

"You can't tell them."

"They'll find out eventually." Ratcher peeled Geth's hand gently off. "But I wouldn't tell them anyway. This is the best way, traveling light. If we want to get your son back in one piece, this is how we'll do it."

Geth nodded. Ratcher hopped the gunwale and disappeared into town. Geth only thought to ask why he'd gone at all once he was gone.

Ratcher didn't make him wait long for the answer. He was back before nightfall, arms loaded down with baggage.

"What's all that?" Geth asked, seated on the deck.

"The things we'll need," said Ratcher. "But forget all that for now. That's not what I was really after."

Geth's eyes narrowed. "Well?"

"The note." Ratcher threw the bags down and settled into a seat across from him. "It's arrived."

Geth squeezed the hilt at his waist. "And?"

"I didn't get to read it, but the gist of it is this: The lilies are holding their contests in two week's time."

"The Games?"

Ratched nodded. "Elius and Lyanne have invited Umbel to send an ambassador."

"Well, that's nothing—"

"This year's Games are being dedicated to their 'newly adopted infant son'."

Geth's swore. "Sneaking, low-down, shit-stinking..." He clamped his mouth shut before the stream of curses could turn into a flood. He breathed in and out. "Well, what else? The Honorus is a baby. Is that all?"

"That's it."

Geth swore some more. "Isn't there a demand? Aren't they supposed to ask for my head, or for me to surrender, or I don't know? I mean—"

Ratcher shrugged. "How much can you write on a note that's attached to a pigeon?"

"So, I'm just supposed to show up at the games? That's it?"

"Under most circumstances, I'd say that's just the first step, that there will be further instructions once we arrive. But in this case, that's all a formality. There's no negotiating once you've already climbed inside the lion's jaws."

Geth wanted to pace, but there wasn't enough room on the boat. He forced his hand off his hilt, clutched his knees where he sat. His eyes landed on the baggage Ratcher had brought aboard.

"And what's all that?"

Ratcher grinned. "Everything we'll need, more or less. Coin, disguises. More knives."

"Knives and disguises?" Geth snorted. "I reckon we'll need a lot more than that. For starters, we need a plan."

"As it happens, I've been thinking about that. Couldn't have done more than speculate before we had that note though."

Geth kicked the bags on the floor of the boat between them. "Well, whatever you had in mind, I like the part about the knives."

"Always come in handy. But that note..." Ratcher pursed his lips. "That made me reconsider. They haven't even made a demand, as you said. To me it seems they're just hoping to draw you to Pellon. They're not worried about the details, they're confident they can get what they want if they can get you on Paellian soil."

"I guess they're about to get their wish," Geth said. "But they're about to learn that the wolf can also be a fox. Best I can tell, the only way to get Ethen back will be to sneak in and steal him."

"Well—"

""Damn!" Geth smacked his fist. "I should have asked Amalia to come along. She does this thing with her voice, her singing. She could have gotten me inside the Lion's Den, or wherever, with no trouble at all."

Ratcher shook his head. "I doubt that. Lyanne is a witch as well, remember? She'll have wards, or whatever they call that sort of thing."

"Bloody magicks."

"Right. But now that you mention it, we could have used a practitioner of that sort just to watch our backs. Between Ceter and Lyanne, who knows what they'll throw at us."

Geth rubbed at his jaw, nodding, trying not to curse. "We going by ship? We have to, don't we? To make it in time. But maybe it's better if we didn't come ashore at the Golden City. They'll be watching."

Ratcher nodded. "And that would give us a few days to get a feel for the place. Lyanne's got enemies you know, and Palladine as well, sure as the sun rises and sets. You don't throw your weight around like those two and not rack up a few critics."

But Geth was looking over the gunwale. The boat had begun moving again, pole men pushing them off into the muddy brown flow of the river. Erehan keep flashed white from atop the bluff cliff of Umbel Hill's north face.

Ratcher's voice turned him. "That's another reason they didn't leave a demand with the note."

"What's that?"

The assassin flicked his chin toward the keep. "They didn't want to alert Hadean. They know he'd do everything in his power to help get your son back. Or to dissuade you from heading east at all."

"Well, I can't get Hadean involved anyway. Last thing he needs is another war. And I can't be talked out of going east either. What I don't understand, is how is it even worth the effort? Does Palladine hate me so much?"

"Evidently he does. And between him and his mistress, they've tried every living assassin except Number Three."

"Still..." Geth paused, halfway through his thought. "Do you think they expect me to turn myself in? To stop a war?"

"Geth—"

"I'd rather die fighting. But they weren't wrong either. This is my problem. He's my son. And the vengeance part, that will be mine as well."

CHAPTER ELEVEN

They boatman took them only so far as Umbel's port. Geth wore his hood up lest he be recognized. A few silvers encouraged the boatman and his crew to keep their lips sealed about their passengers as well. Ratcher disembarked but came back to fetch Geth within the hour.

"Found us a ride." He flashed a grin, yet another bag slung over his shoulder. "An Iyric trader, headed to Pellon with a load of glasswear and furs, something like that. They'd also be willing to ferry a traveling swordsmith and his understudy back home."

"What's in the sack?"

"Well, if we're swordsmiths, I figured we'd need a few extra swords." Ratcher dropped the bag with a clank, rummaged through it to produce a pair of leather aprons. "Here, just like the old days."

Geth took his, put it over his head and fastened the ties. "At least I don't have to shave my head," he muttered.

By sea, the journey would take ten days, not longer. Their ship captain was a no-nonsense Iyrund trader. His beard hung almost from his eyes down to his considerable stomach, gleaming black and silver, and dripping with oil. Ratcher must have paid handsomely. He didn't ask them to row. He planned to put in at Old Crown, a few days ride from Paellia.

"It's perfect, Ratcher said. "Even if Lyanne somehow learns of our arrival, she'll have a hard time coming at us in Old Crown. Familae Kion holds sway in those parts. No one would be happier to see the Leyai thwarted than Lord Ryrus and his lot."

Geth grunted. "I try to stay out of politics."

"Do you? I'd say you jumped in headfirst when you enlisted Prince Gahalus to help in Umbel."

"Had no choice, did I? I won't bother the lad this time though. I reckon we got him in enough trouble already."

Ratcher nodded. "Either way, Old Crown is a perfect place to make a soft landing. You know, get the feel of things before we firm up our plan."

Geth had no plan, that was the truth. He clutched Ethen's little sword to his chest, thought of his son, of Vriana, of the best way to make things right. The waves carried them south and east, out of the bay of Umbel and across Longsea. When they put in at Old Crown, he was no closer to knowing how.

"Perhaps I should have told Hadean," he said, gathering up the various bags Ratcher had brought aboard. "You said yourself he'd gladly lend his weight. And I don't doubt it."

Ratcher shrugged. "You could have. You know, cut to the chase, kick things up big between the two realms."

Geth swayed as the ship's hull rocked into the bumpers. Sailors scurried, throwing over lines, stowing oars. He managed to contain a curse.

"You wanna' know what I think?" Ratcher said. "I don't think Lyanne would balk at a war against little old Umbel. Not if Hadean started it. If she could get him out of the way, she could install some crony in his place, establish favorable trade agreements or some such. That wouldn't do any harm to her support here at home."

Geth muttered a curse. War with Umbel? How could Pellon lose? Twelve great hosts, ships by the score, forts and walls—

"But she didn't want to," Ratcher went on. "Otherwise, she would have sent a different kind of note, made sure Hadean knew how she'd slighted his famous war-captain."

"I don't like it," Geth said.

Ratcher shook his head. "Me neither."

"How long before Hadean finds out about Vriana and Ethen?" Geth asked. They picked up their baggage and climbed onto the quays.

Ratcher frowned. "He's probably heard by now. But he may not know you've left. I supposed he'll be sending his birds up to Towerrock and waiting for an answer."

"An answer he won't get."

Geth nodded, more to himself than to his friend. Ratcher made his goodbyes to the ship captain and they started off, through a gate in harbor wall and into the city. Lilies leaned against the stones in the shade, waving merchants, sailors, buyers, and sellers, in and out of the city.

The sun was low in the sky and they took lodgings at an inn a few streets from the port. A placard with an image of a bull's head hung above the pitted stone lintel of a building that had to be about as old as the city itself. A mixed crowd of locals and travelers sat the tables in the common room. Ratcher led them to a pair of seats square in the middle of them.

"Good place to get our bearings," he said out of the side of his mouth. "A few outlanders, but not too many. We don't need news about the Dominion." He turned to the man next to him to flash wide smile. His neighbor, a leathery old grey-hair with paint across his pants and shoes scowled and turned the other way.

"Don't worry," Ratcher flicked his head toward the old man. "They'll come around."

Geth waved down the barman for two drinks.

"It's good to be back." Ratcher sighed, leaned back in his chair. "Even if it's only for a short while."

"I'd just as soon have stayed home."

"You don't want to see Phelan?"

That brought a wry smile to Geth's face, thinking of the little man. "Wouldn't mind that. Wouldn't be terrible to see Eora either. Even Brega, assuming she's still a half-wit."

They shared a chuckle at that.

"You know, I brought him some forest fire," Ratcher said. "Phelan, that is. Don't worry, I'll let you take credit for it. And we better drop in on Feru-Lea while we're in town as well."

"The witch?"

"Who else?"

"Just the thought makes me shiver. I still owe her, and I don't want to imagine how she'll make me pay. You owe her too, the way I remember it."

The drinks arrived and Geth took a long pull from a sweet, brown ale. Ratcher followed suit, licked foam from his lips. "It won't be so bad. She's alright, once you get to know her."

Geth eyed him sideways. "More than just business between you and that woman, seems like."

"Me?" Ratcher snorted. "But you know, it *would* be nice to have a witch on our side. We have to assume Lyanne will try to use her talents to find us. If Palladine held on to anything of yours from back in Towdric's cell, she could use it to find you anywhere in the city."

Geth sipped his ale to hide a curse. He hadn't even thought of it. How far did her magicks stretch? As far as Old Crown?

"We can't go to the Oak and Hart, can we." Geth swallowed a curse behind another pull at his drink. "We'll could bring danger down on Phelan and Eora just being there."

"I'd say—"

But an outburst from the old painter cut Ratcher short. "...that's what I have to say about the ball-scratching First. Whoreson's, to a man!"

The painter's companions—a woman with a face as lined as his, and a younger man with almost no neck—laughed heartily. Ratcher didn't miss the chance to cut in.

"Who's talking about the great and shining First Host?" He lifted his tankard. "May the sun scald their bare asses and may the cold sea pickle their balls."

No-neck lifted his drink in reply, laughed some more. But Painter muttered something about outsiders with a scowl.

"What? You're not one of those paper-toting ball-scratchers from the Lion's Den, are you?" said Ratcher.

"Me?" The old man puffed up in his seat, ran a hand over each leg to straighten his splattered trousers. "We called those bastards foe back when I wore the white. But those days are gone, I reckon."

"Gone but not forgotten." The old woman spit, heartily enough to earn Geth's appreciation.

Ratcher offered a solemn nod. "Never that."

Geth sipped from his ale, studied the trio beside them.

It was the Troubled Times the old man spoke of—a stretch of years when the realm found itself torn almost in two between the jaws of the great familae. Geth had spent most of that time outside the borders of the realm, living with the Mog. When he came back, Elius, Lyanne, and the Leyai had come out on top. The enmity between the various regions of Pellon went back centuries at least, from what he'd read in the Omnibus, to a time when dozens of petty kingdoms squabbled amongst themselves. Paellius the Great had pulled them all together long ago, but their differences hadn't been forgotten—among common folk like Painter, the familae, or the dozen hosts of the Paellian army either.

But none of that was news. Except how it related to the Games, where Palladine, Lyanne, and Elius dangled his son as bait.

"You hear what they've done now?" Geth asked. He leaned forward. "Word tell is those bastards have given Honorus of the Games to a newborn babe."

It was Painter who spit this time. "Why even hold 'em if it's going to be a slap in the face?"

Geth nodded. "Back when I was in, they said the whole point was to bring the hosts together. The way I remember it, all we did was tear the Golden City up brawling every night."

Painter grunted.

But No-neck shook his head. "If you ask me, they're long overdue. It's no secret the Affliction threw things off schedule."

"See, this is the problem," Painter said. And the old woman was already nodding. "Younger folk only care about some kind of spectacle. About turning coin."

"Not true." No-neck shook his head "I want to see those First Host toadies embarrassed as much as anyone. And the Second and the Eleventh too. That would be a sight to see."

He sipped at his drink, looking thoughtful.

"I was at the Games once, some years back," Geth said.

"The last one? Before the bad winds?"

"The one before that. A week of madness, but I loved every minute of it."

"You headed that way now?" Painter asked. He eyed the big warrior with some interest now, but it was Ratcher who answered.

"Nah, we're here to smith a few blades." He touched the apron across his chest. "Got a contract with some high-borns on the Avenue."

"How long does that take, hammering a few swords?" No-neck asked. "You might still make it."

"When does it start? Just got off a ship from Rath, I'm afraid I've lost my days."

No-neck nodded. "Well, it's Thram's-day now, so I reckon they'll be rowing the Arm in four days.

Ratcher looked to Geth, but the big warrior was already kicking back his chair to rise.

"Four days."

"Four days, you hear that?" Geth said. "We gotta get to Paellia."

He drained his ale and was already halfway up the stairs to grab their baggage when Ratcher caught him by the arm. "Easy now. Do we even have a plan?"

"You heard the old man, the hosts still hate each other. With these Games, it's gonna be a free for all. The way I see it, that's just the sort of mayhem we need."

"That doesn't sound like a plan. In fact, that sounds like the opposite of a plan, relying on the chaos of the week to somehow deliver us the child."

Geth waved Ratcher to follow, closed the door to their room once he was inside. "Look, there's a reason they only hold the Games every three years. It takes that long for everyone to recover. Remember that year Iron-top won the duels?"

"How could I forget."

"The old scratch killed three of his opponents in the process. You know how hard it is to kill a man in armor with a wooden sword?"

"Not that hard if you're Iron-top, apparently."

"And that kind of chaos, that's not just in the Games themselves. Think of the spectators! All the hosts gathered inside one city's walls on top of that. The gold-bands will have their hands full. The Firsties too."

"Sure, but you really think Palladine won't have thought of that. He'll be ready. Lyanne too. They're the ones that invited us into this, not the other way around."

"Well why the hell did we come all this way if we're not going to get my son?"

"Just think, Geth, that's all I'm saying. What if they nab us at Paellus's Gate before we ever make it inside the walls?"

Geth waved that off. "With all the fresh bodies and shiny coins flowing in for the Games, you reckon that'll happen?"

"What if Lyanne's got some witchery waiting for us?"

"Then we head straight for your friend, Feru-Lea. You said she'd help."

Ratcher sat on the edge of the bed, frowning, one hand rubbing his jaw. "Alright, it's something. We'll need horses though. And white tabards."

"We done with these aprons then?"

Ratcher raised an eyebrow. "Sounds like you've got plenty of experience wearing white anyway. I never did ask which host were you with. Sevens? Gotta be Sevens."

Geth snorted. "Sixth."

"Bloody Sixes. I should have known. That explains the tattoos."

"Speaking of which, see if you can get some more of that cover-up. We're like to get jumped on by some Seconds—"

"Or just about anyone."

"That's right, if they catch us two alone."

Ratcher patted the mattress as he rose. "Your turn to take a rest. I'll go see about those cloaks and horses."

Geth nodded. "The only thing we need after that is your witch."

CHAPTER TWELVE

T hey didn't have to search for Feru-Lea, the witch found them. She came to Geth as he closed his eyes to sleep, waiting for Ratcher. He couldn't say how long he slept, but it was long enough for the woman to enter his dreams.

She didn't speak, just looked at him with those dark, sultry eyes. He sat straight up in bed, breathed in a sharp breath. He knew what he had to do.

Filthy, reeking, bloody magicks!

The door opened to admit Ratcher before the big warrior could so much as rise. "Fera," the assassin said. "She—"

"I know." Geth swore. Out loud this time. "What did she do to us? One look from her—in a dream, no less—and my feet are itching."

"I think they call it a compulsion. We swore to help her and she's using some king of...*spell* to make sure we fulfill our oath."

"I don't like it, Ratcher. You hear me? I feel like...like I won't be able to eat or drink or sit down even, not until, well, I don't know when."

Ratcher frowned. "Me neither. And I've never felt that. But we were headed to see her anyway, weren't we?"

"Will we be safe?"

Ratcher didn't answer. They gathered up their things without speaking, saddled the horses the assassin had bought, and rode straight out into the night. Geth's brow didn't unfurrow until they'd made some miles toward the Golden City.

Feru-Lea's spell seemed to ease as they drew closer to her. On the second day, without warning, the pressure on Geth's temples lifted. The big warrior sighed like he'd just taken off his boots after a long day's hike.

Ratcher seemed to feel it too. They exchanged a meaningful look. The crumbling arch of Paellus's Gate appeared around the next bend, a long line of travelers lined up to enter the city beyond that. Among the throngs and wearing Paellian white now, the pair marched under the gates with little more than a glower from the watchmen on the walls.

Snatches of conversation drifted in and out of Geth's ears, just above the god-awful noise of the masses.

"...and I says, well..."

"...ha ha! I bet he did!"

"What's that smell?"

"Hey! Watch your elbows, man!"

"...careless ball-scratch!"

Geth shook his head. Paellia was like an over-stuffed meat pie, bursting with humanity, her stink, her fluids, the oppressive, heavy air of so many bodies. Thankfully, they weren't out on the streets long, they had a place to stay. There wouldn't have been an inn, brothel, or boarding house with so much as an empty patch of floor to sleep on, Geth reckoned.

"There it is." Ratcher pointed out Feru-Lea's candle shop amid the jostling foot traffic. The witch answered the door after only one knock, ushering them in with an urgent wave.

"Hurry!" She looked both ways up and down the street and closed the door behind them. "They're looking for you."

The same dark eyes Geth remembered from the dream flicked from him to Ratcher and back. She rested a hand on the assassin's arm, but she had a smile for Geth as well.

"I wasn't sure you would be here, Wolf of Umbel."

"I couldn't resist," Geth answered flatly.

The witch frowned. "Yes, I found you in the dream, but I couldn't have been sure in the waking world if you were halfway across the realm or sleeping in my cellar." Her brow pinched. "Let me see."

She stepped toward the big warrior, stretched her hands in front of him like she was soaking in the heat off a campfire. She raised them toward his neck, then brought them further down, paused near his belt.

"There."

Geth followed her eyes. The tip of Ethen's little sword poked out from the end of his belt pouch.

"Forest magic," Feru-Lea said. She nodded. "And strong. It probably saved your life."

"Agrem..."

The witch nodded. "Of course. Without this, Lyanne would have known as soon as you landed in Pellon."

Geth and Ratcher exchanged a look. The witch turned to the assassin next. "And you still wear the charm I gave you?"

Ratcher reached under his white tabard to display something like a piece of ivory hung from a leather cord. "Always."

Geth shook his head, swore. "If you knew the queen would be after us, why did you lure us here, practically into her lap?"

"You were already in Pellon." Feru-Lea spread her hands. "I warned Birg not to come, but he didn't listen."

She turned a stern eye on the assassin—Birg was it now?—but the man shrugged.

"I couldn't let him go alone, could I?"

Feru-Lea sat them at her table, produced a joint of cold mutton, salty Paellian cheese, olives, bread, and wine. Proper wine, even if that berry stuff from Ilia had begun to grow on Geth. He tore into the meal, feeling half-starved now that he remembered to eat. No one spoke until the meal was done.

Feru-Lea eyed Geth from across the table. "You aren't happy to see me," she said finally.

"I appreciate the plate and the roof over my head," he replied, "but I have more important business."

"Like what?"

"You don't know, with all your magicks?"

Feru-Lea made a face. "There have been many strange comings and goings lately. But I couldn't say where you fit in."

"The Honorus of the Games, the child," Geth felt this throat tighten up, start to crack. He swallowed down hard. "That's my son. Palladine and a warlock called Ceter stole him."

Feru-Lea's eyes widened. "The gods are merciful."

"The what?" Geth growled.

Ratcher rested a hand on his arm though. "Just listen, Geth."

"I summoned you as soon as I knew you were in Pellon. For your own protection. I knew Lyanne and her champion were after you."

"Oh, is that right?" Geth said. "Just looking out for some friends, eh? No favors to call in."

The witch frowned. "I do have an errand for you. And now I see that it's more important than ever that you do not fail."

"As I think I've mentioned," Geth said, "I have business of my own. And Ratcher here—or Birg or whoever—came along to help me."

"Yes, your child." Feru-Lea shook her head. "There's been much speculation about this child among the covens. This makes great sense."

"You already knew about my son?"

"The Honorus? Everybody knew. But some few of us wondered at the significance."

Geth leaned almost double over the table. "What do you know?"

"She doesn't just hate you, Lyanne. She fears you."

Geth ignored that. "My son—is he...Where is he?"

"He's alive. I believe he's inside the citadel, with the captain."

"The citadel. How do we get in?"

Geth looked to Ratcher, but the witch answered first. "You don't. Not yet anyway. You owe me, remember?"

"Uro's puckered ass, woman! You said you called us here to protect us."

"And I am protecting you. From yourself. You can't get to your son in the citadel. Do you think they won't be waiting for you?"

"I—"

Ratcher cut in. "What do you want us to do?"

Feru-Lea rested both hands flat on the table, studied the surface like she was thinking what to say first. Or which parts to tell them.

"We only have one more day before the Games start," Geth said. "We don't have time for this."

"You'll make time, Geth green-cloak."

Feru-Lea's face went hard, but somehow that only made it more lovely. *Gods all be damned!* That was part of her magicks, Geth reckoned. Her *compulsion*, Ratcher had called it.

But it wasn't going to work, not this time. "Listen woman, this whole debt thing—"

"You will complete this task or you will die." The witch met his eye. "Do you think Agrem of the Duei is the only one with the Sight?"

Geth felt his mouth open and close. Ratcher gave his arm a squeeze.

"Just hear her out."

"Fine." Geth waited. Feru-Lea breathed a sigh.

"Have you heard of the Garden?"

"The Garden?" He hadn't.

Beside him though, Ratcher leaned back in his chair, raised an eyebrow. "As in *the* Garden?"

The witch gave a nod. "The place where the Queen stows her most dangerous enemies." Geth must not have been faking it as well as he thought, for she turned to him, added, "Think of it as the opposite of the Tower of the Moon."

"They say," Ratcher put in, "that Lyanne enchants her prisoners with music and wine so that they never care to leave. If the rumors are true, she's got Ryrus's daughter there, held hostage. That's how she got the upper hand during the Troubles. They sing and dance and—"

"Don't believe everything you hear." Feru-Lea sniffed. "But there are, what the Wolf would call, 'magicks' about the place."

"And you want us to go in and steal Ryrus's daughter, take away her leverage so he can unseat Lyanne?" Geth said.

"And touch off another civil war?" Feru-Lea laughed. "Ha! Far from it."

"What then?"

She looked from Geth to Ratcher and back. "You aren't the only one to lose someone to the queen and this captain. I do indeed want you to sneak into the Garden. And I do want you to steal someone out."

"Who?"

"My mother."

CHAPTER THIRTEEN

The little room fell silent. The smell of Feru-Lea's spiced candles made Geth's stomach turn now that it was good and full. He muttered a curse and rose, loosened his collar for some air.

"Alright, supposing I do owe you. And supposing we all want the best for your poor mother, why can't this wait until after the Games? Once I have my son back safe, I'd be glad to stick it to Palladine and Lyanne, anyway I can."

"You swore you would do a favor for me," Feru-Lea answered. "When and where I asked. I have not compelled you, though I could. Do you not live up to your oaths?"

"Thram and bloody Awer."

"This errand helps us both, Geth Green-cloak. And if we set out tonight, you'll be done before the start of the Games."

Geth eyed her sideways. "The part about how it helps me, how it helps my son, did you plan on explaining that?"

Ratcher cleared his throat. "I think that's obvious, isn't it?"

"It will hurt Lyanne," Feru-Lea said. "And it will distract her. I think you know she is as much your enemy as the captain."

"That's it?"

"She's a witch too, Geth," said Ratcher. He looked to Feru-Lea. "Your mother, I mean. She has to be. It runs in the blood."

"She is a witch." Feru-Lea nodded. "A powerful one. And she holds secrets that could turn the entire Sworn Realms on end. She will know what must be done."

Geth held his tongue. He flicked a glance to the windows at the front of Feru-Lea's chandler's shop. The shutters were half-drawn, the light filtering through had faded. Night was falling. The Games would begin in less than twenty-four hours.

"You can't just charge in with the opening of the Games," the witch said, reading Geth's mind. "The rowers will come, the winners will deliver their gifts, and the wreaths will be hung. You've seen it all before. Even if it takes longer than a night to steal in and out of the Garden, you won't miss a thing."

Geth frowned. "What if they think I haven't got the message? What if they start sending me..."

He couldn't bring himself to say it. But Brega had once delivered a debtor the ring-finger of his wife in order to get his attention. He'd heard of ransomers that sent one body part after another to the family of the captured man until they collected their sum.

Geth closed his eyes to dispel the thought. He squeezed his hilt, cursed out loud. He'd sworn to Vriana to get their son back.

And every fiber of his being howled for revenge. He just didn't know if helping one witch free another would get him any closer to that end.

"We can do this, Geth." It was Ratcher who spoke. "At the very least, Lyanne will have to turn one eye toward the Garden when we're done. And we'll have a second witch on our side."

"I will go to the opening of the Games myself," Feru-Lea added. "To watch, and listen, and learn whatever I may. And although it is *you* who owes *me* at present, so important is this task that I swear I will do everything in my power to help you get your son back after."

Were those the words that sealed it? Did he really believe Feru-Lea wanted to help get Ethen back? Geth wasn't sure. There was always the chance it was some pull of her magick, something subtle, more delicate than the compulsion he'd felt earlier.

But even before he voiced his agreement, Geth knew he was decided. They needed Feru-Lea, like Ratcher said. He just wasn't sure how dearly he'd pay for her help in the end.

"I'll do it."

They laid down for a few hours of sleep before heading out. Geth rolled out his bedroll beside Ratcher's on the floor. Sometime in the middle of the night, however, a creaking noise overhead woke him.

"Is that..." He rolled over, found Ratcher's bedroll empty.

It was.

"Thram's balls."

The creaking continued, accompanied by a soft but rhythmic moaning from above.

Geth kept it to himself—for now—and they left the witch's shop, all three of them, a few hours later. Feru-Lea led them down night-quiet streets toward the port. A few drunks lolled in doorways and the odd cutpurse slithered among the shadows. No one wanted to have a try at two big men with swords at their hips though, especially with lily white on their backs.

Except other lilies.

"Ho there, boys!" A stumbling throng in white crowded the front porch of a tavern just a few blocks short of their destination. "Looks like we got us some Firsties, lads!"

Slurred laughter from puffed out chests answered, but Geth was quick to reply.

"Firsties? None of the First here, unless it's you prim bastards."

One of the drunken soldiers snickered and slapped another on the shoulder. "Told ya."

"Well, who you boys betting on, eh?" the first soldier said, a crusty old scratch with half of one ear missing. "And don't say Mylo or I swear I'll have your liver out."

"Bloody Mylo," someone spit. A few other soldiers had swung down from the porch, blocking the way. Geth rested one hand on his hilt, aimed a practiced glare at the lilies ahead, but Ratcher stepped past him.

He snorted a derisive laugh. "Looks like we got some Sloppy Sevens here. Gotta be. Outta the way, lads. You got a problem with a scratch making a little extra shine? The lady here needs to be at the port."

The half-eared soldier knuckled his brow at Feru-Lea. But that didn't mean he was done.

"Don't worry about us. But you never answered my question. I know some Seconds when I see 'em. Thieving bastards, slinking along your walls."

"So says Vorda's Own." Geth spit. He dug back in his memory, searching for names. "I bet you're under that fat shit, Feldan. Am I wrong? Is that bastard still robbing the Mog for sheep and passing 'em around for you boys to hump?"

"Fat shit!" the snickering soldier echoed. "You haven't heard? Captain Feldan's one of Vorda's own for real now, dead as dirt." That got him snickering again.

"I told you they were Sixers," another soldier said. "Bloody Sixes!"

But the tension had eased. Several of the drunken soldiers ahead turned back toward the tavern. A few others remained in the street, but none of them spared another glance for Geth or Ratcher.

All except that first loud-mouth.

"Well, I don't see why you two sonsabitches should get all the extra shine. We could escort the lady to her ship better than any one-nut ball-scratchers from the Sixth."

Geth ground his teeth, about ready to break the man's nose. But this time it was Feru-Lea who stepped in, graceful as a swan on the water.

"Dear sergeant—" Her forehead pinched just slightly, between those beautiful brows "—I'm sure you and your men hold the honors of the hosts in a place of great importance. But I assure you, a lady may have matters of great import to handle this morning as well. I shall pass now, if you please."

Geth wasn't sure what she did, but the crude bastard went all wide-eyed, mumbled an apology, and stepped back. With the wave of one hand, Feru-Lea parted the remaining soldiers neatly and swept past. Geth hurried to follow, Ratcher right behind him.

Only when they were half a block away did the big warrior turn. "If you do see some Firsties," he called, "kicked their asses for me, would ya?"

The soldiers laughed.

Geth felt his shoulders loosen as they left the men of the Seventh Host behind. "Bloody magicks." But this time he said it with an appreciative shake of the head. They reached the water of Fisherman's Port a few minutes later.

The wooden quays of Paellia's smaller, fisherman's port bustled with activity even in the predawn hours. The habits of trawlers were the same everywhere, even Geth knew that. A boat had to be on the water before the sun was up if the fishermen inside hoped to bring in a good catch.

Feru-Lea led them to a little rowboat nestled among the others, climbed in and motioned toward a pair of oars. resting at the bottom. "Take us due west, away from the city."

Geth and Ratcher exchanged looks. "I'll row first," the assassin said, "But Fera, there's nothing west—"

"Just row."

Paddles splashed and water slapped against the hull. They hadn't gone half a mile, however, before a fog seemed to rise up off the surface. Geth frowned, started to curse. Dank air swallowed the noise. Within moments, they couldn't see more than a few feet in any direction.

"Just keep rowing," Feru-Lea breathed.

"Gods all be damned," Geth muttered.

"You're wondering what's next," the witch said. She wasn't wrong. "The Garden, that's what."

"It's an island?" Ratcher asked.

"Yes. A very small island. And very well hidden."

"So, this fog..." Geth raised a hand, as if he could catch a piece of it, stuff it in a pocket. "This is the queen's doing."

"An enchantment. But not raised solely by Lyanne. No one woman—or man—could do such a thing. Not for more than a few moments."

Geth swore.

Ratcher shook his head. "Dear gods. I didn't know there were such sorceries at all."

They rowed in silence, the sound of the paddles dipping in and out of the sea strange in Geth's ears. The drip of the water, the scuff of a boot on the hull of their boat had the hairs on the back of his neck standing on end. But within a few minutes, the fog melted away.

A dark cliff wall appeared ahead, grey and black. The sky had begun to brighten with the break of day, and from its pale light, Geth made out the walls and towers of a fortress atop the low bluffs. A narrow strip of beach received them, their boat grinding to a halt.

"We're here," said the witch.

Best Geth could tell, that island couldn't have been more than a hectare of dry ground, just a knob of rock, thrust up out of the sea, like the tip of Uro's little finger. That narrow beach stretched to either side, hugging the cracks and cervices of the cliff as far as he could see. But just a little further down, a couple of skiffs had been tied to a post. A set of wooden stairs zigzagged up from there toward the fort walls.

"There," Feru-Lea said, pointing toward the steps. "Bring her down to me."

Geth frowned. "You're not coming? What about the queen's magicks?"

"You are each protected, hidden from her, by the token you carry. But Lyanne will know it the moment I step foot on her island."

"How will we find your mother then?"

"You'll know her."

Ratcher was already out and on the beach, boots tracking up sand. With any luck, the tide would rise high enough to erase their footprints. Then again, if they made it in and out as easily as Feru-Lea seemed to expect, a few tracks wouldn't matter anyway.

"I'll be waiting right here," she said.

Geth followed Ratcher. He flicked one last glance over his shoulder. The witch met his dark eye with one of her own, then pulled the hood of her cloak over her head.

Geth turned back to Ratcher. "I know what you did last night."

The assassin never halted in his climb, but there was a pause before he replied. "What do you mean?"

"With the witch. I know you went upstairs to get sideways with her. I heard you."

Ratcher wagged a finger over one shoulder but didn't turn. "No way you heard me. I move like a shadow. A shadow in the dark."

"Well, maybe I heard *her.*"

The assassin finally turned. "What can I say, I never do anything halfway."

"I'm serious, man," Geth trudged up the stairs behind him, boots creaking on weatherworn wood. "She's got a hold on you. Did you ever stop to think that about that? I'm mean, what has she got us walking into, while she waits all cozy down there in the boat?"

"I hear ya." Ratcher nodded. "But this is different."

"Different? Thram and bloody Awer..."

"She wouldn't send me into danger, that's what I'm saying. Not unless she thought I could handle it."

They'd arrived almost at the top of the steps. A gatehouse loomed above them. One bored looking guardsman leaned up under the entrance.

"Well," Geth said out of the side of his mouth. "How you plan to handle this one?"

"We're wearing white, aren't we? Just play along."

Up ahead the guardsman perked up at the sight of them. "Ho there! Wasn't expecting a delivery this morning. And who are you two anyway?"

Ratcher shook his head, pretended to wheeze a few breaths as he reached the top of the stairs. "Bloody cliff," he muttered. "Delivery though? Nothing like that. She's sent us to fetch one of those old hags."

The guardsman looked dubious. "Well, I wouldn't put it that way if I were you. Considering who we work for. And which one is she after anyway?"

Ratcher shrugged. "I asked the same question. I thought that bastard Palladine might have my hide just for opening my mouth."

That seemed to put the man at ease. Some, at least. He grimaced, offered a commiserative nod.

"He said we'll know," Geth added. "Witcheries, and what not."

"Good because If you need to talk with Lucean, you can do it—"

But Ratcher was already walking past. Geth clapped the guardsman on one arm, followed right behind him.

The sun had only just begun to peak over the waves to the east, but what lay inside the plain yellowy curtainwalls of that fort caught the big warrior's breath in his chest. A curving stone path wound gracefully among manicured bushes and flowerbeds, interspersed by fruit trees lush with produce and flowering species already buzzing with pollinators. A fountain gurgled somewhere ahead, and as they walked a wide green of perfectly sheered grass opened up to the right, a vineyard and orchard stretching for some distance off to the left. The island must have been longer than it was wide, and the opposite wall reared up some fifty paces ahead, not more. Up against it, columned galleries ran in either direction, connecting a high-roofed hall with a good dozen other edifices, two stories each, shutters brightly painted but closed still against the morning chill.

"I wouldn't mind doing a stretch in here," Geth murmured, forcing his jaw closed lest one of the guardsmen stationed atop the walls catch him gawking.

"How do you suppose we'll find her mother though?"

"Let's walk."

Even along those winding paths, it wasn't far from the gatehouse to the center of Lyanne's 'Garden.' They moved in plain sight of the lilies on the walls, but no one looked at them twice.

Among the fruit trees and flower beds, several plain-clothed men and women worked, filling baskets, pruning, digging. If not for the lethargy in their movements, Geth might not have realized these were the prisoners.

"Hey Ratch—"

But a pair of eyes on them froze Geth mid-sentence. Ratcher came to a stop right there on the path. Up ahead of them, on a cobbled expanse, the queen's fountain came into view. Sitting on the lip, eyeing them patiently, sat an old southland woman, skin as dark and aged as mahogany.

"That can't be..."

The woman rose at the sight of them, started in their direction. Instinct, or something more subtle, drew Geth up alongside her, one arm out for her to lean on.

That's nice. Help your mother.

Her lips didn't move, that voice sounded directly in his head. Geth swallowed. Beside him, Ratcher's mouth opened and closed.

"Well, perhaps it was a metaphor."

They led the old woman back the way they'd come. Geth walked stiff-backed, awaiting the cry of alarm, but none came. His eyes scanned the lilies on the walls, the shuttered windows. All were closed except one, where a man with thick dark hair watched them intently.

"Is that...?"

Geth swore.

"No time for anything now." Ratcher took the old woman's other arm. "Got to keep moving. Got to get you to your daughter, don't we, Mame?"

That earned a pat on the arm from 'Mother.'

"It's just," Geth muttered. "I thought I saw..."

They'd made it to the gatehouse. The same guardsman as before nodded as they passed, leaned up against the wall under the arch, arms folded. Arriving at the steps, Geth hoisted the old witch up into his arms like a child, carried her down ahead of Ratcher. He spared one last glance over his shoulder as they reached the sand below. Sure enough, the dark-haired man stood atop the walls, watching their exit.

"Gods all be damned," Geth said. "It *is* him."

"It's who?" Ratcher squinted back the way they'd come. His jaw dropped as his eyes found the lad.

"Gods all be damned. That's Prince Gahalus."

Chapter Fourteen

"She's imprisoned the bloody prince." Ratcher said.

But as Geth looked up and down the beach, he realized they had more immediate concerns. Feru-Lea was gone.

"Shit!"

Almost at the same time, a shout rang down from above. "Hey! Come back here!"

It was Ratcher's turn to swear. "Lyanne must have figured out we're here. Damn it all! She must have been forced to flee."

"Flee? And ditch us here?"

The assassin hurried toward the skiffs tied up a few paces off. "Get her inside. Hurry!"

If Geth needed further encouragement, a shout of alarm from above provided it. "C'mon, Mother. In you go. It's what your daughter wanted."

Once she was inside, he started pushing. The boat lurched free and he stumbled down to one knee, cursed, and rolled unceremoniously over the side and in. Ratcher jumped the gunwale last. He found the oars and started rowing.

As before, the fog swallowed them within moments, muffling the cries of the guardsmen on the walls. Soon, the only sound was the splash of the oars, the drip of seawater. And a low hum from the old woman.

"What's she doing?" Ratcher asked.

Geth reckoned he knew. "Bloody magicks."

He took a turn at the oars to keep them moving as fast as possible, even if the witch's tune hid them, like Amalia's song had done back in Umbel. If the guardsmen did launch any boats, they never caught up. The old woman didn't stop humming as they rowed into port.

Geth loosened his sword in its sheath, wondered if the queen would have men waiting on the docks. But they saw nothing suspicious as they rowed in among the other ships. Most of the fishermen were still out to sea, the port less crowded than it had been in the morning. Ratcher lashed their stolen boat up and with Geth's help, they lifted the old woman out, back onto dry land.

Geth's eyes scanned the harbor, the white-clad guardsmen on the towers, the odd gold-band walking the quays. But it was like the time Amalia had sung them right past everyone, inside Towdric's dungeon. Not a soul seemed to notice them.

"So, what now?" he said, starting the old woman away from the water, into the walking traffic and among the shops and tenements of the city.

"Back to the candle shop," Ratcher said.

Geth stepped in front to lead the way. The streets were crowded with foot-traffic, beasts of burden, hand-carts, and men and women on horseback or wagon bench. But no one tried to bar their way this time. They arrived within sight of the candle shop before long, even with the old witch in tow.

"Wait," Geth said as they drew near. He halted them down the street, steered Ratcher and their ward under the awning of a broom-peddler.

"Easy now," the broom-seller raised his hands. "I don't have anything worth stealing."

Geth ignored him. His eyes were on Feru-Lea's front door. It looked to be hanging ajar. As he watched, several wary-eyed gold-bands stepped through and outside, followed by a silver head Geth could never forget.

"Thram's balls."

Ceter. He'd almost forgot about him. He'd placed all the blame on Palladine and Lyanne, but here was the creature that had nearly killed his woman and stolen Ethen besides.

A vein on the side of Geth's head started throbbing. Every inch of him begged to charge down the street, hack the warlock to pieces. But not before demanding to know what they'd done with Ethen.

A small but firm grip on his wrist, froze his hand where it had strayed, on his hilt. The witch didn't have to speak her warning, in his head or out loud.

"You're right."

Geth breathed in and out, long and slow. He muttered a curse. Killing the bastard—if he could even manage it—would only tell Palladine and Lyanne where he was, and where he'd been. That wasn't the way to get his son back.

"Let's go," he said.

Ratcher stood in silence, rubbing his jaw. Geth could see the fear in his eyes, even if he tried to mask it. That fear had nothing to do with Ceter.

"She's fine," the big warrior said. "They'd be hauling out at least a few dead soldiers if they'd caught up with her here."

Ratcher smoothed the front of his white tabard. "She's in hiding somewhere. We'll catch up with Fera sooner or later. That's it."

Geth resisted the urge to spit. He wasn't so sure they would. They'd broken her mother out. That's all she wanted. What did a witch like Feru-Lea need with their problems anyway?

"But what do we do with the old woman now?" he wondered aloud. He wasn't sure what Feru-Lea would have wanted, but there really was only one option.

He took the witch gently by the elbow and started her back the way they'd come. "C'mon mother. We gotta' get you off the street."

Ratcher fell in stride with a frown. "Where we headed then?"

Geth kept walking and didn't look back. "To Phelan and Eora, the only friends we have left in this town."

It was going to take a good while to cross the city and reach the Oak and Heart. Geth eyed the old witch as they walked. Her mouth hung open, her gait shuffled. She looked tired. And she didn't hum anymore either.

"We need to get your mother-in-law on a wagon. She can't keep up this pace." Geth said.

"This way." Ratcher flicked his head toward a side street. "We've got to make a stop first."

The assassin led them on a winding course through Paellia's crowds until they reached a narrow door set between a cloth-ier's shop and a shoemaker. A rusty iron lock held it shut, but Ratcher picked at it with a slim tool from his belt pouch until it opened. A foul air wafted out to Geth's nose.

"Thram and bloody Awer. The Tribs? Again?"

Ratcher nodded. "Claw wasn't the only one to make use of the place."

"You think it's a good idea we take the old lady into a sewer?"

"I wouldn't be here if it wasn't necessary, would I?" The assassin shivered. "Last time I was down in the Tribs, I had to take a swim. You may have forgotten, but I haven't."

"But the woman, Ratcher? She's got to be tired. All those steps, the dark..."

"Don't worry, no one's going down but me. I just need to get some supplies." Ratcher leaned in close. "And some shine."

Geth's eyes narrowed.

"I've got a stash-house down there. We'll need to change out of these whites. Lyanne and Palladine know we snuck into the

Garden as lilies. And we're gonna' need coin to rent a cart or wagon, like you said."

Ratcher started down the stairs. Geth waited with the old witch, but the assassin didn't take long. Soon they were changing their army-issue whites for leather-trimmed fleeces, cut in the fashion of Bronland.

Geth fiddled with the cuff of his shirt. "Why Bronian? I'm already sweating."

"The gold-bands will be looking for two big bastards wearing swords. But nobody will look twice at a couple Bronians with a blade or two."

With the kind of shine Ratcher was holding, it didn't take long to convince the first passing wagon driver to make room on the bench for Mother. Walking beside her, they started off toward the Oak and Hart. It was nearing midday and traffic on the streets was all headed in one direction, north, toward the river. The Games were about to begin.

"She was wrong, you know," Geth told Ratcher as they walked. "Your witch. We should have been there."

"At the river?"

Geth nodded. "The Honorus will be there. He has to be. And with all the crowds lined up over the water, we could have snuck in and grabbed him."

"We'd need one hell of a distraction. With the river to the north, we could only come at them from the south."

"Not if we had a boat. We could—"

"C'mon, Geth. We've got a week of events. We don't need to risk everything on day one."

"Well..." Geth sighed. "Thram's purple cock."

He wasn't wrong. Geth didn't say what he was really thinking though, that Feru-Lea had duped them both. They marched in silence until the wagoner had brought them within a few blocks of Phelan and Eora's inn.

"You still think we could be bringing trouble down on the place?" Ratcher asked.

"They're tracking me, I reckon, not you. And I still have whatever magicks Agrem put on Ethen's toy sword."

Ratcher rubbed his jaw. "Do you think she can hide us? Like she did at the fisherman's port?"

Geth felt the old woman squeeze his hand. He looked down, met those rheumy old eyes. She smiled. It was a motherly gesture indeed. That was enough to decide him.

"I reckon she can."

They crossed the street toward the front door of the inn. A man with a bandaged leg almost limped into them coming the other way, but Geth just snorted a laugh. *Eora; always helping someone or other.* He held the door for Ratcher and the witch and stepped into the sparsely occupied common room behind them. He didn't see the innkeep, but there behind the counter stood Phelan, jaw about down to the surface of his bar.

Vorda's withered tits.

Geth couldn't hear the words from across the common room, but he read the little man's lips. Phelan fumbled the tankard of ale in his hand, recovered it before more than a slosh hit the counter. But he didn't come around the bar to greet them. He turned toward a serving woman, sent her in their direction instead.

It was Brega. She wended slowly past the tables until she stood in front of them. "This way," she mumbled, almost too low to hear. Her mouth hung open. A little fleck of white spittle clung to the corner of her lips. She turned without waiting and started up the stairs toward the guest rooms.

Mother watched her, shook her head, and followed. Geth and Ratcher exchanged a look, then trailed them up the steps.

Brega took them to a room and left. They seated the old witch on the bed. Ratcher pressed a flask into Geth's hands with a nod. The big warrior tucked it away inside a pocket just as Phelan came through the door.

"Dear gods!" He smashed into Geth with a hug.

Geth clutched him back fiercely. "I never thought I'd miss your skinny carcass."

"I could say the same about your hairy ass." Phelan leaned back, frowned at him from arm's length. "Uro's wrinkled sack though, Ilar leathers weren't enough? Had to go Bronian?"

"It's a long story."

Ratcher cleared his throat.

"Oh, right." Geth produced the flask, passed it over. "Speaking of Ilia, this is for you. Go on, give it a whiff at least."

Phelan chuckled. "Forest fire."

His smile vanished though as he unstoppered the liquor. Heaving a sigh, he sucked down a healthy swallow.

"Alright, I'm ready," he said. "What god-awful reason can possibly have landed you on my doorstep, dressed like a foreign bonebreaker, with an assassin in tow on top of it all."

Geth reached for the drink and took a long pull. "Where to begin?" He needed the excuse of burning liquor on his throat to mask the tremble in his voice. "Palladine and Lyanne... they've got my child."

Ratcher did Geth a solid favor, relaying the tale to Phelan for him. From the attempt on Mother, to Ceter's attack on Vriana and Ethen, right down to their arrival in Old Crown.

"And this one?" Phelan hooked a thumb toward the old witch.

"A friend of a friend," Ratcher said vaguely.

Geth snorted. "There's no point keeping it a secret." He turned to face Phelan. "Ratcher and I racked up a debt last time we were in town. With a witch. She called in the favor. The queen had this woman held prisoner, until we busted her out."

Phelan stepped toward the door, flicked the latch. "They're looking for you, aren't they." It wasn't a question.

"They were looking for us already. But she's no ordinary grandma, this one."

"Course not." Phelan muttered a curse, ran a hand through those blond locks.

"There's more, Phelan." Geth waited til the little man looked up. "They've got Prince Gahalus too."

"Gahalus? Well, that would explain why nobody's seen him."

Geth nodded. "On a nearby island. Lyanne's got it hidden by mist, but it's so close, I swear you could swim there on a good day. And it's no ordinary prison either. It's beautiful. They call it the Garden."

"Poor bastard," Phelan said.

"Wish I could have busted him out too. And everyone else for that matter, reasons be damned."

Ratcher shifted where he stood. "She's keeping more prisoners than just her son and this old witch, that's for sure."

Phelan arched an eyebrow. "I thought our dear king and queen liked to stow their enemies in the Tower of the Moon?"

"Only the lucky ones," Geth put in. "Like you and me."

Ratcher stood nodding. "Makes you ask yourself who else they're keeping. You ever wonder if that's what really became of old Iron-top? And what about the Lady Talayne, Ryrus's daughter?"

"Well, she's not in the Tower," Geth said. "I can tell you that."

Phelan reached for the forest fire but the door rattled behind him, and he whirled with a frown. "Who is it?" he said through the crack.

"It's me, you fool!" came a muffled voice. Geth smiled as Phelan unlatched the door to admit Eora.

"Geth." She hugged him almost as warmly as Phelan had. "And I see—"

The innkeep's eyes widened as they rounded Ratcher to land on the old southland woman seated on the bed behind him. Eora smoothed the front of her white apron. "Mother Oedelia," she breathed.

The old woman smiled, nothing more.

Eora stepped closer, knelt down to take her hand. She held it, eyes closed for several moments. Geth reckoned there were magicks at play, but he didn't ask what.

With a sigh, Eora rose. She laid Mother Oedelia's hand back in her own lap and turned back to Geth and the others. "Poor thing."

"Is she alright?" Geth asked. "We had to move quickly, but we tried to be mindful."

"Where did you find her?"

"The queen had her," Ratcher chimed in. "In the Garden."

"It's real?" Eora asked, "the Garden?"

The assassin nodded. "Feru-Lea sent us to break her out."

"Feru-Lea."

Eora's tone was flat. Geth didn't ask if, or how, they knew each other, but it seemed the innkeep held reservations of her own regarding the witch.

Maybe that wasn't the reaction Ratcher had expected. His chin went up. "That's right. She said the mother here could help Geth and I."

Eora blinked, she looked back toward Geth. "I guess you have some things to tell me."

The big warrior heaved a sigh. This time, he told the tale himself.

"...and that's why we're here, to find my son." He looked from Eora's face, down into his hands as he finished. Eora hugged him. Gods but it felt good not to be feared or hated sometimes.

"You've come to the right place," she said. "I'm sorry what they've done to you. Sorry and angry. I'll help, you know that. In any way I can."

"I know. Seems like you're always helping me, but never the other way around."

"You don't need to worry about that, Geth. What you need is a plan."

The gods can be kind. Sometimes. Before anything else, Eora and Phelan disappeared downstairs to fetch a hot meal. There was magick in her stew, that crusty bread. Geth swore it. Or there was no such thing as magick at all.

When he had sopped up every last drop, Eora settled on the edge of the bed beside the witch Oedelia, looking down at Geth where he'd settled with Ratcher and Phelan on the floor.

"So, what we know is this," she said. "Palladine and Lyanne will have the baby at the Games each day." A few wisps had come loose out of her braid, but her eyes flicked from one face to the other, fierce and bright.

"He's the Honorus," Geth replied. "He has to be there."

"And that was the point of the note they sent to Umbel. They've told you where to come and meet them. And that's where they plan to catch you."

"So don't go," Phelan said. "We'll nab the kid from the Lion's Den. Late at night maybe, whenever we see a chance."

Geth frowned. "Wherever we do it, we'll need a distraction. There will be thousands of people watching each of the events. I gotta' believe there's an opportunity there if we can think it up."

"Sure, but half the spectators will be lilies."

"Lilies that hate each other."

Ratcher perked up. "He's got a point. We could use that to our advantage, given some proper planning."

"What event is being held tomorrow?" Geth asked. "I don't want to waste any time."

"Let's not be hasty," Eora said. "We need time to think things through. No sense poking the lion if we haven't charted a way out."

"The Games are only seven days long. What happens when they end? What happens if we haven't got my son back by then?"

"Geth—" the innkeep started, but the big warrior cut her off.

"We don't have time."

"Well—" This time it was Phelan, but Geth spoke right over him too.

"What event are the holding tomorrow, damn it? Because whatever it is, I need to be there."

Phelan looked from Ratcher to Eora and finally back to Geth.

"It's the duels."

CHAPTER FIFTEEN

P helan left to scout the set-up for the duels. Where would it be held? Where would the dignitaries like the Honorus be seated? Geth paced the room like a caged animal, but thankfully the little man was back with the answers before nightfall.

"It's going to be right there in front of the Leonine Gates," he said. A few chairs had been brought in and Geth, Ratcher, Eora, and even old Oedelia watched the little man from their seats. "A head table of sorts has been set up on a raised platform under the center archway into the citadel. They've got a cradle there already."

Geth pulled at his mustache. "I reckon the lot with the shine will be up on the ramparts for a better view."

"That's right. But they've built a raised surface for the actual fighting space as well. About waist high, just tall enough to give everyone else a better view from the ground."

"And the fighters? Where will they be before each duel? They put up some tents or something?'

Phelan nodded. "Right up against the wall, to either side. That way they don't obstruct anyone's view."

Geth looked from face to face. Could a swordsman, an assassin, a thief-turned-innkeep, and a healer contest an enemy with the weight of an entire realm behind them? They had to try.

He considered the battleground. His son would be right there, at the center of things, beside the king and queen. Palladine would be keeping watch close by, he was sure. Not to mention the usual retinue of lilies and watchmen that could be expected to protect the lords of the realm.

"A bloody brigade," he muttered under his breath.

"What's that?" Phelan frowned.

"We've got to create a distraction."

"No kidding."

"If we can get Palladine, Lyanne, and all their muscle looking in one direction, we can sneak in from the other and get Ethen back."

"I'm all for taking risks," Phelan said, "but—"

Eora cut him off. "We can do it. With Mother's help, I can get us right up to the platform."

Geth reckoned it was that singing spell she was counting on, but Ratcher answered before he could say as much.

"I can go with the women, for protection, while you two—" he looked from Geth to Phelan and back—"well, while you two do whatever it is you plan to do."

"We'd better have a ship waiting as well," Eora said. "I can't hide you for long at the inn."

Geth nodded, but Phelan rose from his seat, finger raised. "Hold on now. How are we supposed to create a distraction big enough to swipe the kid from right under the nose of a witch and a decorated war-captain?"

"How did you switch the dice right under the nose of the other gamblers all those times?" said Geth.

"Switch dice? I wouldn't know anything about that. But if I *did* want to get everyone's attention, there's one sure way to do it."

Eora folded her arms, eyed him sideways. "Pray tell, how is that?"

"Raise the stakes."

Maybe it was crazy. Maybe it was all driven by the anger that had been smoldering inside Geth since...well, forever. But he had an idea. And no one could say it wouldn't catch Palladine's eye.

He laid out his plan as his friends listened. "Everyone will be looking at me," Geth said when he was done. "They won't be able to resist."

Phelan had been silent through much of the discussion, but Geth knew the objections were coming. Eora and Ratcher were willing to give it a try at least. The little man waited until the others had left to prepare sleeping arrangements before speaking his mind.

"You really think this is going to work?"

The big warrior sat on the edge of the bed. He pulled his boots off with a sigh. "Eora and Ratcher aren't trying to talk me out of it."

Phelan shook his head. "That's because they don't understand the risks. They don't know your history like I do."

"If you're scared, you can stay back, Phelan. I'm not forcing you to help."

"Vorda's saggy tits, man, that's not what I'm saying! How do you even plan to get up there? You think you can just march in wearing white and that's that?"

"I'll sneak in among the Sixes."

"The Sixth Host?" Phelan swore some more. "You're crazy, you know that?"

"Well, I won't last five minutes pretending to be Fourth or Fifth."

"They'll recognize you! And me too, probably. Half those bastards were lifers, even back when we were in."

"Sure, but most of them will be worm food by now. That's why the call them the *Bloody* Sixes, Phelan."

The little man rolled his eyes. "No shit. But what about Urian? Awer himself couldn't kill that old prick, and I reckon it's him that'll be closest to the duels."

"The Hammer," Geth spit. "Hard and cold, the bastard."

"You didn't leave him on the best of term, did you? If no one else remembers us, he most definitely will."

"I'm counting on it."

Geth left him with that. He wandered downstairs in search of Eora. Her voice echoed out of a laundry room where he found her directing Ratcher around, the big assassin's arms piled high with bedding.

"You'll two will have to fit in one room," she was saying. "Mother can have her own, of course."

"Of course," Ratcher said. The pair of them turned at Geth's entrance.

"While we're talking, what's all this 'Mother' business anyway?" he said.

"Oedelia?" Eora nodded. "She's a great woman, even if time has taken its toll. She helped plenty of us along the way, did her best to steer us in the direction of Neyna's compassion. We appreciate her for that."

"We?" Geth raised an eyebrow. "You mean the local garrison of witches?"

"Witches, sorcerers, magi—they're all just names. But yes, we all share certain...talents. Mother Oedelia, she's about the oldest...*practitioner*, shall we call it, I've ever met. The wisest, the shrewdest. And the kindest."

Ratcher listened with a frown. "Why would Feru-Lea want to break her out?"

"Why wouldn't she?" Eora looked from the assassin to Geth and back. "But why would she take the risk? That's the question to ask."

Geth could think of one answer.

Maybe Ratcher could too. He licked his lips, turning upstairs without another word. He waited until he heard footfalls reach the top step.

"I don't trust Feru-Lea," he told Eora, voice held low. "She's got a hold on Ratcher, if you understand my meaning."

"She wasn't wrong to free Mother."

"You questioned why she'd take the risk though. Isn't it obvious? There's no risk at all if you send someone else to do your dirty work."

Eora shook her head. "That's not true. Lyanne will figure out it was her. She's the only one capable of pulling it off. The only one left, that is."

"So, what do we do with her? The Mother, I mean."

Eora went silent for a moment, thinking. "Tell me about the Garden," she said finally.

Geth relayed all he'd seen, from the concealing mist, to the groves and fountain, to the sight of Prince Gahalus. Eora listened, eyes narrowed the whole while. When Geth was done, she nodded slowly.

"I think I have an idea what Feru-Lea's after. I don't think she's working against you, although you're right; she could judge it worth risking your lives."

"That's what I was afraid of." Geth muttered a curse. "Well, what does it mean?"

"It means she's finally chosen a side."

Eora watched Geth expectantly, but the big warrior just looked back at her.

The innkeep huffed impatiently. "Haven't you ever asked yourself how Feru-Lea was able to operate on Lyanne's front doorstep with impunity?"

"I didn't even know who she was until a few months ago."

"She's been careful to remain neutral all these years, that's how. Lyanne's first order of business once she'd hoisted Elius onto the throne was to destroy anyone who might challenge her."

"Challenge her magicks, you mean."

Eora nodded. "But Feru-Lea was somehow able to convince the Queen she didn't pose a threat to the throne. Even though she wields great power."

"Not sure I like where this is going," Geth said.

"That's right. It's not hard to wonder if she bought her freedom in exchange for betraying the others. Like Mother Oedelia, for instance."

Geth couldn't help but glance toward the stairs where Ratcher had disappeared. How much of this did the assassin know? And how firm was her hold on him?

"You think Lyanne's got her now?" he asked.

"It's possible. But I think it more likely she ran at the first hint of danger. As I said, Lyanne will know the break-out was her doing."

Geth heaved a sigh. "I just hope she doesn't get my friend killed."

If Eora was about to say anything, the sound of footsteps and Ratcher's return cut her short. "Get who killed?" he asked.

"Me and Phelan," Geth said quickly. "See, the reason I came down here wasn't to help with the linens, truth be told. I need something from Eora."

The innkeep gave a soft snort. "Of course you do. But I said I'd help, and I meant it."

"Good, because a woman with your...*talents* is about the only person who could help me."

Ratcher raised an eyebrow, but Eora didn't flinch. "Well? Say it."

"I need you to brew me a poison."

All was ready in time to start out a few hours after dawn. They joined the throngs marching east toward Cistern Plaza; three soldiers in Paellian white, a young local woman, and an old southlander. The duels would begin an hour before midday.

"You know the rules," Phelan said as they walked, more to the others than to Geth. "Three touches, or until one man can't rise. There's going to be a bracket posted, but everyone's betting on some scratch call Mylo."

"Which host is he with?" Geth asked. "Fourth? Eighth?"

Phelan grimaced. "First."

"Bright white bastards."

Ratcher chuckled behind him.

Eora watched Geth with a frown though, leading Mother Oedelia by the hand as they wended toward Cistern Plaza. "Why does everyone hate the First anyway?" she asked.

"Everyone doesn't hate the first," Geth said.

Phelan snorted. "Just about."

"Well?" Eora asked.

"Because they're a bunch of ink-fingered parchment-scratchers, that's why." Geth looked to Phelan but the little man left him to it. "You already know there's plenty of mistrust between the hosts after the way things went down during the Troubles. But no one hates the First more than the Sixth and the Seventh."

"Because they never have to fight?" Eora asked.

Geth nodded. "You spent some years in the Lows, you know how it is. Bandits, gangs, Mog raiders. The peace doesn't keep itself, if there ever was any peace. There's always some unsavory job needs getting done. And it seems like the orders always come down from those sonsabitches in the citadel, sending some unlucky file from the Seventh or Sixth out to get bloody."

"Bloody Sixes." Phelan spit.

"And you think this old rivalry will be enough?" Eora didn't look convinced.

"It runs a lot deeper than what you'd call a 'rivalry.'"

"'Feud' maybe?" Phelan offered.

"Or just say it plain," said Geth. "They hate each other. Either way, Phelan says this Mylo scratch from the First Host is set to duel some bastard from the Sixth in the second round of bouts. There's sure to be problems. It's perfect."

The crowd grew thicker as they neared the citadel and Cistern Plaza. The mood was festive, the shouts friendly, the songs lively. Geth rested one hand on his belt pouch out of habit, the other on his sword hilt. Eora and Mother Oedelia moved at the center of the three men in white, just in case.

Lilies in twos and threes dotted the throng. On this occasion, most wore some insignia to denote his or her host, usually an armband. Gold, of course for the Twelfth, the city watch. Three dark hash-marks on white for the Third. All blue for the Eleventh, the navy. Black for the Seventh, headquartered in Vordae, in the Lows. Red for the Bloody Sixes, their neighbors. Soldiers in every color of armband eyed everyone else sideways. But for now, they kept their weapons at their belts.

"This is gonna be a shit-storm," Phelan muttered as they marched.

"Aren't the Games like this every time?" Geth snorted. "Does nothing to foster brotherhood, or whatever it's supposed to be about. Gods only know why they still hold 'em."

"Tradition?" Ratcher offered.

"Coin," Phelan corrected.

Both of them were right. For all the brawls that could be expected, the excitement, the pageantry, was infectious. The scent of fresh-baked bread-twists and sweet wine filled Geth's nose as local vendors shifted their wares. Children rode parents' shoulders. Gamblers and bet-takers argued over odds in doorways and under awnings along the way.

A little voice in Geth's head wondered what *his* odds were. Would he survive? Would he be holding his little son against his heart again in a few hours? A pain burned in his chest thinking of it. He'd get the boy back, he swore it. If he had to burn the entire citadel to the ground.

The sound of horns echoed over the chatter of the crowds. Rounding one last corner, the great, wide plaza with its lake-like cistern at the center opened up before them. The sun glistened off the water, gleamed dully on black basalt statues of men and strange beast, splayed out on islands or rearing up from the surface itself.

"What now?" Eora asked, shouting to be heard above the din.

Geth pointed toward the three arches of the Leonine Gate, the main entrance to the citadel and the Lion's Den, the palace, behind it and above. "He'll be under there. Be ready."

"How will we know when to move?"

Geth looked from the innkeep to Ratcher and back. "You'll know."

With a flick of the head for Phelan, he started off on a wide circle of the plaza, the little man in tow. They passed locals and outlanders of every description. Some had climbed up on rooftops surrounding the court to get a better view. Others crowded balconies. Shopkeepers stood in doorways, offering passersby the chance to watch from second or third story windows for a fee. Street urchins begged for coin or bread. Pickpockets slunk through the crowd as always, invisible if you didn't know what to look for.

"So, Eora's supposed to have a boat waiting at the river marina after this?" Phelan asked.

Geth nodded. "She sent one of her people ahead to hold it for us. The cook, that scratch with the lisp."

The closer they moved toward the fighting stage, the seedier things got. Laborers, laundresses, craftsmen and housewives gave way to knots of rough looking men and troops of soldiers in white. Sliding a ring of cloth up to his bicep, Geth put on a gold armband, compliments of Ratcher. City watchmen were about the only folks who could move unmolested between the various knots of lilies. And even then, only with caution.

"Gold-tooth bastards," a woman with the blue band of the eleventh sneered as they passed.

"Watch it," Geth growled, but kept moving.

Up ahead, he could see the bracket Phelan had mentioned, a great wooden board with a tree-like design displaying the line-up of coming bouts. One line of script read 'We Honor the Gods' at the top, above moveable round plaques pegged in place accordingly. There were painted with slash-marks in the various colors of each host. There was no point listing anything more; even in the Golden City, only half the populace could read more than a few words.

They moved deeper among the bands of lilies. Phelan flicked a glance over his shoulder, reached forward to tap at Geth's gold band. "It's time."

The big warrior slid it off, stuffed it into a pocket. Phelan passed him a replacement, little more than a scrap of red cloth.

Geth glanced both ways, moved along several steps before slipping it on.

"Swore I'd never wear this damned rag again," Phelan cursed. "I must really love you."

"I'd never ask you to do it for me," the big warrior told him. "I'm not worth the trouble. We're doing it for my son."

A bout was getting set to begin up on the fighting stage, and a deafening cheer went up as the arbitrator bent under the stretched rope enclosing the space. He straightened, raised one hand overhead, three fingers up. Circling in each direction so all could see, he waved his hands. He waited for a cheer to rise and fall, then raised both hands together, five fingers displayed on each.

"Third Host against Tenth," Geth said. "For anyone too drunk to read the board, I guess. But hey, what do you suppose the bastard does when someone's dueling the Eleventh?"

Phelan chuckled. "He uses ten fingers," he said, "and then he flashes his cock."

They'd arrived among the Sixes, a motley band of several dozen white-clad soldiers arrayed to the south of the stage. Beyond the fighting platform, the head table stood, shaded by gold and white awnings, overshadowed by the high arch of the Leonine Gate. To either side, against the walls, tents had been raised.

"That's where the fighters prepare before each duel," Phelan said.

But Geth was hardly listening. The king was already seated on his dais, Lyanne right beside him, the pair chatting idly with a young man that had to be their son and heir, Eachus, Gahalus's older brother. Palladine was there as well, standing at the top of the stairs leading up. Geth felt a surge of white-hot rage fill his chest.

"Not yet," he told himself. "Not yet, not yet..."

He wanted to charge up there, hack limps apart until he had his thumbs in the bastard's eye-sockets. But then it would all be for naught. As they moved closer, he saw what he'd come for. Between Elius and Lyanne, almost too low to make out, a bassinette rested, gently rocked by a serving woman sitting behind it.

"Ethen—"

A horn sounded, followed by a cheer that rumbled the pavers under Geth's feet. Phelan pushed until they were at the back of the men of the Sixth, a cursing, shouting mass of about the dirtiest sonsabitches ever to wear white.

"It's starting," the little man said.

Geth looked up in time to see the two fighters, fitted with close-faced helms and armed with small round bucklers, crash together with wooden swords. The crowd roared. It'd started alright.

CHAPTER SIXTEEN

They'd pushed themselves up to within a dozen yards of the fighting stage. That was as close as Geth could get. Lilies of the Tenth and Third crowded right beneath the duel, separated by gold-bands but already spitting insults back and forth. Geth turned his eyes back to the flashing wooden swords on the stage. The champion of the Tenth landed the first touch and someone hurled a cup of wine overhead, splattering spectators and contestants alike.

Geth found himself clapping along with the men beside him. The fighter from the Third had failed to raise his buckler in time, receiving a whack across the cheek-guard of his helm for his troubles. The arbitrator leapt between them before the champion from the Tenth could get in a cheap strike. He turned to make sure both fighters were ready before stepping back out of the way.

Hickory wasters clattered against one another and the fighting resumed. Geth remembered training for such duels himself. Any man deemed worthy to represent his host was one hell of a swordsman; strong, experienced, technical. But it was endurance and speed—especially with that buckler—that won most matches.

As Geth watched, the scratch from the Tenth snuck in another touch. This one came in *under* the buckler, a whack on the top of the thigh. The crowd cheered and cursed. The sneaky bastard managed to get a second, cheap blow in across the forearm of his opponent before the arbitrator could separate them.

Spectators cursed or heckled the contestants.

"You better get moving," Geth told Phelan through the side of his mouth. "This duel's almost over."

The little man turned and disappeared into the crowd, headed in the direction of the tents beside the citadel wall.

Geth forced his hand away from his hilt and mouthed a prayer. "This better work," he muttered. He turned his eyes back up to the duelers, separated to opposite corners in the wake of the extra strike the champion of the Tenth had snuck in. A runner was sent up to King Elius himself, the final judge. When the lad returned to relay the king's ruling, the arbitrator pointed to one corner, raised two fingers, then pointed to the other and raised one.

"What?" some cried.

"That's right!" others hollered.

In keeping with the rules, Elius had penalized the Tenth by awarding the champion of the Third a touch.

Not that a king could always be counted on to make a fair ruling. Many a cheat had been known to go unpunished. Sometimes a duel was fixed by an extra touch being given 'in error.' But such were the Games.

The champion of the Tenth didn't seem to mind the penalty either. His tactic was simple by Geth's reckoning; injure the opponent if he could and win that much easier with a final touch on the next exchange.

And by Geth's estimation, the Tenth was, indeed, about to clinch the win. The way the fighter from the Third rubbed at his sword-arm, the gambit seemed likely to work. Geth blew out a steadying breath. This would be over soon.

It wasn't. Maybe it was indignation, but the champion from the Third somehow rose to the occasion. Wasters clacked back and forth, bucklers absorbed blows, elbows and fists flashed when the chance arose.

But neither fighter managed a touch. At one point, the champion of the Third charged his opponent with such force, the pair of them went down with the contact, wooden surface of the fighting stage bouncing with the impact, helmets jarred sideways. The crowd shouted for all they had, worked to a froth, just the way Geth wanted them.

When the two men finally rose—the arbitrator between them—the hang of their shoulders and the heave of their chests told Geth this match couldn't last much longer. The duelers were exhausted. He edged back out of the crowd, toward the citadel wall.

He didn't see how it ended, but by the jeers of the men nearby, he could tell it was the Tenth that had pulled it out in the end. The arbitrator raised the winner's hand and the pair ducked under the rope to exit that stage. The loser had to be carried out.

Spectators and stewards began preparing for the next bout. The Sixes to either side of Geth displaced the men of the Third to crowd close to the fighting surface along the south edge. Lilies from the First moved in to occupy the north. Gold-bands filled the space in between to keep them apart.

But Geth moved in the other direction, toward the row of tents set up to the south of the Leonine Gate, up against the rampart. A few other Sixes milled about outside one of them, but with that red armband, no one paid Geth any mind. He slunk around to one side, away from the flap, leaning close to the canvas to have a listen. A familiar voice reached his ear.

"...this is it, man. Get yourself together."

"I don't know." A pause. "Ah! Damn, that hurts!"

"What? What is it? Your stomach?"

"Ah!"

"Gods all be damned, get up! Awer's twisted balls! Did you just shit yourself?"

That was Geth's cue. Puncturing the canvas carefully with one of Ratcher's knives, he cut downward to create a makeshift entry into the tent. He ducked inside, across from the two men who'd been talking. The first lay on the floor, moaning. The second stood over him, but turned at the sound of Geth's arrival.

"What the.."

Geth raised both hands before the old man could reach for his blade. "Not here for trouble, Captain."

The old man blinked. "You." He shook his bald, sun-spotted head. "Not dead, eh? What are the odds?"

"A lot better than this bastard winning today for the Sixth."

Geth flicked his chin at the man on the floor. That one had curled up in a ball. Judging by the horrid smell, Geth was pretty sure he'd shit himself indeed.

"Well, what do you want? I should have you charged with desertion and hanged. But even a dumb half-breed can see I've got bigger concerns on my hands."

Geth bared his teeth in something like a smile. "That's why I'm here. To save the day for a poor downtrodden captain and the bloody bastards in his charge."

"Are you cra—" The old soldier halted mid-sentence. "Gods all be damned, it's you alright. *You* did this."

"What's the use pointing fingers?"

"Listen, Half-breed, I'll be damned if—"

The tent flap opened, and for the second time the captain cut himself short. A messenger-boy peeked his head in. "Captain, its time."

"Damn it all to hell!"

The boy beat a hasty retreat.

But Geth was already reaching for the helm that rested on a table to one side. "Help me get into his armor," he said.

"What the hell is this all about, huh? I knew you had a chip on your shoulder, Half-breed. But I didn't have you down for a snake."

"Snake? Because I break the rules and play for keeps? It's you that taught me that. Or didn't teach me different anyway."

"You knew how to break rules before you ever slid into a red armband."\

"Maybe. But what's this is all about? Well, that part you'll appreciate."

"Awer's nuts, say it, Half-breed."

"It's about revenge, Urian. So don't deny me. Revenge against a certain bright-white from the First."

Geth had never wanted to be a champion, not for the Paellian army anyway. But walking through the crowd with Urian at his back again recalled a time when he almost was. Through the tunnel-like vision of his helmet, the faces of cheering warriors of the Sixth flashed by on either side. The air shook with cheers and curses. Wearing the armor of the real champion, the men of the Sixth Host shouted and clapped his back all the way to the stage.

"I hope you haven't forgot how to swing a sword," Urian said as they reached the fighting platform.

"I've been keeping one close by."

Urian muttered a curse. "This Mylo scratch is gonna' eat you alive."

"Don't worry, Captain. I'll do the Sixth proud. I'm prepared to do anything."

"Just keep an eye on his feet. He's a stringy bastard. He'll try a sweep if he can. And for the love of the gods, keep your left arm up!"

Geth nodded, climbed up to the fighting stage and under the rope. Wood flexed beneath his weight. Across from him, Mylo, champion of the First, swung his wooden blade in an intricate pattern, drawing scattered applause from the spectators, jeers from the Sixes. Geth would have spit if his helmet allowed it. Glaring at the bastard while he rolled out his shoulders and neck would have to suffice.

Soldiers hooted down beside Urian, but others looked from one to another. "Is that Barand?"

Hearing that, Geth turned back to face his one-time trainer. "Oh, by the way, no need to worry about our friend in the tent. He'll be fine in a few hours."

Urian cursed some more. "Just kick that peacock's ass, Half-breed. And watch his feet!"

In the center of the fighting space, the arbitrator had his hands up, signaling with his fingers for anyone daft enough not to know who was dueling already. Geth adjusted the borrowed armor he wore, the knee-high leg greaves, the wooden sword in his grasp. He stole a glance at the raised dais where Elius and Lyanne sat in their padded chairs, shaded by awnings and attended by servants. There between them, a kneeling woman rocked little Ethen in his cradle, hidden in blankets.

Could he somehow know his father was near, that he'd come for him? Did he cry? Geth wondered if he was close enough to hear it if he did.

"My boy," he mouthed. Emotions rose in his chest, and he sucked in a steadying breath. He forced his eyes from that little cradle to the edge of the dais. Standing there at attention, bald head gleaming almost as bright as his cuirass, was Palladine.

"Evil, gods-damned, bastard son of a..."

Geth forced himself to face that Firstie bastard Mylo ahead of him, channeling his rage to the fight at hand. The crowd hooted and clapped. Elius leaned forward in his chair on that dais. The arbitrator motioned the two fighters to come forward, touch blades. Geth could hear his heart pumping in his ears. No sooner had their wooden blades clacked than he charged.

Wooden swords clattered one another, clanked off iron bucklers, jarred arms and shoulders as two true masters exchanged blows. Geth came at his enemy with a strength fueled by hate, by desperation, and with a skill honed by years of every kind of combat.

But Mylo was equal to it. His sword and buckler matched the blows that came at him. As if by agreement, Geth and his opponent broke contact, circled, considered one another. The crowd signaled their appreciation with a hearty round of applause.

Across the fighting platform, that fool Mylo twirled his waster in his hand and raised his buckler sideways, like a discus. The men of the First cheered.

"Sonofabitch really is a bloody peacock." Geth shook his head. "C'mon, Brightie, time to get your feathers plucked!"

Mylo reacted smoothly to Geth's attack. A straight thrust from the big warrior clanked off his buckler, a slash clattered away off his wooden sword. He was a limby bastard indeed, just as Urian had warned, those long arms impossible to breach.

And quick on his feet. He danced and circled, sword arm whirling, buckler up high. The men of the First fairly climbed on top of one another, hooting and shouting, jeering a lowly opponent from the lowest part of the realm.

Mylo's buckler deflected a slash and a thrust and Geth stepped back. The two fighters separated again, circling warily. This wasn't going to plan.

"Thram's purple cock."

He needed to put this bastard down and have done. This wasn't the fight that was going to get him closer to rescuing his son. This was only part of the plan. And it wasn't going to work if he let it drag on. Especially the way it was going so far.

"Gods, I'm a fool."

Had he really expected it to be so easy? Did he really think he could just show up and thrash some of the best swordsmen in all of Wide Eria? Did he—

Mylo came at him before he could finish the thought. A high slash from left to right met his buckler, followed by an arcing chop from overhead. But that was just a distraction. Geth's eye caught the movement of Mylo's foot too late. A low sweep of the leg tripped him up, sent him windmilling backwards into the ropes. With both arms out, the bastard's wooden blade met no obstruction as it thrust forward to jab Geth's middle.

"Damn!"

The arbitrator tried to step in, but with Geth up against the rope, Mylo managed a second thrust, this one quite a bit lower.

"Sonofabitch!"

It missed his cherries, but the jab struck hard into the big warrior's upper thigh. With a shout, the arbitrator finally separated the pair. He didn't miss the extra blow either. His boy was sent up to Elius for a ruling.

But the prim bastard threw up his hands, tapped the side of his eye.

"What? Didn't see it?" Geth mouthed. "Thram and bloody Awer!"

The crowd clapped or hissed and the two fighters squared up again.

"I told you to watch his feet!" Urian shouted from down below. At the old captain's back, the men of the Sixth howled for blood. They were a motley band already, and angered as they were, looked ready for some real mischief after the king's ruling.

But that's what Geth was after. Mylo had played right into his hands.

Still, he couldn't let this fight go on forever. He circled the enemy, eyes burning holes into him, or trying to. Mylo's sword flashed in those absurd twirls, his feet bouncing on their wooden stage. That spawned an idea—that and the calls for blood echoing down below. This man was a fencer, champion at that. But Geth, he was a killer.

Skipping forward to end it there, Geth raised his sword high. Mylo tracked the motion, braced for the blow, but Geth jumped hard in place where he stood, sending a wobble down the wood, like Cald had done to him an age ago, fighting off the log. It didn't have the same effect on a wide, flat surface, but it upset Mylo's balance enough to allow Geth to press. He hacked and swung and never let up. Mylo parried, backpedaled furiously, until it was the Firstie against the rope. A final swing smashed through his waster, to clang hollowly off his helmet.

The Bloody Sixes went bloody mad.

Wine cups flew. An ear-ringing ruckus shook the plaza. Geth riled them up even more with the pump of his fist. The arbitrator signaled one touch a piece.

Geth flicked a glance to the dais again, to his son's cradle. He needed to end this soon. But as he squared up with Mylo yet again—still two touches away for either man to win—he realized he could only lose. To win would simply take too much time, and tire him out in the process, if he could even manage it.

As if to emphasis the fact, Mylo rushed in with a series of cuts, sneaking in a second touch with a blow that skipped off the top of Geth's buckler and just barely rang off the pauldron protecting his shoulder.

"Shit!"

The bright-whites behind Mylo jeered Geth for all they were worth. "You're no match, filthy bastard!

"Slink back over the hills with the rest of the good-for-nothings!"

The arbitrator signaled the score: two touches to one.

You're a killer, Geth told himself. *You're a real warrior. This is working!*

Whether or not he was wasting time, Geth realized he *wanted* to win this duel. Nothing would infuriate the First more. And that would certainly get Palladine's attention.

The way to win became suddenly obvious; that buckler. Geth cursed himself. He'd told himself the buckler was key before the duel had even begun, and just as soon he'd forgotten. Mylo was too quick with the left arm that held that shield. But how quick was he with his right?

The arbitrator had stepped out from between the two contestants and before Mylo could give his sword another frivolous twirl, Geth flung his own buckler right at his face. The move stunned his opponent, but that wasn't the point. With the toss of his waster from right hand to left, Geth changed the point of attack to come at Mylo from his sword-side.

He gave it everything he had. He had no choice, he had nothing to defend his right. Wood clacked against wood. Mylo circled, tried to position himself so he could use his buckler as a weapon, but Geth kept up the press. He swung with all his strength, knocked Mylo sideways, and thrust home with a jab that might have broken ribs even under that armor.

"Ahhh!" Mylo cried.

Geth didn't let up. The arbitrator tried to step in, but Geth threw him aside to crack Mylo yet again, this time across the side of the helm, laying him out flat.

That did it. The men of the First howled and went for their swords. Something thrown from down below whizzed past Geth's head. Gold-bands wrestled with the men right below the fighting stage, but more Firsties were already charging in that direction.

Geth turned toward the raised dais just a few dozen feet away, stripped off his helmet, and hurled it at the pompous lot of them.

"Palladine!" he screamed. "Palladine! I'm here! This ends now, Palladine!"

No one had seen that coming. No one except the captain himself.

Perhaps it was the way Geth had switched hands to fight with his left, or perhaps it was something else. But the bastard was already down off the dais and charging before Geth howled his challenge. His sword flashed in his hand.

He wasn't the only bright-white on the charge either. Down below, Firsties cursed, pushing through the thin rank of gold-bands trying to hold them back. One of them broke free, then another, climbed on stage, steel flashing.

But the Bloody Sixes didn't let Geth down. From behind him, they gained the stage as well, surging past him like a wave up the beach. Swords met one another as they crashed into their opposites. Steel rang off steel.

It was chaos. Geth looked to the dais. Elius and Lyanne were gone, so too most of their servants and even the cradle itself. But the woman who'd been rocking it still knelt, eyes wide, shaking in place, hands on her head.

Had they done it? Did they have him?

Geth couldn't think on it. Palladine was nearly there, a half dozen gold-bands pushing a way through for him, hauling fighters off the fighting stage. Geth was alone again up there as fighters from both hosts made their retreat lest they end up in the dungeons. As Palladine slid under the rope a few paces away, Geth looked down at the practice sword in his hand and realized a gaping hole in his plan.

"Thram's balls."

"You're mine!" Palladine screamed.

But a bump against Geth's ankle turned his eye downward.

"Take it!" Urian cried.

The pommel of a naked sword rested beside Geth's foot, three feet of gleaming steel eager to do the work it had been forged to do.

CHAPTER SEVENTEEN

Palladine tried to rush before Geth could arm himself, but the big warrior dove under the swing, snatched up Urian's blade, rolled, and came to his feet, sword in hand. The captain was on him with another ferocious cut before he could think, followed by two more, low then high.

Geth felt the shock up his arm as he deflected those strikes. Apparently any plan to imprison or torture him had gone by the wayside. Palladine wanted blood.

"Come and get it!" Geth told him.

Swords clashed again, the two men locked in contest surrounded by a riotous mass of brawling lilies and watchmen. Up on that platform, they smashed together and apart like a pair of walruses on a scrap of rock, surrounded by a stormy sea. A contest worthy of song raged on the planks, but with so much chaos all throughout Cistern Plaza, who even saw it?

No one except the gods.

Palladine cursed. Geth roared in fury and desperation. He was going to have his revenge. Eora and Ratcher may have had

Ethen, but he wasn't leaving until Palladine could never haunt them again. His anger burned as hot as ever, matched only by the merciless hatred in the cold blue eyes of his enemy.

"You thought you could get away with it?" Palladine hissed. "You think you're above the law, above the king and queen of Pellon? You, the lowest, meanest, basest stray?"

Geth swung for him. Steel shrieked against steel as his blade slid down the length of the captain's sword and off again. They pulled apart, momentum sending them past one another to regroup at opposite ends.

"You're the low one, you sonofabitch! A *child*? My boy will have your dried up balls in a baby-rattle when this is done!"

"You'll have to find him first!"

What the hell did *that* mean?

Palladine's mouth twisted into a grin. "That's right. Did you think I'd really bring your child here, where you'd surely strike? Only a madman would put a baby in harm's way."

Geth felt his stomach drop.

But the cradle? He swore he'd seen a little foot in there among the blankets. Had they slipped him away? Or switched little Ethen with someone else's son?

Geth didn't waste another thought on it. He charged. Urian's sword whistled through the air as he swung, smashed against Palladine's blade, once, twice, three times. The captain skipped and backpedaled, flowed around the fighting space in retreat.

But never did he stumble or allow himself to get cornered. And Geth had begun to tire. He'd already fought one blade-master after all. Palladine, he had to concede, was every bit as good as Mylo. No, better. This man was no mere fencer. The captain knew how to take a life as well as anyone.

"It ends now," Geth growled.

He didn't have the energy, or the time, for anything else. Tossing his weapon from right hand to left, he used a familiar tactic to press. Swords clanged off one another as Palladine parried, dancing to his own left to create space. Before Geth could close again, he'd switched his own grip, matching the big warrior's left-handed pose with a left-handed grip of his own.

A look of triumph lit the bastard's face as he copied Geth to launch a left-handed attack. He wasn't as good with it as his right, but it caught Geth by surprise. Only a desperate flick of the big warrior's sword deflected the first strike, allowed Geth to get his bearings.

And Palladine's swordsmanship wasn't the only problem. A flash of motion out of the corner of one eye turned Geth in time to meet a pair of gold-bands climbing onto the stage behind him. He swung his sword in a wide arc to send them scrambling away, turned just in time to parry another onslaught from Palladine.

"Shit!"

The captain came at him with a reckless fervor. Geth deflected a reaching lunge, skipping backward at the same time. Those two watchmen would be at his back in another second, but Palladine was hacking at him, driving him right toward them.

Geth ducked a wild slash at his head, thrust home with Urian's blade. But the captain twisted so the edge only scraped against that bright cuirass. Momentum carried Palladine forward to shoulder-barge the big warrior rather than skewer himself as Geth had hoped.

"Oof!"

"Argh!"

Geth teetered, struggled to regain balance, push back. They wrestled chest to chest, swords useless up close, arms tangled, legs heaving. Geth was the bigger man, but Palladine's blue eyes bulged with hatred. A footfall sounded behind the big warrior and that look of triumph lit Palladine's eyes again.

"It's...over!"

Something whooshed past Geth's ear. A man cried out from over his shoulder.

"Run, Geth!"

The big warrior looked up. From the parapet above the Leonine Gate, Phelan reloaded his sling and turned it in a circle over his head. Another stone whipped past, clanked off Palladine's armor.

"Ah!"

The captain stumbled. With a heave, Geth untangled himself, pushed the bastard off, brought his sword around, readied for a thrust. Palladine let that shove take him out of reach though, leveled his guard to match Geth's.

"I said *run!*" Phelan shouted again.

Gold-bands were everywhere. They swarmed the Bloody Sixes, those that hadn't fled, or been killed, or dragged away. Geth flicked a glance up, saw there were lilies on the walls now as well, closing fast on Phelan from both sides. The little man's eyes went wide as he spied the nearer group, but without warning, the first soldier in the bunch turned to punch his fellow straight in the nose.

"Ratcher!"

But where the hell were Eora and Oedelia? Was it true what Palladine had said? Had they failed? Across the fighting stage, the bastard just watched with an evil glint in his eyes as the last of the Sixes were driven off, replaced by watchmen and bright-whites on all sides of the platform.

Palladine's lips curled into a smile.

Geth's jaw clenched, a wordless noise of fury and frustration foaming through his teeth.

"You're mine," Palladine said. "All the pain you've caused us, everything you've ruined, all of it will be made right again."

"You won't take me alive. You won't survive to enjoy it either."

But Palladine didn't so much as flinch. He'd already proved he could hold his own. And his men crowded the fighting stage, just waiting for the order.

Geth's eyes searched for a way out. His enemies were half a dozen thick in every direction. He tightened his grip on Urian's sword, sucked in a breath, cursed the Red God and all the rest.

"Run, dammit!"

This time it was Ratcher who yelled. Geth looked up to find his friends hemmed in by lilies, back-to-back on the wall. But like the damned fool that he was, the assassin actually winked at him. Geth's jaw dropped. Ratcher reached under his cloak. Lifting one arm, he lobbed something down at the stage. His voice rang above the din.

"Lights out, Wolf!"

CHAPTER EIGHTEEN

Geth got his eyes shut a split second before Ratcher's blinding dust hit the fighting surface. He turned, covered his face, felt the burn on the backs of his hands as it exploded outward. A cacophony of curses, spluttering, and coughs rang out. The big warrior crouched there in place, counted to five, then cracked his eyes.

Blinded men clawed at their faces, bumped and stumbled into one another, swearing like sailors, crying, yelling from one to another. Geth searched for Palladine, found him off the stage, staggering away, deep among his blinded gold-bands.

He wasn't wrong to beat a hasty retreat. Geth could have still caught up to him, killed him then and there, but he never would survive himself. Ratcher's dust could only drift so far. A dozen yards from the stage, lilies blinked and wiped their eyes, or looked about in confusion, wondering what the hell had happened to their fellows.

Geth's only option was to flee. Stripping off his dueler's armor, he was down to Paellian white, just like everyone else. He stuffed his red armband behind his belt and slid off the stage, among the cursing, stumbling enemy. Hiding his face in his elbow and navigating with half of one eye, he wended right through the lot.

Away from the press of the crowd, he craned his neck, scanned the walls. By the look of things, Ratcher had thrown his dust up there as well. Men rubbed at their faces, gripped the crenels, eyes shut tight. Geth felt his heart leap. Had they made it? His eyes found the assassin a moment later though, clutched at each arm by lilies, Phelan right beside him.

A head of white hair among the soldiers told the tale. "Gods all damn you, Ceter!"

Maybe it was the distance, or the heat of the moment, but Geth hadn't even felt the fearspell. He swore again. There was nothing he could do, for now at least. They were alive, even if Lyanne and Palladine had them.

What had become of Eora and Oedelia, he couldn't begin to guess. He crossed the plaza, past the wreckage of shops, vendors carts, and overturned wagons, in the wake of what must have been a stampede of human flesh. A few injured lilies leaned up against edifices, dumbstruck. Wide-eyed gold-bands wandered the streets in knots of no less than three or four.

"Hey, you," one of them asked. "What the hell happened?"

Geth ignored him, hurried in the direction of the river. Maybe Palladine had been bluffing. Maybe Eora and Oedelia were there already, waiting at the ship. With Ethen.

The smell of the river hit Geth's nose as he rounded the last corner, but the docks were quiet. News of the fighting, of the chaos, had spread, he imagined. Folk had locked themselves indoors.

"Math-ter Geth!" a lisping voice called.

Geth turned to find Eora's cook crouched down beside a boat. "Where is she?" he asked. "Are they here? Do they have the baby?"

The man frowned, shook his head.

"Thram and bloody Awer."

"What do we do now?"

Geth's fist clenched and unclenched on the hilt of his sword. "We wait."

The sun crossed the sky, faded from yellow, to orange, to a ruddy pink as it slipped beneath the horizon. A purple, star speckled night wheeled overhead. They waited all the way until dawn.

But no one ever came.

"They've been captured," Geth told Lisp as the sun rose again.

"Are you thure?" The cook asked. Neither could bring themself to raise the possibility they'd been killed.

Geth led the man through the thin morning traffic of water-carriers and laborers back to the Oak and Hart. They barred the front door and Geth collapsed into a chair, head down on his arms on the table. He was alone, out of ideas, and if he was honest, afraid.

"I'm sorry, Vriana," he muttered. "I'm sorry. I'm so sorry."

Lisp nudged Geth's elbow with a plate of cold ham and bread. A few bites brought him back from the edge of despair, but even with his emotions reigned in, he couldn't begin to imagine what to do now.

A knock at the door sent one hand to Urian's hilt. "We're closed!"

"Let me in!" a muffled voice said.

"Gods all be—"

But before he could speak his mind, Geth found himself crossing the space and opening the door. Out in front of the Oak and Heart, cowled and flicking glances up both sides of the street, stood Feru-Lea.

She pushed her way inside as soon as the door was cracked. "Goddess be praised."

Geth cursed her roundly. "Thram's pimpled ass, woman. Where the hell have *you* been?"

The witch settled heavily in a chair, threw her hood back. Her hair fell out, disheveled, coated with what looked like plaster-dust. She sighed. "If I told you, you wouldn't believe me."

"Lyanne finally decided you'd outlived your uses, eh?"

Feu-Lea directed a glare at him. "She decided it was finally worth coming after me. I made her regret the decision."

Geth sank down in the chair across from her. It was only then he wondered if it had been the woman's compulsion that had made him open the door in the first place. He muttered another curse.

"You're alone?" the witch asked. "Perhaps Lyanne isn't the only one with regrets."

She wasn't wrong. He should have listened to Phelan. He'd rushed things. They done it his way and he was no closer to rescuing his son. And it was his friends who'd paid the price.

"They aren't dead," the witch said.

Geth looked up to meet Feru-Lea's gaze. "I didn't say they were."

"She won't kill them. Not while you're still free, not while she can use them against you."

"Against you too."

Did he imagined it, or had Feru-Lea flinched? But that didn't make him feel any better.

"You used me," he said. "You used the both of us. Is it true you sold those other witches to Lyanne? Why the hell are you here anyway?"

"I need—"

"Muscle? Protection?" Geth couldn't help himself. All his anger, his frustration, it needed a way out. "I've been used enough already for one lifetime. Gods all damn you, woman, I won't have it anymore!"

Geth didn't know when he'd stood, but there was no question the witch was flinching now. He leaned over her, one hand gone to his waist. But it clutched the little toy sword Agrem had made him carry, not his blade. If she tried her magicks again, he prayed it might protect him.

Whether she did or didn't, Geth felt nothing. He forced himself back down into his seat. Feru-Lea composed herself, ran one hand over her hair to smooth it.

"I never betrayed anyone. To Lyanne or to anybody else. If I made a truce with the queen, it was only in the interest of self-preservation. I was never an ally or a friend."

"Why did you wait until now to free Oedelia then? Speak the truth."

Feru-Lea regarded him flatly. "Because she told me it was time."

Geth frowned, thinking that through. *Bloody magicks.* He exhaled, long and hard but managed to hold in the curse on his lips.

"What do we do now?" he said instead.

It was the witch's turn to blow out a sigh. "We rest. And then we go rescue our friends."

A few hours of sleep did Geth a world of good. If he failed at everything, if couldn't get his son or his friends back, he could still do one thing. He could raise hell.

But he didn't intend to throw it all away lightly. And he had a direction now. Palladine's words had made one thing clear to him; he'd been doing things all wrong.

"They never even had my son at the Games," Geth told Feru-Lea.

It was evening, they sat at a table in the common room, picking over a cold chicken carcass Lisp had provided. The witch frowned down at the bones on her plate but didn't speak.

"They invited me to come. And like a half-wit, I made a grand entrance."

"Well," the witch shrugged. "From what I heard, it was something to see."

Geth eyed her sideways. He had no choice but to work with the woman—he had no one else. But that didn't mean he trusted her.

"What I'm saying is this," he told her. "They want to trade my life for my son's. And now they have even more lives to hold against me. But what do we have to bargain with? What can we do except rage like idiots, a few fools against an army. Eventually I'll be dead or in irons and they get what they want."

"That wasn't my idea," said Feru-Lea, "the rage part."

"We need something to hold against them. Otherwise, we have nothing."

The witch pushed her plate away, looked up to meet Geth's eye. "One doesn't require special talents to surmise you have something in mind."

"I do. I can't believe I didn't think of it before. It was right there in front of my eyes when you sent us to the Garden."

"The other witches?"

Geth shook his head. "Gahalus."

Across from him, Feru-Lea blinked. Geth could see the wheels turning behind her eyes, but he couldn't have said what exactly she was thinking.

"You don't think that's something we could use against Lyanne and Palladine?" Geth asked.

"No, no, it's something." She shook her head. "I'm just wondering if I can slip us past her wards a second time."

"Well? Can you?"

"I can try. But even then, it will be more difficult just to get past the guards. No one had troubled the Garden since, well, ever, before we free Mother. They'll have their eyes wide open this time."

"The guards." Geth nodded. "I think I have an idea where that's concerned."

Feru-Lea raised one delicate eyebrow.

"Gahalus has friends in this city. Friends that would do anything for him."

"And?"

"And that makes them our friends too, if we're planning to break him out."

Night had fallen, the cover of dark welcome. Geth had no doubt the watch would be looking for him, the men of the First and the Second Hosts as well, most likely. He could only hope the

Games and all its chaos would be enough to keep them distracted.

He slipped into Ratcher's Bronian fleece, pulled the hood
low over his face. Urian's sword went through his belt, and he
started for the door.

"If I'm not back by sunrise, they've caught me," he told
Feru-Lea.

"Where are you going?"

Geth ignored her, left through the back, headed for the
Sable Dragon. Aside from that first alleyway, he avoided narrow
streets and the thugs they hid, steering wide around gold-bands
and lilies as well. It would be a miracle if he could get in and out
of the inn without being recognized, but he had to try.

Lilies and gold-bands overflowed from the common room
when he arrived, milling about outside the doorway to the Sable
Dragon, cups in hand. They slapped each other's backs, cursed
and laughed, pissed against the wall, no one paying any heed to
the lone outlander passing by. This once, it would have been
worse to wear white. He kept moving just in case, right on by.

A snatch of conversation floated to his ear along the way.
"...and threw that stick about a damn mile."

"I saw it. Awer's rock-hard prick, the bastard had it sealed. Am
I right, Bronlander?"

Geth knuckled his brow and continued past, eyes down lest
he be recognized.

So, the Games were still on. He snorted a laugh. Of course
they were. Who cared if a few lilies cut each other up at the

duels? No one was about to let something like that interfere off the flow of coin.

Geth counted off days as he walked. The javelin throw would have taken place that afternoon, that's what they'd been talking about. He reached the end of the street, turned right at the crossway, then down the first alley, headed for the Sable Dragon's back door. As with the front, patrons spilled outside the place, but Geth hurried past them and inside.

Pangs of guilt, fear, and anger struck Geth as the back hallway opened up to reveal a common room he and Phelan had visited not a year ago. More than likely, many of the same soldiers and watchmen that had witnessed their arm-wrestling contest were there among the crowd. Geth leaned up against a wall well away from any lamps, scanning the tables and chairs until he found the big bald head he was looking for.

Tham sat by himself in a corner, surrounded but ignored by groups of white clad lilies and gold-bands. He had one of the only chairs in the place—one of the only tables too—even if he had no one to share it with.

"You there," Geth said, moving up close to stand over the big bodyguard. "I'll arm wrestle you for that chair."

Tham looked up. The snarl on his face turned to a scowl as his eyes met the big warrior's. "You got some balls on you, Turncoat, coming in here."

"Turncoat?"

"You wear the green now, don't you?"

"I tried wearing white, but it didn't stick."

"Well—"

"Doesn't look like it did you so well either."

Tham scowled into his drink. "They're looking for you, you know. After that stunt you pulled yesterday."

Geth moved closer, voice low. "And here I thought you of all people would appreciate what I've done."

"Starting a riot?"

"Kicking Palladine's ass."

"The way I was told—"

"And Mylo's."

Tham snorted. "Well, that scratch might be nursing a thump or two, but Palladine gave as good as he got from what I heard."

"And what *did* you hear?"

Tham rolled his eyes. "I'm six cups in already. You really need to ruin my drunk?"

It was Geth's turn to snort. "I'm looking at the ruins of a man alright. You just gonna' sit in this place and drink yourself to death while the prince rots away in his mother's dungeon?"

"What the hell would you have me do? No one knows where he—"

"I know where he is."

Tham's eyes narrowed. But he only loosed a wry laugh. He lifted his cup for a long drink, set it back down. "Sure you do. So does everyone else. But nobody knows where this bloody 'Garden' is anyway."

"That's because they haven't been there."

Tham had started to raise his drink again, but his hand froze halfway to his lips.

"That's right," Geth said. "Ask around if you don't believe me. I've been there, broke one of the prisoners out already. With a second set of arms, I reckon I can break out another."

For a good long moment, the bodyguard met Geth's eye.

Did he think he was bluffing? Did he reckon it all a lie? After a moment, he shook his head. Muttering a curse, he drained his cup to the dregs and hollered loudly for a refill.

Geth waited for the harried looking barman to slosh wine from a pitcher into Tham's cup and retreat again. "Did you hear me? We can get him out, you and me. Tonight."

"You and me?" Tham muttered another curse. "You really are crazy. First the queen's favorite pet and now the bloody Garden? You know, you keep tempting the gods, eventually they're gonna' squash you flat."

Geth clamped down a curse of his own.

Tham kept on muttering, directly into his wine. "Crazy bas tard..."

Geth forced his jaw to unclench, swallowed his curses. The big bodyguard's slick head gleamed faintly in the dim light. This wasn't the reception Geth had expected. He would have bet everything he ever owned the bastard loved Gahalus. Everyone else did. There had to be something holding him back.

"You can't be scared, can you? Big bad Tham, the strongest arm in the Golden City?"

Tham just sighed. "It's not about being scared, Sellsword. It's about what happens after. And that's if we can get to the boy in the first place."

"I have a witch who can get us there and away. It'll take more than a few guardsmen to stop the likes of you and me once we make land."

"They'll be ready for us." Tham scowled at the sound of his own words, even in the noisy common room. He leaned forward, lowered his voice. "They'll have doubled the guards, seeing how you already got in once. Tripled maybe."

"She—"

"She's waiting for you, man, do you hear me? Her hounds are off the leash. In the Garden and everywhere else."

The big bodyguard flicked a meaningful glance around the room. With another shake of the head, he raised his cup to his lips. Geth had his back to the rest of the low-ceilinged chamber, and the place was crowded and loud anyway. Still, those words made him nervous.

"Well, I'm going after him. Alone if I have to."

"You aren't listening, man. Uro's wrinkled cheeks, I thought I was the drunk one."

"I swear on Awer's red soul, we can get to him."

"But even if we could steal him away, what then? Lyanne won't stop until she has him again. You can't protect him from the queen. No one can."

"No one except a king."

CHAPTER NINETEEN

T hey left out the back, the way Geth had come, out onto moonlit streets.

"I want to hear you say it, Sellsword; King Hadean will protect the prince if we can break him out?"

Geth nodded, waved Tham down the alley and out onto the streets. "After what Gahalus did for him back in Umbel City, you doubt it?"

"We did save his ass."

"And Hadean doesn't forget his friends."

They walked in silence for half a block. Geth couldn't remember if Tham had accompanied Prince Gahalus to Umbel that summer, but either way, he knew he'd heard of Geth's relationship with King Hadean. And he clearly knew how things had gone.

"Are you in?" Geth asked. "Or are we just walking off the drink?"

Tham put one foot in front of the other for a several more strides. "What's the place look like?" he said finally. "How would we do it?"

Geth licked his lips to hide a smile.

Walking and talking, he told Tham all about the island in the mist, the walls, the gardens within the Garden. "I reckon the witch gets us to shore and we march up like I did last time, like we belong. If they try to block our path, we smash our way in. One shout and Gahalus will come running. And then we're out."

"What if the gate's barred? And who's to say they don't have a dozen swords in the gatehouse."

"Hey, I'm open to suggestions if you're scared of a dust-up."

Tham let that slide, frowning as he walked. "They'll recognize you this time around. Maybe what we need is a fresh face or two, some fresh arms to help carry the load."

"And maybe a fresh idea."

They kept walking. Geth wasn't sure where they were headed, he just let the big bodyguard lead the way.

"There's one scratch I can think of that might help," Tham said finally. "Him and his brother."

Geth nodded. "A man like Gahalus has got to have more friends in this city than just you and me."

"That boy makes friends everywhere he goes." The big bodyguard actually smiled. "He—"

"Well, here's the men we're looking for."

It wasn't a familiar voice that cut Tham off, even if Geth had grown well-accustomed to that sort of scornful tone. His hand went instantly to his hilt, a curse on his lips. Had Tham betrayed him, led him into a trap?

But before he could draw, the big bodyguard stepped in front of him. He raised both hands, gestured for peace. The two shapes that materialized out of the shadows ahead already carried naked steel.

"Ho there, good men of the watch. Took you long enough. Well, here he is, all wrapped up. Everything but the bow. If your lot still wants him, he's yours."

Despite those words, Geth relaxed. The two gold-bands looked from one to the other. The first stepped closer, frowned down his nose at the pair of them.

"You expect me to believe you weren't plotting some kind of trouble with this whoreson? Everyone knows he was thick with your lad, the prince."

"I'm just trying to turn him in," said Tham. "You think I'm crazy?"

"Crazy? Sure."

"Not crazy enough to get between a mother and her son. Not when that mother is the queen."

Tham chuckled. The noise was forced, but the two gold-bands relaxed a hair. No sooner had the first man lowered his blade than Tham punched him square in the jaw.

Geth went after the second. Urian's sword slid out from behind his belt, but Tham had grabbed the first watchman and swung him into his fellow before Geth could strike. Another punch sent that one down to the pavers.

Geth stepped in, drew back his weapon.

"Wait!" The big bodyguard threw an arm up in the way. "You may be full-fledged green-back now, but I'll be coming back someday. The prince too. He wouldn't take kindly to the likes of you and me spilling blood where we didn't have to."

"Huh." Geth reckoned Hadean would have felt the same way. "Fine. But we better find those brothers of yours and get moving. These two aren't gonna' lay here on the cobbles forever."

Tham nodded. They started off at a jog.

"You sober yet?" Geth asked.

The big bodyguard just snorted, shot him a sideways glance. "I bet you dribbled some piss back there, eh? Thought I was really gonna' turn you in?"

"Me? Never. But it did give me an idea. I think I know how to get inside the Garden now."

Tham's eyes narrowed for a fraction of a second. Then he smiled. "You want to pretend I'm bringing you in as a prisoner."

"Yeah, I'd say you've walked all the drink out now."

"You know what, Sellsword? With the help of the brothers, I think it might work."

"Good. All we need is my witch."

Tham left to get the brothers while Geth headed in the opposite direction, back toward the Oak and Hart. He raised a hand to knock when he arrived, but the door wasn't barred. Inside, Lisp stood behind the bar, patrons scattered in ones and twos around the common room.

"What the—"

"It's alright," a man with a bandage on his knee said. "If she needs us, we're here for her."

If Geth wasn't mistaken, it was the same man he'd seen limping out the day he'd arrived. He looked around the common room. A couple at the next table nodded. Lisp smiled from behind the bar. Brega swept the back hallway, dull-eyed as ever.

Geth stepped over toward Lisp. "What is this? You think you can run this place with just Sleepy and her broom? And what if someone brings the watch down on us?"

Lisp shook his head. "Theze people love the Lady Eora. They don't mind to help."

"And the witch was alright with you opening back up?"

Lisp spread his hands. "She's gone."

Geth swore. Where the hell had Feru-Lea gotten off to? Straight to the citadel to turn him in, win back favor with Lyanne or trade him for Ratcher? He scanned the room, thinking.

"Alright," he told Lisp. "I'll be in the kitchens. I need to eat something. Let me know if anyone shows up, especially if it's the watch."

Geth found himself a loaf and some dried fruit, but it wasn't a half an hour before Lisp burst through the door, eyes wide. "They're here!"

Footsteps sounded. Geth threw Lisp out of the way, drew Urian's sword. It was Tham who came through the door though, trailed by two lilies with the same dark hair on their blocky heads.

"Uro's shriveled nuts," Tham said. "You need a better look-out." He hooked his thumb over one shoulder. "These are the brothers. Now where's your witch?"

No one was happy about Feru-Lea's disappearance. But for the time being, there was nothing they could do but wait, hope she'd only left for supplies or something of the like. Geth stretched out on the floor, caught a few hours of rest. The witch returned with the dawn.

But she wasn't alone.

"Ratcher!" Geth had risen with the noise of some commotion in the common room to find Feru-Lea shadowed over by the assassin at the bar. Something wasn't right though. Ratcher's head hung on his shoulders and he didn't turn at the sound of his name.

The witch did, however. She met Geth's eye, her face ashen, stunned.

"What the..."

Ratcher still hadn't turned, hadn't so much as acknowledged anyone, from Geth to Lisp, even to Feru-Lea, holding him by the hand. Lamplight flickered off glassy eyes. His jaw hung a limp as his head.

"What have they done to him?"

The witch opened her mouth and closed it again. She cleared her throat, straightened, tried to compose herself, but she couldn't find the words.

She didn't need to. Geth's eyes went to Brega, sweeping mindlessly again, over and over across the same stretch of floor.

"Dear gods." He rubbed his jaw. He moved close to rest a hand on Ratcher's stubbly cheek, tried to meet his eye. The assassin pursed his lips, nothing more.

Geth turned back to Feru-Lea. "What can be done?"

The witch sank heavily into a seat at the bar. "I...I don't know."

"Something can be done," Geth said. "I know it. Eora did the same thing to Brega, but by accident. With her singing and that tea. She could undo it too she said. We just need to—"

"They have her, Geth. Eora I mean. And I'm no healer."

"You can try!"

"There's more."

The witch looked up with those pretty eyes, but the fear in them only made her look like a child, small and helpless. She reached into a pocket and pulled out a folded note. Geth took it and read.

"Thram and bloody Awer." He blinked hard and read the note a second time. "And she has them all."

Feru-Lea nodded. "Three more days of the Games, not counting the feast. And she has three of our friends, not counting Mother. She's going to release one each day, the same way she released Birg—"

"I read the damn note!" Geth turned halfway, swore, turned back. "I'm sorry, I...hold on, you said three. Eora and Phelan, that only makes two."

"Your son."

"Gods..."

Geth sank down into the seat beside the witch. His hands went to his head of their own accord, ran through his short locks. He looked up at Ratcher's witless expression, flicked a glance at Brega and back. "He's just a child."

"Counting today, we have three days," Feru-Lea said. "Two really. We can't let this happen to a babe. If you don't turn yourself in to Palladine and the queen, they all end up like this."

"And there's nothing that can be done?"

"I tried. But Lyanne didn't do this alone. It will take something special, more than anything I can conjure by myself to undo the queen's touch."

"What about the other witches? If the queen is using magicks to hide the Garden, I reckon she's got all those other witches in there alongside Gahalus. With one stroke—"

"It won't work." Feru-Lea's eyes went hard. "We can't free them. Not yet."

"You just said you couldn't heal our friends alone."

The witch scowled. "And what might Lyanne do with Eora and Phelan once she knows her plot's unraveled? If she can't use them, might she not just kill them all and have done?"

But that scowl was a little forced. Geth knew a lie when heard one. He could only guess at what Feru-Lea's real angle was.

One thing was clear though, she'd finally chosen a side. She had no choice. Ceter's arrival at her candle shop left no doubt she'd fallen afoul of Lyanne. Where she stood with those other witches, however, Geth couldn't say.

What he did know, watching her hold Ratcher's hand, was that she really did love the man. Perhaps he could trust her because of that. Either way, he needed her. He knew that as well.

"Alright." He stood, straightened that ridiculous Bronian fleece. "Back to the original plan then. We free Gahalus, use the prince to get to his mother."

Feru-Lea nodded. Footsteps sounded as Tham and the brothers arrived, right on cue.

"This the witch?" the bodyguard asked. He frowned at Ratcher. "What's wrong with him?"

Geth didn't bother explaining. He turned back to Feru-Lea. "These men can help us get Gahalus out of the Garden. If you can't heal Ratcher, we may as well leave now."

CHAPTER TWENTY

The usual foot-traffic clogged the streets as they marched out into the morning air toward the same little port Feru-Lea had used on their first expedition to the Garden. Geth heard folk talking about the Games, the disc-throwing competitions that would be held that day. Hopefully that would keep Lyanne at least partially occupied.

She'd released Ratcher in the evening, according to Feru-Lea. By Geth's reckoning, they had about twelve hours before Lyanne and Palladine bewitched the next one of their friends. *Twelve hours.* Plenty of time to get to Gahalus.

"How'd you find him anyway?" Geth asked Feru-Lea as they stepped into her boat. As before, no one paid them any mind; a trio of lilies, a big foreigner, and a high-born lady.

"We have a bond. I could feel he was in trouble. I went to him."

Bloody magicks. Geth shook his head. "Did she have eyes on him? To try and catch you?"

"She did." Feru-Lea smiled. "But they weren't hard to...redirect."

"Redirect?"

"I don't ask you to explain your business, do I? Don't ask me to explain mine. We don't have the time. Now, let's review the plan."

The brothers started rowing. Oars dipped in and out of the water as they left the port. The pair of them wore white, their usual uniform. Tham had donned the white tabard Geth had used earlier, but the big warrior himself still wore his Bronian fleece. He had a set of manacles as well; they would be the captors, he, the captive.

"Take these," Feru-Lea said, producing two pendants, made of braided reeds best Geth could tell, and hanging from cords. They were set with something whitish, not unlike the carved ivory amulet Ratcher wore, some kind of bone or tooth.

"What are they?" the first brother asked.

"They belonged to the queen's men. You are known as soldiers of the First Host, but these will mark you as Lyanne's chosen."

The second brother slipped one over his head, but the first frowned down at his. If Geth wasn't mistaken, blood had dried on it.

"If we're not asking questions," the big warrior said, "I won't ask how you came upon those either."

The witch sniffed. "They came after me, not the other way around."

The boat rocked and swayed, carried forward stroke by stroke toward the Garden. The tang of saltwater filled Geth's nose. The sun had only half risen, the day still hushed with morning. As the fog rose around them, the quiet became a thing of itself, heavy, ominous.

Feru-Lea's eyes were closed. She held something like a handful of dried herbs in one fist and she shook it gently at her side. Perhaps Lyanne's dank air swallowed the sound, but it looked like she was humming.

"I haven't seen the whole island," Geth said, as much to break the silence as anything. "But I reckon the prince must be in one of those houses against the far wall."

Tham grunted. "You said he saw you last time. He'll be looking for us."

The brothers plied the oars and the dark shape of a cliff materialized ahead. The fog thinned to something like a natural morning mist, seawater lapping up against that little strip of brown beach.

They ran the rowboat onto the sand alongside a few others.

"Are you coming ashore?" Geth asked Feru-Lea.

The witch cast a glance up at the walls, pulled her hood over her head. "Tell them I'm your boatman. I'll stay here."

"Will you still be here when it's time to get scarce?"

"Just get the prince. I'll be here."

They stepped over the gunwale and started up the creaking, zig-zagged, stairs. Atop the cliff, at the gatehouse, the portcullis was down, a pair of wary-eyed guardsmen watching their approach.

One of the brothers went first, followed by Geth, wearing those manacles, then the second brother. Tham came last, hood drawn up over his bald head. Geth bent his neck downward as they drew near, tried to look defeated.

"What's all this?" the first gateman asked, an old, scarred-up soldier with sharp, bird-like eyes. His hand gripped his hilt—his fellows did too. Several more lilies backed them up from atop the walls.

"It's done," said the first brother. "We got him."

"Who?"

Tham chuckled from behind Geth, maybe a little too loud, but the brothers played along. "The scratch that snuck past the lot of you, that's who."

The scarred gateman muttered a curse.

"Well, open up. He's here for a longer stay this time."

The second gateman looked to Scar, his sergeant, Geth reckoned. "Show us his hands. Right? We need to see his hands. You got those irons on tight?"

The first brother jerked Geth by the fleece until he lifted his hands. The pin was only stuck in place with a bit of resin, but without a close inspection, there was no way to tell if the manacles at his wrists were well clamped or not. Perhaps the two gatemen were thinking the same thing. Neither moved to raise the portcullis.

"C'mon, man, the second brother said. "I don't know how you let a stranger in last time, but you know us. We've been with the First since before the Affliction."

Scar spit. "Sure. but we weren't told to expect anyone or anything. Anything but trouble, that is."

"Queen's probably busy with the Games," Tham put in.

"And who are you?"

Tham drew his hood back. "I'm the one who caught this turncoat bastard."

The younger gateman shook his head.

But scar only cursed. He leaned close to his fellow to whisper something. The soldier nodded, hurried off.

"You," the scarred sergeant said. "I heard about you, none of it good. They say you're on the outs. They say you had a hand in all the mischief that landed the prince in here. That true?'

Tham shrugged. "That's why I had to pull this off. How else was I gonna' get back in good graces?"

"She gave us these," the first brother offered, gesturing to the amulet hung on his chest. "Gave us the call up."

Scar frowned. The younger gateman returned, another half a dozen lilies at his back, but those little trinkets seemed to be enough. He waved a hand at someone on the other side of the wall, out of sight.

"Go ahead, lift it." He turned back to the brothers. "Well? C'mon then. Bring the big bastard in. These boys will walk you to his cell, just in case."

CHAPTER TWENTY-ONE

T he portcullis groaned upwards. With a clang it stopped, and the brothers pulled Geth roughly inside the Garden. *Damn!* He cursed under his breath.

But not at his friends. He eyed the lilies to either side of him. How were they supposed to get Gahalus away now? With Tham and the prince himself at his side, Geth reckoned they might hack their way through Scar and his boys, but not without making one hell of a racket. By the time they made it back to the gatehouse, the whole of the fortress would be coming down on their heads.

They walked the curved pathway, past that immaculate lawn, the shrubs and flowerbeds. Geth flicked glances ahead and either way, desperate for ideas. Sergeant Scar led the way, three lilies with him, three more bringing up the rear.

"Wonder why she wants him here?" he said, only half turning as he marched. "Tower of the Moon seems a more fitting place for the likes of this traitor."

Tham grunted. "Seems he's already been there. Broke out, the slick bastard."

Scar whistled. "Well, I don't see how he deserves fine wine, music, and the rest. I mean, all they have to do is a little...well, gardening. How's that a prison? Now, you got the fog. Sometimes it rolls over the island. That'll curl your whiskers if you understand me. But aside from those hags under Lucean, you're living pretty good inside these walls."

Geth's ears perked up, hearing that. He slowed his pace to drop back beside Tham.

"Tell them to take me to the one called Lucean," he said out of the side of his mouth.

"I hope you got a plan," Tham whispered back.

He moved past the big warrior to get closer to the sergeant at the lead.

"This Lucean fellow, what'd he do? Captain Palladine mentioned that name. I think that's the one supposed to take our man here."

"Lucean?" Scar swore. "Well, why didn't you say something. C'mon, this way."

They'd arrived at the fountain, the center of the Garden, best Geth could tell. Ahead, those buildings with the painted shutters and shaded galleries peeked out. But the sergeant turned them left, through the orchard and vineyards. The ground rose gently until another wall appeared, this one of plain weathered stone. No paint or columns here. A fort within the fort, Geth surmised.

"I reckon this makes more sense," Scar was saying. "Nasty sonofabitch, the Witchmaster. I shudder to think what he has in store, but then again, it's not me getting dumped in there."

The guardsmen shared a laugh.

A single heavy door marked the only entrance Geth could see. Their path took them right to it. The hairs on the back of his neck went up as they neared. The scarred sergeant hesitated before pounding on the door with one fist.

A tense silence settled over them until noises sounded from inside and the door opened. A slight, balding man that looked like nothing so much as a scribe frowned down the length of his nose at them.

"What is this?"

"A prisoner," said the sergeant. "For your master."

Geth could just see past the man into a small ward, encircled by buildings. There were no shutters at all on these, painted or otherwise. The windows were barred.

But the little man made no move to let them inside. He wore an amulet much like the ones against the brothers' chests, but his frown only deepened, spotting theirs.

"Well?" said Scar. "I can't just leave him out here." He pushed his way through, waved Tham and the brothers to follow. They pulled Geth in alongside. If the hairs on the back of his neck had been standing before, they were trying to jump off him now.

"Thram and bloody Awer."

At the center of the ward, garbed in rags, two women and one man sat cross-legged in a circle, chained at wrist and ankle.

Mouths worked soundlessly and one of the women swayed gently where she sat. There was nothing else to be seen, but Geth could feel...*something* sweeping off of them, like the tension in the air, in your ears, and on your skin, when a storm was about to break.

This was it. He needed a distraction, needed to raise enough hell to occupy the whole of the Garden and get Gahalus out of there in the confusion. Those three chained wretches were the answer.

Before Geth could think of anything to do, however, a voice sent a shiver down his back. "Who are you? What is this?"

Scar cleared his throat, gathered himself visibly. "This one's for you, Master Lucean." He turned to Geth. " Don't worry, turncoat. It won't be so bad. You won't remember a thing."

He forced a weak laugh. None of his men could manage even that.

But the one called Lucean looked like his eyes might bulge out of his head, stalking on long legs toward them, robed all in black like a servant of Vorda.

Scar hurried back out the way they'd come, waving his men to follow. The brothers stood dumbstruck, but Tham had the composure to knuckle his brow, dip his head in a half-bow.

"The queen..." he said.

"You fools! Who is this man? Lyanne would have—"

Geth heaved against his manacles. With only a sliver of wood in place of the pins, they burst open. "Bar the door!" he shouted.

Tham sprang toward the wooden entry, slammed it shut and dropped the bar. The brothers drew steel, but Lucean swung an arm like he was throwing something and the pair of them stuck fast where they stood. Geth charged, twirling one end of his iron manacle like a mace on its chain. The witchmaster motioned toward him next and Geth felt something like wind buffet against him, but that was it. He crashed headlong through the man's magicks, coming around with his makeshift weapon in a lethal arc.

Somehow, the blow flew high. Lucean's upraised hand snagged the weapon, his other gone back in a fist, but Geth dropped a shoulder to ram him right off his feet. They landed in a flailing tangle of arms and legs. Geth got an elbow up across the witchmaster's neck, drove down with all his strength, but suddenly he was up in the air, weightless for a split second until the ground rushed up to meet him.

He sucked air, curled up, trying to get his wind back. Gods be praised, the old sorcerer must have been too stunned himself to pounce on Geth while he was down. Across the space, Tham and the brothers shook their heads to clear them, tried to come to his aid, but Geth waved them off.

"The witches!" he yelled, pushing up to all fours. "Get them free!"

Lucean launched himself at the big warrior with a snarl before he could say more.

He landed on the big warrior's back, clawing like an animal. Lanky as he was, the man was impossibly strong. Hands like iron found Geth's throat, but the big warrior bucked like a colt, flung the witchmaster straight forward and off.

A flash out of the corner of one eye turned Geth just in time to roll out of the way of Tham's sword.

"What the hell?"

Past the big bodyguard, standing in the doorway to one of the buildings, the sorcerer's scribe hissed and frothed, hands raised, twisting and pulling like a puppetmaster. It was Tham's eyes that bulged now. He couldn't stop himself, lifting that sword for another swing.

Something unseen struck the scribe and he doubled over with a shriek, convulsed, and fell flat. Tham staggered, collapsed to one knee. One of the women in rags had risen, a vengeful light in her eyes.

"Lucean!" she howled.

Geth had gained all fours himself, he turned toward the sorcerer as well. "Lucean!"

But the old sorcerer just laughed, hands rising slowly at either side. The air shook. The ground trembled under Geth like he was in the middle of a stampede.

He gritted his teeth and crawled forward, but across the ward, the rag-clad witch went over like she'd been run down by a herd phantom steeds. Lucean laughed again, stepped toward her. Geth pushed up to one knee, threw out his hands for balance against the shaking earth, and stood.

"I'm here, you bastard!"

He staggered forward, no weapon to hand but his fists. The witchmaster turned, glided forward effortlessly. As another tremor forced Geth's arms wide for balance, Lucean cocked an arm back to slap him across the face.

Stars streaked across Geth's vision. He stumbled, hit the ground hard. But swinging one arm as he landed, he managed a chop at the sorcerer's ankle.

It wasn't enough. Lucean grunted, but didn't go down. Teeth bared, he drew a hatchet from his belt. Before he could get it overhead though, Geth tackled him around the knees, pitched him straight backwards.

"Agh!"

The witchmaster cursed and spit. Geth squirmed up toward the hand with the hatchet, caught it near the elbow, just in time to stop the skull-splitter Lucean had lined up at his head. An iron claw grabbed a handful of Geth's hair. Thank the gods it hadn't grown out very far and there wasn't much to hold on to.

They grappled, scratched and pulled, as savage as mountain cats, nothing like a master swordsman and a wizened sorcerer. Geth had his weight on the witchmaster, but Lucean still had that hatchet. Wriggling like a fish, he twisted a bony arm free of the big warrior's sweaty grip. He couldn't leverage the blade end, but he hammered down with the handle. Carved wood thumped the dome of Geth's head.

His vision shook. Lucean pulled and twisted, rolled until he was on top. It was all Geth could do to shake his head clear as the witchmaster sat up, hatchet raised high in a two-handed grip.

"No!"

Geth's hands went up in a desperate defense. The triumph in the sorcerer's eyes turned to alarm as his back arched, sticking him fast, weapon still raised.

He shook in place, still straddling, Geth, as froze as the brothers and Tham a moment before. The big warrior reached for his belt, drew the first thing his hand touched; Ethen's toy sword.

He gripped it blade-down, stabbed desperately with the blunt wood at Lucean's thigh. Gods all be damned if Agrem hadn't put some potent magicks into it. Like a razor through velvet cloth, it cut through black robes, slid into flesh all the way to the little crosspiece.

Lucean gasped. Geth pulled the makeshift weapon free and aimed higher, slammed it into the witchmaster's gut, up near the liver. The ground trembled once and went still. A wind Geth only then noticed quit, dropping twigs and leaves and dust. Like a straw man blown over, Lucean groaned and teetered sideways, arms out to either side, stiff as a board.

Geth rolled out from under the sorcerer, looked up to find old Oedelia standing there outside one of the doorways. She teetered herself, lowered slowly with a groan to sit with her back against the wall.

"Up, warrior!" a woman's voice called.

Geth turned, found the woman in rags striding towards him. Tham and the brothers moved like they'd just rolled out of bed after a night in their cups. But several more rag-clad women had appeared from inside the buildings, along with at a couple of ragged men.

"What do we do, Catriona?" a woman with wild yellow hair asked.

The first witch smoothed down her own matted curls to frown at the doorway leading back out to the orchard. The door shook on its hinges as she watched, the sounds of cursing soldiers echoing over the walls. Turning back toward Geth, she extended a hand to help him rise.

"We make them pay."

CHAPTER TWENTY-TWO

G eth took stock. A good dozen rag-clad men and women had cast off their irons, led by the curly-headed witch called Catriona. Lucean and his underling lay twisted, dead, but guardsmen massed outside the door, hurling threats and hammering at the entry. He'd wanted a distraction to steal away with the prince. He reckoned he'd overshot the mark.

"Tham, the door!" Geth said.

The big bodyguard knew what to do. He shook his head clear, hustled over, set one brawny shoulder against it to brace against the next impact.

"We can't stay here forever," Tham said. "They've got a ram."

"What now?" That from one of the ragged men, a stringy old bastard with a face as cracked as a fallen autumn leaf.

"Where's your anger, Asaac?" Catriona said. "They imprisoned you, beat you, used you."

"Lucean's dead—"

"Lyanne isn't!"

The fury in Catriona's voice was enough to make Geth flinch. Then again, maybe these witches could do more than just help him get to the prince. What was it Feru-Lea had said; anything that hurt the queen, was a help to them?

"She's right," Geth said, stooping to take Lucean's hatchet. He straightened, looked from face to face. "Find your anger. That might as well be my motto."

Catriona nodded. "Use your talents. It's the only way out."

"But what about the amulets?" said the witch with the yellow hair.

Catriona ignored her. "Are you ready?"

"I'm ready," said another witch, a tiny woman with fierce brown eyes.

"Good. Now open the door."

Tham looked to Geth. The brothers moved up beside the big warrior, swords in hand. But Catriona and the fierce little one shouldered past them.

"Now," she said.

The big bodyguard nodded. With a grunt, he lifted the bar and jumped back out of the way. The door swung open. Two lilies sprang through with a yell, but they hadn't gone a yard before first man's legs went out from under him. He collapsed like a drunkard just over the threshold. The second lifted his blade until Tham clubbed him down with a bare fist from behind.

Catriona charged out through the door with a scream. Geth started to follow, but the rest of the witches and warlocks, rushed past him in a throng. They'd found their anger alright.

With Ethen's toy back at his waist, and Lucean's hatchet raised, Geth joined them. Tham and the brothers hurried to get their swords in front of him, but it was the witches who met the enemy first. What met Geth's eyes as he leapt through the door on their heels was a battle like nothing he'd ever seen.

There were no shield walls or lines. There was no clash of sword and spear. But there was plenty of mayhem. Shrieks and whimpers replaced battle-cries. Imaginary barbs—hurled from empty hands—did as much damage as slings or arrows. Whatever those witches were doing, it was working.

"Snakes, snakes!" one lily shouted, stripping off his helm to tear at his hair and run away. Others stood stock-still, eyes wide. Some just looked at their fellows, confused, clutching an amulet like the ones the brothers wore. One man touched his chest, slid down to a knee, then keeled over right there.

"Hold your ground!" Scar shouted, his hand on one of those necklaces. "Remember your training! Remember—"

Thos words died in his throat as one of soldiers staggered like a drunkard up behind him, ran him through from the back.

"Run!" a toothless lily cried. "Run for it!" He waved a hand and led the way in hasty retreat through the orchard, crashing through the trees. Most of the guardsmen followed. The remaining few, not more than a handful now, looked from one to another, cursed, and hurried to join them.

They'd won.

"Bloody magicks." Geth lowered Lucean's hatchet.

But the fight had taken its toll on the witches as well. A man came limping back towards them through the trees. Geth blinked. It was the stringy old warlock Catriona had called Asaac. He collapsed in the grass once he reached them, breathing hard.

To either side, witches leaned on one another, sweat rolling down their faces. The yellow-haired woman trembled, but the little, brown-eyed witch pushed herself up straight.

"Let's go. We aren't out yet."

Geth nodded. "She's right. And you better put on a brave face for the next round. They'll be waiting at the guardhouse."

"Stand tall," Catriona agreed. "Fake it if you must. But summon that anger again. Wear it in your eyes."

Geth, Tham, and the brothers moved to the fore. The freed witches came behind them with deadly purpose in every stride. They started down the path through the orchard. It was only then the big warrior realized Oedelia wasn't with them.

He hurried back the way they'd come. There in the door she stood, watery eyes watching him.

"Mother!" Geth beckoned.

The old woman raised one solemn hand.

But she didn't come. She turned instead, went right back inside her prison.

"Sellsword!" Tham called out.

"Damn it!" Geth hurried to catch the group up. He fell in alongside Catriona, who seemed to be leading the freed witches and warlocks.

"The Mother," he said. "She's still back there."

Catriona frowned but didn't break stride. "That's her choice. She can walk out of here any time she wants. Like she did a few days ago."

Geth swore. "Bloody magicks."

But he reckoned Catriona was right, even if Oedelia was halfway senile. From what he'd seen, she could fend for herself better than any of them. He rejoined Tham and the brothers at the front.

Emerging from the orchard, they strode toward the fountain at the center of the ward, its waters still. To their left, beside the bright-shuttered buildings, a throng of men and women cheered at the sight of them. And there was Prince Gahalus, hand in hand with a young woman with straight black hair.

The prince led Lyanne's prisoners of state out to join them. Tham meet him halfway. He swallowed the lad in a hug and cursed him roundly, grinning all the while. The brothers followed after, but the prince led them all forward again, toward Geth and the others.

Gahalus bowed low to the witches. "You've freed us. You have my thanks. This is not a thing I'll soon forget."

The fine attire of Gahalus and his cohort stood in sharp contrast to the rags the others wore, and Catriona wasn't the only one to eye him askance. "We aren't free of your mother just yet."

The prince frowned past her at the gatehouse. "No, not yet."

Lilies hurried to form up in front, others taking up positions with bows from atop the walls. Gahalus turned back, his eyes finally landing on Geth.

"And here's the famous Wolf. I knew you'd be back."

"Did you?"

"Did you ever desert a friend?"

"Well, no." Geth grimaced. "But I'm afraid I'll have to ask a favor in return this time."

The prince just smirked.

"Be ready," Catriona said. "Mind those archers."

"They have wards," Asaac wheezed. "And I'm already spent."

"Me too," someone else said.

Catriona shook a fist. "Find that anger again! Wear it on your face if that's all you can do. Let them see us and be afraid!"

She turned back toward the guards at the gatehouse. Ahead of them, the captain shouted an order and bowmen knocked their shafts. Geth cursed himself for not snatching up Scar's sword along the way. Before the first blows could be exchanged though, Gahalus stepped between the two battle lines.

"Wait!"

Raising both hands in a call for peace, he walked slowly forward, followed at a healthy distance by Geth and the others. From the gatehouse, the guard captain came forward as well, sweating under his helm.

"My prince, go back to your quarters. No one needs to get hurt. These are your mother's orders, not mine."

Geth didn't miss the amulet hanging around his neck.

But if Gahalus knew anything about that, he didn't let on. "You're right, there's no need for bloodshed. Or worse. I won't have it. Are we not all Paellian? Are we not brothers?"

"Tell those witches to stand down."

"I'm sorry, captain, but it's you who must stand down."

The lily frowned. He shouted past the prince, directly to Geth, Catriona, and all the rest. "Go back! You're outnumbered! Go back before it's too late!"

Catriona cackled like only a witch can. "Numbers? We don't need numbers!"

The guard captain cast an uneasy glance over his shoulder at his men. Geth hefted that little hatchet. Catriona spoke to her fellow witches out of the side of her mouth.

"Whatever you've got, throw it at those...What's this?"

Her words trailed off as the air suddenly went still. Geth shivered, the hairs on the back of his neck standing up, not for the first time on that god's forsaken island. The sun slid behind the clouds and a mist began to rise from the ground, swirling until it rose like a thin blanket to obscure their feet. Beside him, Catriona had closed her eyes, started to hum.

The fog thickened.

"Dear gods," the captain mouthed.

Geth shook off his surprise, stepped up beside the prince. "This is your last chance!" he shouted. "We won't be able to call them off!"

"Please!" Gahalus said.

If the captain had been sweating before, he was dripping now. "Your mother will have my hide!"

"She'll forgive you," Gahalus said, loud enough to be heard by all. "How could you stand against such sorcery? It's impossible. No one knows better than her."

He moved forward without waiting for a reply until he'd reached the line of guards. He squeezed the captain's shoulder, offered a solemn nod, and walked right past him. Soldiers in white made gestures to ward off evil and retreated to either side.

The mist held where it was, cool on the skin, but not so thick as to obstruct Geth's vision. He waved the others to fall in and hurried to follow the prince. All in a knot, the Garden's captives filed through the gate and down the zig- zagged stairs to the beach.

Feru-Lea was still there among the boats this time. From a standing position, she sagged down to her seat at the sight of them, eyes sunken. Geth kept a snide comment to himself, but Catriona stormed past him.

"You," she hissed.

"Hello, Catriona."

"I should drown you right here."

"You'd rather I had left you in that place?"

Catriona's fists shook at her side, but Geth stepped between them. "Enough! We have to go. Lyanne will have ships on the water any minute now."

"Ships?" Catriona frowned.

"Look."

Geth pointed. Grey hills, gleaming yellow-orange, peeked out across the water. The mist was gone. Boats dotted the sea not a mile away.

They piled into Feru-Lea's rowboat, stole two others besides, and pushed off the little beach. Geth took the oars beside Fera, but Catriona stepped in the same boat, seated herself right across from her.

"This isn't over, woman."

CHAPTER TWENTY-THREE

They arrived back at the Oak and Hart, wet and exhausted. Lisp and Eora's patrons-turner-helpers whipped up food and drink for all. Something like a celebration ensued.

But Ratcher's slumped form, seated like a dotard in a chair by the fire, reminded Geth they had so much more to do.

He took a seat beside Feru-Lea. "You've got help now, can you heal him?" He flicked his chin toward the assassin.

"That remains to be seen."

Geth didn't miss the wariness in the witch's voice. He wondered, did she doubt they could pull it off? Or was she skeptical about getting any help from the witches they'd set free?

Geth rose to ask them himself, but Catriona was already coming the other way. She passed the big warrior like he wasn't there to stand over Feru-Lea with a hard stare.

"We are away and safe now," she said. "Let's hear your account of things. How exactly did you, alone of all of us, stay clear of Lyanne's claws while we were hunted down, one by one, enslaved, and tortured?"

Feru-Lea returned the curly-haired witch's glare with one of her own. "Once we have Lyanne on her knees, you can ask her."

"There will be a reckoning!"

"Why? Because I outwitted the queen?" Feru-Lea cast a scathing glance around the room at the others. All conversation died, replaced by a tense silence. "You fell into her trap, each of you. While I avoided the cat's claws, as you say. If I kept my head low, it was out of necessity. Which of you would have risked your life for mine if things had been different?"

"You betrayed us. Or at the least, you stood by and did nothing. What's right is right."

"Right?" Feru-Lea snorted. "There is no code. This is no sisterhood. You're as guilty as anyone, Catriona. The webs you spun are legendary. And now—"

"Speak plain! Did you help Lyanne? Did you serve her?"

"Never."

This time it was Catriona who snorted. "Lies. We'll have our retribution."

"It wasn't me that imprisoned you, Catriona."

"And yet you're as guilty as the queen."

"I didn't owe you anything. And still I freed you all in the end."

"You didn't save us, we saved ourselves," someone said. "The storm-bringer was already dead by the time you lifted that fog to help."

Geth turned, it was the little woman with the fierce eyes. He didn't think it the right time to point out that he was the one that had killed the old sorcerer, not anyone else. And Feru-Lea didn't bother to point out that they wouldn't have ever found the Garden without her.

"Storm-bringer?" she said instead. "Ha! Lucean couldn't raise a drizzle without your help. Mother Oedelia told me everything. And where is our Mother now?"

There were some shifting feet and guilty looks, but no one spoke.

"You left her in that place. All of you. You left Mother Oedelia in prison, and you dare to cast blame on me?"

"Don't turn things, Feru-Lea. You and that bitch..."

But Catriona frowned suddenly, letting her words hang. Geth followed her eyes back to Feru-Lea, still seated, her own stare gone far away, mouth slightly open.

"What is it?" Catriona breathed.

"It's...her," Feru-Lea blinked. "Lyanne." She turned to Geth. "She's left your friend Eora in Cistern Plaza."

The big warrior's hand went to his waist where Urian's sword hung, back in place. He gripped the hilt and swore. "Thram's balls. Let's go."

Feru-Lea rose but Catriona leaned in close. "We'll be waiting for you when you get back."

It was well past noon, the sun high, blazing down on the city even in autumn. Foot traffic flowed mostly toward the great square known as Cistern Plaza, another round of competitions soon to begin. It was the wrestling, Geth thought. And after a day of rest, the crowds would be sure to get rowdy.

"We've got to find her quick," he told Feru-Lea. "If the queen has witched her dumb like she did Ratcher, Eora could be in real danger. Any bastard could grab her."

He didn't have to explain what could happen to a vulnerable woman in a rough city like Paellia.

They marched at a clip, hoods low over their faces. They'd left Gahalus and everyone else behind lest they be recognized. Feru-Lea had brought a spare cloak for Eora to ease her escape. Geth's eyes scanned every passing lily and watchman but no one had any care except for the Games.

"She'll be followed," Feru-Lea said. "Lyanne can't do it herself, but she'll have a net of soldiers cast to catch me if she can."

"Will that work?"

"No." Feru-Lea eyed Geth evenly. "But they might catch you."

"What?"

"She has no apprentice, no help, not that I know of. No one with enough talent to trouble me, at any rate. But if you don't do as I say, you'll be in danger."

Geth forced his hand off his hilt. "Alright. What do we do?"

"We don't go to Eora, we let her come to us. And no matter what, we don't show ourselves."

Geth nodded.

They came within sight of the wide plaza but turned down an alley running parallel instead. Feru-Lea led the way. Spectators in twos and threes hurried along the cobbles even here. The witch halted a few yards past a pair of drunks pissing against the alley wall behind some watering hole or other.

"This is the place," she said. She pointed to the back door.

Geth pulled it open, motioned her in. "If you say so."

Feru-Lea cast a searching glance up and down the alley once more before stepping through.

Inside, the tables were full. The witch went to the bar, ordered wine, leaving Geth to study the clientele. Eora wasn't among them.

"I don't see her," he said.

Feru-Lea scowled. "I told you, she will come. Now keep a watch for a moment. Let me call her."

The witch closed her eyes, breathed deeply. Geth cast glances either way. But no one else seemed to notice anything amiss. The place was lively, full of light from the two huge front windows, and noise from chatty patrons. It was only a few moments before Feru-Lea opened her eyes again.

"Let's get closer to the windows," she said. "She'll be here soon."

It was several minutes before Geth saw anything, but when he did, he couldn't contain a curse. "Its...gods all be damned."

It wasn't just Eora moving dumbly through the crowd. Phelan came right behind her, holding her hand by the looks of it. But something wasn't right. As they came closer, Geth saw there was blood dripping from the little man's nose and his eye was purple. Even Eora had a swollen lip.

"Sonsabitches!" He rose from his seat, started toward the door.

"Wait!" Feru-Lea snatched him by the shirtsleeve. "We can't be seen, that's the whole point."

"I don't care!"

"Yes, you do! This isn't the way to get your son back."

She was right of course. Geth couldn't see the watchmen trailing his friends anyway. Then again, he didn't have to see them, as long as they saw him.

"No, you're right." Geth breathed in and out. He squinted into the plaza until the tail became obvious, two grim-faced bastards dressed in ordinary tunics. There would be more, no doubt. Palladine knew a pair of toughs wouldn't be enough.

"They're almost here, be ready," Feru-Lea said.

"What's the plan?"

"Once they're in, run and bar the door. We take them out back, down the alley, and through a back door up the street. I'll try to steer Palladine's men in the wrong direction, but Lyanne may have them warded."

Geth nodded. He moved up near the front of the little tavern, to the side of one window. As his friends staggered in, he pushed the door shut behind them, flipped the latch, and tugged them toward the back.

"C'mon, Eora. Phelan, c'mon!"

They didn't answer, as dumb as Ratcher. But Lyanne had tied them together at the wrist so pulling Eora's hand dragged them both. They hit the back door just as the sound of curses echoed from the front. Down the alley a few yards, they ducked inside a building on the other side and started through a dim-lit tenement.

"Who are—"

Feru-Lea waved a hand and a frowning oldster shuffled out of their way. Through a hallway and they were out on the street again, one block from Cistern Plaza. Feru-Lea found another shop across the street, repeated the process by witching the shopkeep aside. Through another back door, across the alley, through another, and they were two blocks away and safe.

The witch halted long enough to throw that extra cloak over Eora's shoulders. "Give him yours," she told Geth. "And throw up the hood. If they see us from a distance, they won't recognize us. You'll have to keep your eyes low though, in case they know your face."

But Geth's hand was on Eora's cheek. He touched that swollen lip. "What if I want them to see me?"

Feru-Lea arched one of those delicate eyebrows.

Geth was already headed back the way they'd come already. "I'll meet you back at the inn!" he called over one shoulder.

"Wait!"

He didn't.

Reaching the edge of the wide plaza, Geth scanned the crowd for the two grims tailing his friends. There were plenty of lilies. But he was looking for men faced *away* from the Leonine Gate, away from the center of the action where the wrestlers would compete. A roar went up from the crowd even then as one of the matches began. Geth found the men he was looking for coming out of the tavern they'd hidden inside, cursing one another, shooting desperate glances all around the square.

The eyes of the first one landed on Geth. A smile touched his lips to reveal a set of crooked front teeth. It was a smile Geth was about to wipe from the face of the Wide Eria. Crooked reached back, tugged at the arm of his fellow as Geth loosened Urian's sword and started toward them.

The gold-bands drew, charged with a yell, scattering spectators and trampling one poor fool down. Geth met the first one with an arm-shuddering blow to send him reeling to one side. The second tried to step in before the big warrior could reset himself, but Geth let his momentum spin him, coming full circle with his blade low, to slice the bastard below the naval.

"Aggghhhh!"

Geth didn't wait to watch his guts slide out. He turned back to the first gold-band, Crooked. The watchman sent a straight thrust at him, but Geth parried, jabbed straight forward with a fist to crumple the bastard where he stood.

It was all too easy, especially after the fight against Mylo and Palladine, true blade-masters. Geth raised his sword then lowered it with a sniff, shoved it back in his belt. This bastard didn't deserve a quick death.

"Come here, you sonofabitch." With a kick, he disarmed Crooked, dragged him up, only to punch him back down again. The bastard climbed to all fours, groaned, coughed one of those crooked teeth into his hand.

But he was laughing when he looked up to face Geth.

"You think it's funny to abuse a woman?" the big warrior said. "You think you can lay hands on my friends?"

"He said you'd say that."

The man flicked a glance over Geth's shoulder. Following that gaze, the big warrior's eye landed on another dozen lilies, pushing through the crowd. Palladine marched at the fore.

"Thram's balls."

Leaving Crooked there, Geth sprinted for the same tavern they'd hidden in earlier. He barged through the front and exited the back, aiming for the same trick Feru-Lea had used earlier.

But soldiers were already coming down either end of the alley, in plain sight of which building he ducked into next. With another curse, he slammed through a doorway, down a hall and out into the next street.

A furtive glance both ways revealed more lilies. They'd figured out his game. He could only cut through taverns and bakeries for so long before they cornered him somewhere. "Damn you, Thram and Awer!"

They hadn't seen him yet, but he was stuck where he was. And more soldiers would be following behind him in moments. He drew Urian's sword, mind working, still ducked in that doorway. Up and down the street, soldiers closed the net, moving from shop to shop, peering inside each. The nearer group was only a couple doors down. Geth heaved a breath, cursed the gods, readied himself to step out, until a triumphant shout echoed from the first group of lilies.

"I see him! He's here!"

Geth slunk back under the doorframe just in time as one troop of soldiers ran past him to join the others. A yell echoed down the street as they piled inside what appeared to be a tinker's store, bellowing a challenge. Geth just stood there blinking until a fierce whisper reached him from across the street.

"C'mon, Green-cloak!"

Feru-Lea. She waved at him from inside the threshold of a shoemaker's store. Geth flicked a glance down the street both ways then crossed the space at a run. Inside, he joined the witch and his two dumbstruck friends. They dragged the pair by the arm, breathless, away and to safety.

"Dear gods." Feru-Lea shook her head. "He said you had a temper, but I didn't take you for a fool."

Geth rubbed his jaw. "Seems like everyone knows about that. Even Palladine."

Thankfully, the witch didn't twist the barb.

But Geth didn't need her to. He really was a fool. Palladine knew him better than he knew himself. He looked to Phelan, that vacant, purple eye, Eora's busted lip. Geth knew it was because of him they'd been roughed up, a ploy that had almost worked.

"At least we've got them back," he muttered. The cobbles passed under foot as they neared the Oak and Hart. But dragging the pair along raised another question.

"What's her play?" Geth pulled up short a block from the inn. He frowned at the rope binding his friends at the wrist, wrestled it off to free them.

Feru-Lea's eyes narrowed, but she just shook her head. "She's cunning. I couldn't say with any certainty."

"I thought we'd really done something," Geth continued, "stealing the prince, I mean. I thought that gave us leverage, raised the stakes as Phelan would say. But here we are, a few hours later, and Lyanne has released two of her hostages, not one. And beat them up on top of it."

"We've got her attention," Lyanne said, "there can be no doubt about that. We've destroyed the Garden, freed a source of her power, not to mention more than a few political enemies. Perhaps you're not the only one with a temper. Perhaps we've made her mad."

"I reckon that could work to our advantage, if she's really anything like me. A hasty move, a mistake... That could be the thing we need."

Feru-Lea's brow pinched up. "She's spiteful, the queen. Remorseless. I don't know about her enforcer, Palladine, but I fear what Lyanne could do in anger."

Geth blinked. His mind went to his son, in the queen's hands even now. He shook his head to dispel dark thoughts before they could gather. He took Phelan's hand in one grip, Eora's in the other. He had all of his friends back at least. That was something.

"That young woman with the straight hair, the one with the prince," he said, thinking back to the fight at the Garden, "could that have been Ryrus's daughter?"

"The one with Gahalus?" The witch frowned. "If the rumors are true, it has to be. What that means for Pellon—indeed for all the Sworn Realms—who can say? The ramifications of setting her free could play out for generations."

"Well, that's good, isn't it? Anything that hurts Lyanne could help me get my son back."

"This is bigger than your son, you know that. Lyanne, the whole of Pellon—"

"Ethen is the only thing that matters to me."

Feru-Lea snorted. "That's not true, Geth Green-cloak. You're not a man to let down your friends."

"Pellon's problems are none of my concern. This place chewed me up and spit me out. How do you think I ended up wearing the green?"

"And Gahalus? What of his problems? What will you promise him? You can't just use him to get the child back, then leave him to the mercy of his mother. What exactly do you intend to do with the prince? Do you really think you can trade one son for another?"

Geth didn't answer. He didn't know. It didn't sound good the way she said it either.

Maybe it was her magicks, but Feru-Lea read his mind. "Whatever you do, you'd better do it quick."

Geth frowned. "What do you mean?"

"Your friends." The witch flicked a glance at Phelan and Eora. "Lyanne said one hostage at a time, but it seems she's moved things up."

Geth swore as realization hit him, but Feru-Lea spoke first.

"That's right. By my reckoning, we only have one more day."

CHAPTER TWENTY-FOUR

They walked in silence until the inn appeared up ahead. Feru-Lea pulled the door open and Geth ushered his slack-jawed friends inside.

But the common room was empty. Lisp looked up from behind the bar and Ratcher drooled beside the fire. Aside from the whisk of Brega's mindless sweeping, the place was silent.

"Where is everyone?" Geth asked.

"The prince left," Lisp said. "I think they went to the river."

The man came around his counter to look Eora over with a frown, but Geth just rubbed his chin. It made sense; the girl—Ryrus's daughter—and the others would need to leave Paellia or risk being rounded up by Lyanne and thrown right back into a cell. Tham and the brothers, no doubt, had gone along to help Gahalus get them away. That didn't explain what had happened to the witches though.

No sooner had the thought crossed Geth's mind than the whole troop came marching down the stairs, almost in lock-step. Catriona led them. Geth didn't like the look on her face.

He went on the offensive. "Right on time," he said before anyone else could get a word out. "My friends need help. Together you can heal these people of whatever magicks Lyanne's laid on them."

Catriona's eye flicked to Phelan and Eora. She sniffed. "In due time, perhaps. But first, Feru-Lea of the Bronlands is coming with us, to answer her sisters and brothers."

Geth's hand went to his hilt. "No one's going anywhere. You hear me? Not until you've healed my friends."

His eyes flicked from one witch to the next, hard and menacing. He'd stepped in front of Feru-Lea, but the witches and warlocks fanned out behind Catriona, undaunted.

"We only want *her*. Step aside, warrior." The witch waved a hand.

Geth shivered, but if those words were supposed to do more, they failed. "Keep your magicks off me, woman. This is the last warning you'll get."

After what he'd seen in the Garden, he didn't doubt they had some nasty tricks up their sleeves, but he wasn't taking no for an answer, not with his friends lives on the line.

Feru-Lea must have seen the shift of his weight. She pushed past him. "Stay your hand, Green-cloak. I'll have no bloodshed on account of a misunderstanding."

"First things first," Geth growled. "My friends. *Now*."

Catriona opened her mouth, but Feru-Lea beat her to it. "We can't do it without Mother Oedelia. Together, Catriona, Mother, and I could lift Lyanne's curse, but without Oedelia, none of these practitioners are strong enough in the arts of healing."

Across from Feru-Lea, more than a few of her fellows scowled, but none muttered anything loud enough to hear.

"This won't take long," she said. "I'll be back."

Catriona's eyes flicked from the witch to Geth and back. "We shall see."

Feru-Lea laid a hand on Geth's arm, gave it a reassuring squeeze, then followed behind Catriona back out onto the street. Where they were headed, he couldn't have guessed. The others fell in behind. He watched them disappear around a corner.

"Thram's pimpled ass."

He exhaled a sigh, ran a hand through his hair. He looked from Ratcher to Phelan to Eora, the three of them arranged around the fire like dotards indeed. For all he'd been through, he realized he hadn't accomplished much at all.

And yet he hadn't even begun to play the new piece on the board. He turned to the barman. "How long ago did the prince leave?"

"Not half an hour ago," said Lisp.

Geth started straight for the door. "Be back soon!"

It wasn't so far to the river marina, not at Geth's pace. It made perfect sense for Gahalus to help his fellow prisoners escape. And it would be easier to sneak them up the Arm than out through any of the gates or sea-ports. With only one day in hand, however, Geth didn't have the luxury of waiting for the prince's return.

His mind worked as he marched down the streets, foot traffic thin and mostly moving in the opposite direction. What would he tell Gahalus when he arrived? He'd already promised Tham that King Hadean would protect the both of them from the queen. But there had to be some way the pair could help get Ethen back first.

Feru-Lea made a valid point earlier; trading son for son—the prince for Ethen—that was out of the question. But perhaps, as with Gemela in Ilia, he could use Gahalus to lure his enemy out. Before he could think more on that, a familiar chill hit his spine and he cursed out loud.

"Thram's crooked cock!"

Ceter. Geth knew his magicks well. It was only one more block to the marina, but he turned to arrive through an alley, far to the east end of the landing. Even from there he could see a commotion at the mouth of the boatyard, where a large naval galley had been moored up alongside a short, sleek vessel.

Geth cursed again, slid Urian's sword around to the small of his back. He hustled at a crouch as close as he could get to the two ships, crouched down beside a barrel at water's edge. Gahalus, Tham, the brothers, and everyone from the Garden stood in a clump on the deck of the sleek vessel. Gold-bands surrounded them, swords draw.

But they didn't need those weapons. Geth recognized the stiff posture of men and women frozen by the warlock's fearspell. A small boat rowed out to join them. With a hand from the watchman, the queen herself climbed up onto the deck.

"Damn."

Geth bit down the rest of his curses. He hadn't expected the prince to get caught so quickly, but the arrival of Lyanne was the real surprise. Then again, with magicks like hers, could they really expect to hide him? Geth touched Ethen's little sword, cursed some more, and slid into the water.

With the queen's entrance, no one was paying attention to anything else. He swam as quietly as he could until he was up against the hull of the galley. Inching around, he got himself in between the two ships, in the shadowed space beneath the curve of the two hulls which met a few feet above the river's surface, the smaller ship held fast by moorings lashing it to the great galley.

He needed to cut those ropes. Stretching up with Urian's sword, Geth reckoned he could manage it, but he needed a distraction.

Thank the gods, a voice above provided one.

"...don't think I have to tell you that I'm disappointed. Especially after all the things we discussed on the island."

It was Lyanne. Geth couldn't see from there, but all eyes would be on her, he was sure. And if he sawed at the mooring carefully, from the bottom, his blade would barely be visible.

He moved toward the first of three ropes binding the two ships, half-listening to the queen. "...do you understand all we've sacrificed, your father and I? You love the small folk, don't you? Do you want things to be better for them? They can be.

"But they're like children; they need a firm hand to guide them, the rod when necessary, the reward when they've earned it. Your father and I, we're the only ones willing to give them that, not just here in Pellon, across the Sworn Realms. While other kings sip spirits on padded chairs, wage wars of vanity, or ride out for a leisurely hunt, your father and I would make the sacrifices—the hard choices—needed to secure safety for the small folk, which is as much as anyone can really ask."

Geth had cut the better part of the first rope. He left a few strands hanging and moved on to the second, repeated the process. Cold river water lapped up into his face, chilled his arm as he stretched up with Urian's blade. But an even colder voice sounded above.

"We should take them and go," Ceter said. "I sense...something."

Geth slid down the hull to the final rope, began sawing, prayed that he had time to finish. Even then, the easy part would be done, nothing more. But he had a plan for what came next.

"Let us leave then," Lyanne said. "There's little sense standing here, as Master Ceter has advised. There will be no song and wine where we're headed though, I'm afraid. The island is...no longer an option."

Geth finished. He slid around the hull of the war-galley to the opposite side. Another set of ropes secured it to the end of the docks. Quiet as he could, Geth climbed up to the lip of the gunwale, cast a furtive glance over the edge.

All eyes were still on the queen. She stood in front of Gahalus and a knot of prisoners that included Tham, the brothers, and Ryrus's daughter. Sailors in lily-white surrounded them, but Lyanne wasn't done with her son just yet. No wonder the lad hated her.

"These people are our enemies, you do understand that, don't you? Your father's enemies, my enemies, your enemies as well. Her familae would kill us without a second thought. We've kept Ryrus in check all these years, and spared his kin as well. Do you think he would spare you, as I've spared Talayne? For peace?

"Perhaps it's all above the reasoning of your young mind. But I thank the gods nonetheless. If not for this timely intervention, your thoughtless actions could very well have led to civil war."

She raised one hand to her son's cheek, even as he stood there, petrified, frozen stiff by Ceter's magicks. Palladine was nowhere to be seen, but a lanky, stork-like bastard wearing a ridiculous gold-trimmed hat stood alongside the warlock a few paces behind the queen.

There was little sense in waiting, as Ceter had said. And seeing that fool in the gold-trimmed hat, Geth reckoned he knew what to do.

"Aghhhh!"

With a yell, he was over the gunwale, charging straight for Ceter and the ship captain. It was only a few strides across the naval galley and down with a leap onto the deck of the sleeker ship. The pompous scratch got his blade out fast enough, but he had nothing like the strength required to parry Geth's swing. Urian's blade crashed through to batter the man down to the planks.

Geth didn't finish him though, he went after Ceter next.

The warlock was already on the retreat. He bolted left, down the length of the sleek ship and back over the edge onto the taller galley, leaving Geth down below. But Geth had done enough already. Swords rasped out of sheaths as Gahalus, Tham, and the brothers drew steel.

"Eleventh!" the ship captain shouted, struggling to rise.

Geth turned back, ran him through before he could gain his feet. His seamen just gawked, unsure whether to attack their prince, or Geth, or just flee. The big warrior hacked at the nearest mooring, slicing the remaining threads neatly in one chop.

"Hold them!" Lyanne shouted. "Ceter! Men of the Eleventh, hold them!"

But the warlock was already inside the cabin of the galley. And with their captain dead, the seamen followed Ceter's example in retreat. A pair grabbed the queen, hustled her over the side and up onto the big warship. The brothers hacked at the remaining ropes as sailors emerged like bugs from hatches and holes to man the sleek ship.

Tham threw his great arms against the side of the big galley with a roar. "Arrggghhhh!"

Space appeared between the two ships, but Ceter reemerged from the cabin, longbow in hand. Like Ciro Brightbow out of legend, he plied the weapon flawlessly. He didn't loose at Geth or Tham or the brothers, though. Arrow after arrow flew, striking down the men Geth had freed from the Garden until only the straight-haired girl was left, shielded by the prince.

Geth had already climbed aboard the war-galley. Tham heaved again and the sleek vessel was free. Oarsmen pushed her out into the river, but with a wail, Tham lost balance and went overboard in between them. Geth couldn't spare another glance. Ahead of him, Ceter's bow was bent.

"Ceter!"

With a yell, he hurled Urian's sword, sideways, like a disc. There was no chance it would kill the warlock, but it did clatter into him, sending his arrow wide. The warlock cursed, his bow-string cut. Gahalus and his ship lurched away. Someone threw down a rope and they towed Tham along like a soaked water-rat behind them.

It was only then Geth realized he stood on the deck of an enemy ship without a weapon. Lyanne must have ducked below but a dozen seamen turned their eyes toward him.

"Get him!"

"Shit!"

It was Geth's turn to retreat. Two strides and a jump and he was over the side and into the water, thrashing toward land.

Lilies cursed him and shook weapons from the gunwale. The prince's ship moved in the opposite direction, upriver, and away.

The sun was still high in the sky as Geth pushed through the door of the Oak and Hart. But he was cold. And wet. And alone. Riverwater squelched in his boots, dripped from his clothes down to the planks of the floorboards. Lisp had the decency to pass him a cup of wine as he sank into a chair.

The common room was empty except for Brega with her broom and his three friends, arranged around the fire, as before. They spoke to him, even if slack jaws never moved. He'd failed, they said. He'd failed them and he'd failed his son.

"Gods all be damned."

It was no god or goddess that answered him though, just a haughty witch. "There you are."

"Feru-Lea?" Geth looked up as she appeared from the back hallway.

Lisp looked confused behind his counter. "How..."

"Well," Geth said, "seems you managed to clear your name. That's good. But Gahalus and the rest, they're gone."

Feru-Lea strode past him so he had to turn from the bar and his friends beside their fire to face her.

"I'm not concerned with the prince, though others are," she said. "I'm concerned with you."

Something in her tone made Geth flinch. The hairs on the back of his neck went up and he heard the scuff of a shoe just in time to turn. Behind him, his three friends had risen. Eora came at him first, knife in hand.

"What the—!"

Geth swatted the blade from her grip before she could swing it.

Ratcher went for him with bare hands next. Springing from his chair, Geth avoided the assassin's lunge. Ratcher landed like a felled tree on top of that empty seat, tumbled to the ground as Phelan rushed Geth right after him.

As many times as the big warrior had wanted to slap his friend, he took no joy in thumping him now. He leaned back to let a clumsy knife-slash whistle past, then stepped sideways to aim a kick into the bottom of Phelan's pants. His friend went down in a heap, Eora coming the other way to attack the big warrior again.

Geth had figured out what was going on by then. Whatever magicks had turned his friends against him though, it was hampered by Lyanne's previous spell. They moved like they were stuck in the mud. He dodged around Eora easily and made for the bar. Reaching over, he grabbed the first bottle he could find, turned, and hurled it at Feru-Lea.

The witch grunted as the bottle struck, doubled over, stumbled against a wall. "Rise!" she cried, lifting both hands over her head. But Geth didn't wait for his friends to strike again. He crossed the space, took the witch by the neck, and gave her a squeeze.

Before his eyes, her features melted away to leave him holding the skinny old warlock Asaac in his hands.

"Gods..."

Words failed him. The warlock clawed at Geth's hands weakly until the big warrior shook off his astonishment and forced him down into a seat.

"Ahhh!" Asaac wailed.

"Treacherous bastard!"

Asaac slumped in his seat. "I'm sorry! She made me!"

He spoke of Lyanne, it could be no one else.

"Does she know where we are? Does she know about this inn?"

"No. But she has me! Kill me, please! I deserve it!"

Geth swore. He looked over his shoulder. His friends lay dumbly where they'd landed. Whatever spells the man had laid on them, it seemed they were broken.

"Kill me!" Asaac said. "I can't fight it! I tried, but she has me! Kill—"

With a tremendous slap, Geth knocked him out cold. "Oh, shut up."

He led his spellbound friends, one by one back to the fire. Asaac, he thrust into a storeroom, arms tied behind his back with a spare belt. Lisp had run away somewhere, and the common room was quiet. Geth snatched a bottle from behind the bar, un-stoppered it, and sank into a chair.

He was alone.

And what did he have to show for his troubles? His friends had been struck dumb. He'd broken a prince and a troop of witches from a secret prison and lost the lot of them just as quick. He thought of the promise he'd made to Vriana as she lay there, sick, helpless. How he wished he could hold her hand now.

But what would she have to say? He sucked down more wine. Gods, he was tired. He croaked a laugh, to no one but himself. He might have cried if he had the strength.

Geth was dreaming and he knew it. It felt real, except that in real life, he was fairly certainly he couldn't fly.

The wind rushed past him, yellow and orange tiled roofs below, blue sky above. He moved over the city like a bird on the wind, drawn by instinct, or something else, due west. Pigeons scattered as he lit upon the edge of the city walls.

He stood to one side of the arch of the Greater Gate, Paellia's primary entrance. A pair of chatting lilies moved toward him, but they looked right through him, walked on by. Of course they did. It was a dream, wasn't it?

But a mournful howl drew Geth's eye out over the grounds surrounding the city, all the way to the ruins of Paellus's Gate. *A wolf, so close to the city?*

Like a bird indeed, Geth was in the air again, gliding over the heads of travelers on foot or on horse, with or without cart or wagon as they approached the city at the center of the world. A raised hand hailed him as a man with spikey hair looked up with a grin. Geth felt his jaw drop.

"Agrem? Is that you?"

With a jerk, Geth was awake, knocking his empty wine bottle sideways where it spun and threatened to roll off the table. His face was numb where he'd fallen asleep on his arms, but that didn't stop him from laughing out loud.

"Everything alright?" Lisp asked, back behind the counter again.

Geth ignored the cook-turned-barman. He kicked up from his seat, squinted out the window. Best he could tell, he hadn't slept more than an hour. The sun still shined bright outside, as it had on Agrem's face on his approach to the Golden City.

The streets were quieter than expected as Geth hurried toward the Greater Gate, a few drunken spectators hustling home from the Games, nothing more. Wary-eyed lilies and watchmen patrolled the streets in packs, but Geth didn't have time to find out why. He ducked down alleys and side lanes to avoid them, breathing hard by the time he came within sight of the Greater Gate.

And there he was, the Seer, in the flesh. The spikes of his hair glinted in the sun, collar thrown open against the heat, pack over one shoulder, walking-stick in hand. Geth started to call out, until his eyes drifted to the Ilar's left.

Vriana.

"Gods be praised."

Geth's voice came out in a hoarse whisper. Joy and surprise, relief and shame all wrestled inside him. She walked with her chin up, staring down passersby that dared gawk at the outland woman come to the great city, clad in fur and leather, standing taller than most men and girt with sword and dagger. There was no way she'd seen anything close to Paellia's grandeur, and yet she wore a look haughty enough to rival any queen. Joy won out, and Geth laughed from deep in his chest.

At that distance, there was no way the Seer could have heard, but he turned nonetheless, raised a hand in greeting. Vriana squinted to follow the direction of his wave, and another familiar face appeared behind her, stern eyes searching for enemies.

"Hack, you brave fool!"

Geth wended through the traffic coming into the city. He didn't pause for any greeting, didn't stop until he had Vriana clutched against him in a tight embrace. "Thram and Awer, Vorda and Selel, I swear I'll never curse the gods again!" He breathed her scent for a good long second then pulled away to hold her at arm's length.

"I am here," she told him.

CHAPTER TWENTY-FIVE

The catching up would have to wait. Geth couldn't let them stay there, not with so many watchmen about. He started the trio back toward the inn.

Busy as it was near the gates, foot traffic quickly thinned as they got deeper into the city, hastening the trek. But Geth didn't like it, not one bit.

"This place is..." Vriana searched for a word.

"I know," said Geth. "There should be more people. Something's up."

"*More* people?"

Geth did his best to hide a smile.

A few streets further on, he found an innkeep standing outside his establishment, frowning at the quiet streets.

"Hey friend," Geth called. "What's happened?"

The man looked from the big warrior in his Bronian fleece, to the Ilars in their leathers, to Hack's green-cloak. He shook his head. "You mean you're not here for the Games? I was about to ask you the same thing."

Geth just grunted.

"Well, I can tell you this,' said the innkeep, "there was some trouble at the wrestling event this afternoon. So I heard tell."

"That right?" Geth frowned. "I had to leave early. But I didn't see anything worse than a few crooked lilies."

The innkeep shrugged. "Something between the Eleventh Host and the Sixth. You know how those Sixer half-breeds...er..."

Maybe he'd seen Geth's tattoos. The man trailed off, thinking better of whatever he was about to say. But Geth just waved his friends to continue on.

"Wait, I've got an empty table!" the innkeep called at their departing backs.

They dodged soldiers and lawmen until they'd reached the Oak and Hart. Lisp was behind the bar, but his eyes went wide and that tongue of his wouldn't work at all at the sight of the Ilars.

"My friends are hungry," Geth told him. "Do we have anything to eat around here?"

The barman hurried through the door to the kitchens. When Geth turned, his friends stood beside Phelan, Ratcher, and Eora in front of the fire. Hack muttered curses, Vriana grimaced, Agrem knelt to rest a hand on Eora's arm.

"Mmmm."

"Lyanne, she..." Geth trailed off. He didn't know where to begin.

Heaving a sigh, he went all the way back, starting with his arrival and Feru-Lea's errand to the Garden. He moved quickly through the fight at Cistern Plaza and the failed plan that landed his friends in this dumbstruck state. His teeth were gritted by the time he recounted their second expedition to the island prison, the witches' abduction of Feru-Lea, and Gahalus's flight.

"We've only got one more day," he concluded. "And then Palladine and Lyanne will put the same spell on our son."

The room fell silent. Vriana searched his eyes. "Mmmm."

That summed it up, Geth reckoned. He'd come a long way, thrashed around a bit, and that was it. He had nothing—no plan, no ploy, and no ideas.

"I just need to think," he muttered, stepping away from the fire to pace the room. He pulled at the ends of his mustache. If Lyanne was as good as her word, Ethen would be made dumb and left somewhere to fend for himself in less than twenty-four hours. They had to act. And they had to do it quick. Geth looked to Phelan; the stakes had never been higher.

At least he had his friends though, all of them, even if the half of them couldn't do more than drool. Palladine and the queen had his son, but they'd tried to get to his woman too, and failed. He looked to Vriana, pride swelling his chest at the sight of her, fierce as anything.

That gave him a thought, though it wasn't the kind that would get them any closer to Ethen.

"Vriana," he said, "Whatever we decide, whatever we try, there something we need to do first."

"Speak, Gethe."

"It's not for lands or titles, for Ethen or anything else. It's just for us. Right now."

"What is this thing you want?" the chieftess asked. "Tell me."

"I want to marry you."

Lisp must have been the sentimental type. Geth didn't even know he'd been listening, but before he could say 'Thram's balls,' the barman was around his counter with a bunch of flowers. He offered them tentatively to Vriana while Agrem arranged everyone in front of the hearth. They moved the chairs so that their friends could watch, spell-blind or otherwise.

Hack stepped in close at Geth's side, hands composed in front of him. Geth blinked.

"What?" said the green-cloak. "I'm your best man, aren't I?"

Agrem stood before them, cleared his throat, began some prayer or other in the Ilar tongue. He made them hold hands, taking the flowers and walking three circles around them. He dropped petals as he went, chanting something in his language.

Geth mostly only knew the curse words. He didn't recognize a single syllable. But he reckoned it was as good a way to be married as standing before a sister of Neyna or riding off on horseback in Mog fashion. He looked to his left, met Virana's eye. A part of him had wondered if she would have him. The way she looked back though, the glow on her face, he didn't think she'd ever looked happier.

They kissed when the ceremony was done. It was just a touch of the lips—there would be time for passion later—but the embrace that came after...Geth thought his body would've swallowed hers if it could have. He squeezed her hard against him, one hand on her back, the other in her hair, holding her head firm against his. He breathed her again, shuddered as the weight of so many torments came off. He pulled halfway away finally to take her in with his eyes.

"Vriana—"

"You are a brave man, Gethe," she told him. She had a firm hold on the back of his neck and didn't seem likely to let go.

"Am I?"

"Mmmm. Some would say a foolish man, to sleep beside the Chieftess of the Laeri, Sword-daughter to Vather Lonega, devil of the Point-Fort, slayer of her own brother."

Geth smiled. "Slay me in my sleep if you want. I'll die a happy man."

Vriana snorted a little laugh, but just then the door shook as someone rattled the locked handle from outside. Lisp hurried to question the new arrival through the crack. He pulled the door open a second later to admit Prince Gahalus.

But the prince left Lisp doubled over in a bow to march directly up to the fire. His eyes flicked from Agrem, to the flower petals, to Geth and Vriana, still entwined. A smile lit his face and he bowed low to the chieftess.

"Love," he said. "It's on the air, isn't it?"

"Uh—" Geth's mouth opened and closed.

The prince thrust out a hand for a clasp, shook vigorously. "Congratulations. A beautiful couple, really." He eyed the weapons at Vriana's waist. "And a fitting one, it appears."

They shared wine and bread, cheese and cold meats which Lisp produced from the cellar. No one spoke of their predicament until Geth reached behind the counter for a bottle of the strong stuff.

He poured a thimble-full for each of them. "White Adus," he said. "But just a taste. We still have work to do. Dangerous work."

"You don't do it justice," said the prince.

Geth grimaced. "I didn't think you were coming back. You were wise to sneak the others away. And perhaps you'd have been even wiser to stay away yourself."

"I know she has your son. I'm not keen to be traded back into my mother's hands, but I couldn't stand by and do nothing. Not after you risked so much to break us out."

Geth grimaced. "I would have broke you out the first time if I'd known you were there."

"That's alright, Master Wolf. I knew you'd be back."

Agrem waved a hand. "Mmmm." He'd hardly spoken except for the wedding ritual, but he frowned impatiently now. "What to do? The she-cat will come for her son, just as we come for

ours, mmmm? Words laid on this place will not hide him forever."

It was Geth's turn to frown. He didn't know what the Seer
meant by 'words laid,' but he knew who the she-cat must be.
He certainly didn't want Eora's home and livelihood destroyed
because of him.

That raised another concern. He stepped toward Gahalus,
offered Ethen's toy sword. "Here. You'll need this."

The prince took it gingerly, turned it over in his hands. "What
is it?"

"Protection. Like those amulets your mother's guards wore at
the Garden, I think."

"Don't you need it yourself?"

"You need it more."

Gahalus nodded with a frown. His eyes went to Ratcher and
Eora and Phelan last of all. "We still don't have a plan, do we?
I'm sure you hoped to use me as leverage against my mother, but
you know I can't let her have me again. I might end up as they
are, poor souls."

"We're going to fix that," Geth said. "As sure as we're gonna'
get my son back. We just need a few witches."

"Where are they anyway?"

Geth shook his head. "They took Feru-Lea and vanished.
Only one of them came back."

He told them briefly about Asaac's return, drawing a few
choice words in Ilar from Vriana, and more or less the equivalent
from Hack in plain Aturian.

Gahalus hardly listened though. He wandered over to stand beside Phelan's chair.

"Ah, Phinnie. What roll of the dice landed you here, eh my friend?"

"No dice," said Agrem. "A cat's scratch."

Gahalus leaned down to straighten Phelan's collar. "This is an abomination." He looked up to meet Geth's eye. "I'm with you, even against my mother. All the way to the end."

Much as they needed the prince, Geth's feelings were mixed, hearing that. It was no small thing to choose a group of outsiders over your own kin. Who would want to be the cause of that?

But then, what kind of woman abducted babies, turned adults into slack-jawed fools, and imprisoned her own son?

"She won't stop," Gahalus said, reading his mind. "She's got big plans. Stealing your son is just the beginning."

"Then we kill her." Vriana stepped forward, eyes bright. "We take what is ours."

Geth blew out a sigh. "I'm just trying to get Ethen and get away clean." He looked to Gahalus. "Could you even do it, if it came to that?"

Gahalus didn't look up. His eyes were on Phelan again. "She's evil. She loves me, maybe, but that doesn't change it."

And Gahalus loved her too. Geth could see it. He sucked in a sharp breath as the solution came to him.

"This isn't about love, not for your mother," he said. "It's about fear. But your love is the thing to undo her."

Gahalus frowned.

Geth continued before he could speak. "Talayne, the young woman. She's the daughter of Ryrus, isn't she?"

Realization lit the prince's eyes, but a frown followed hard on its heels. "We can't risk her, not like that. And she's gone now anyway."

"She may be gone," said Geth, waving everyone to follow to the storeroom where he'd stowed Asaac. "But *he* isn't."

It could work. Lyanne needed Talayne back. They needed Ethen. And with Asaac's magicks, they could orchestrate a trade. For the first time in a long time, Geth had real hope. But they had to do it quick.

"On that ship, the girl could be back beside her father tomorrow," Geth said. "We have to arrange a meet with the queen before she gets word from Ryrus that he has his daughter. There's no telling what he'll do once he has her safe."

Gahalus nodded, reached around the bar for more White Adus. "A much better plan than trying to use me as bait. My mother would see right through that. If there's one thing she knows about the wolf, its that he's loyal to the pack. That's why she went after your son in the first place, I'm sure."

"Mmmm," Agrem agreed. "But first I must see to this ehlo-sferu."

He disappeared inside the storeroom with Asaac. Geth didn't know much about magicks, but thinking of all Ethen's little sword had done for him, he reckoned it wouldn't be any trouble for the Seer to strip Lyanne's compulsions. Asaac, no doubt, would be happy for the chance to redeem himself.

After a brief inspection though, Agrem shook his head. He frowned over the unconscious warlock. "Mmmm." Without warning, he gave the man a sharp kick.

"Ah!" Asaac came away with a start. He sat up to struggle against the belt holding his old hands behind his back. "You!" he hissed.

Agrem gave him another kick, and the warlock slumped back over with a whimper.

"Need time, mmmm?"

"Can you shake Lyanne's hold on him?" Geth asked. "I know he'll help us if it's up to him."

"I can make him clean again. But the she-cat will see through his—" he frowned, searching for the word, "—change. It will need strong magicks, as you say, to bend her eye around it, to make her believe."

"But it can be done?"

Agrem nodded. "Mmmm."

Geth left him to it. Back in the common room, Gahalus and Hack had circled behind the bar to inspect Eora's liquors. Vriana had pulled a chair up beside their three dumbstruck friends. She looked up at Geth's arrival.

"I know your shield-mates," she said, "but who is this woman?"

Geth blinked. "She's a friend. And Phelan's partner now. We go way back."

"Mmmm." Vriana looked Eora up and down, reached over gently to smooth a strand of hair down. "Then she is my friend too."

"That's...good."

Vriana kicked back her chair, stood. She set one hand on Geth's shoulder. "It is alright that you have...friends in your past, Gethe. She looks like a good woman. And I am happy she is with Phelan now."

"Uh..."

"We must think more of this witch-queen if we are to free them now. And one day, perhaps, we shall sit for *their* wedding."

"That would be something."

Gahalus came back from behind the bar to join them, followed by Hack.

"She's right," said the prince. "There's still a lot to discuss. It won't do any good to draw my mother out if we aren't prepared for her when we do. She'll round us all up and slap on her spells if we don't lay our plans carefully."

Hack nodded with a grunt. Vriana hummed. Geth muttered a curse.

"Where do we meet for the exchange?" he wondered aloud. He tried to think of the meeting like it was a checkerboard match, the players she'd field, how it might play out. There was only one place that would do.

"*The Garden.*"

Geth and Gahalus said it at the same time.

The prince grinned. Hack and Vriana both frowned, but Geth matched the Gahalus's smile.

"If we get there first, we can see her coming," Geth said. "We tell her to bring my son and two oarsmen, no more."

Gahalus raised a finger. "There's only one flaw."

"How to get away. We'll need a fast ship, something like the one that took you upriver."

"The Wasp," said the prince with a nod. "Given a few hours, I'm sure I could find something suitable. But what's to stop my mother from encircling the whole island? She's got the Eleventh Host and all her ships at her beck and call."

Geth pulled at his mustache. They could make demands until they were blue in the face, but he wasn't fool enough to think Lyanne wouldn't double-cross them the moment she had Talayne in hand. The prince was right.

"The Eleventh," Geth repeated.

Prince Gahalus raised a finger. "There may be a solution, something you've already set in motion."

Geth frowned. "Me?"

"Have you heard of the row between the Bloody Sixth and the Eleventh? After the wrestling competition? Everyone's talking about it."

"I heard something, but—"

"Well, when you helped us escape, you killed the captain of the warship that had snared us."

"One captain out of dozens," Geth said. "Hardly enough, I reckon."

"But not just any captain, Master Wolf. Who do you think my mother would call upon to help recapture her most dangerous enemies? Not just any captain at all, but the commodore of the entire fleet."

"Lord Hicrates?"

The prince nodded. "The old boot-licker himself. Killed in action. And a good riddance too. During the Affliction, they say he ordered men thrown overboard if they so much as sneezed."

"Still, he's only one man. And what has this got to do with the Sixth anyway?"

"Well, isn't it obvious? It was you that killed him, Master Wolf. Someone recognized you from the duel at Cistern Plaza—and yes, I heard about all that. Now the Eleventh are saying it was the champion of the Sixth that murdered their man."

"Thram's twisted balls."

"I'd say the feud between the navy and the men from the lows is burning white hot after that."

Geth grimaced, mouthed a few choice ones. Then again, Gahalus wasn't wrong to look for an opportunity there. With the sailors of the Eleventh distracted, there could be a way to stall them when the hour came to make the exchange with Lyanne.

He just needed to figure out how.

But Vriana came up close beside him before he could think of anything. She squeezed his arm, smiled that fierce smile of hers. Hack moved in from the other side wearing a grin.

"You fought another duel?" he asked.

"And killed the boat master of these sun-landers, mmmm?" Vriana's chest puffed out almost as much as Hack's. "I am proud."

"But how are we going to use that? We need to cripple Lyanne's ships somehow. What does it matter how hot the feud with the Sixth burns if..."

Geth's own words supplied him the idea. His mouth opened and closed.

"You're a genius, my prince," he said.

Gahalus frowned, "Well..."

"We only need to distract the fleet for an hour or two," the big warrior said. "And what better way than to send them out to sea?"

"I'm listening."

"It's fire, see? We set fire to as many of the Eleventh's galleys as we can. The last thing a ship captain wants is to be caught at port under an attack. He's a sitting duck. He'll cut ties and launch. They all will. Am I wrong?"

The prince nodded slowly. "There's a good twenty ships in the great harbor—more at anchor around the east side of the city. But we only need to worry about those at port."

"And we only need to hit a few of them. Just enough to sound the alarm, start a panic."

"Once those ships are offshore," Gahalus said. "My mother's messengers will have to row out there to order a move on the Garden. But can we do it? They'll be on the alert. Can we manage to set fire to even one of those galleys?"

Geth smoothed his mustache. "Not without the help of the Sixth."

CHAPTER TWENTY-SIX

They were running out of daylight and they were running out of time. Geth sent Hack with Prince Gahalus to find the sort of ship they would need to make a hasty exit from the Garden. He took Vriana with him to find the Sixth Host.

"I was worried," Geth said, one hand on his hilt, the other clasped tight on his wife's as they started out. "Agrem said you'd be alright, but..."

"I am strong, Gethe." Vriana squeezed his hand. "They told me about the tsook, how you ran the forests to steal Sythme. How you swam the river, for me."

Geth turned his head to find the chieftess's bright eyes on him. He licked his lips, unsure what to say.

That he'd been petrified? That he would have failed if not for Hack? Vriana squeezed his hand again and he decided it didn't matter.

"I've never been so glad to see someone as when I saw you marching into this city. Ha! What a sight!"

Vriana sniffed. "It is a dirty place. Crowded. And it smells. But the roofs are pretty. And the stones. They remind me of..." she paused, thinking. "Bread and butter."

Geth smiled. Gods but her hand felt good in his. They were together. They were married. And they were going to get Ethen back before the night was done.

They kept moving, didn't say much more. They didn't have to. Geth led them south, shadows grown long as the sun dipped. Thanks to Feru-Lea's errand, he reckoned he knew just where to find the men of the Sixth Host.

It was a considerable march from the Oak and Hart to the tavern where they'd run into the soldiers of the Seventh, but at least that brought them nearer the Greater Harbor, where the Eleventh and their galleys waited. Geth had prearranged for Agrem and the prince to meet them afterwards at the Fisherman's Harbor. That way, they could set out for the Garden as soon as they were done.

The last scrap of daylight was disappearing as they arrived on the street where Geth had last seen the men of the Seventh Host. It was a dump of an establishment, called the Lamb's Tail, according to the flaking placard. Doors and shutters were closed on either side. Not a soul could be seen, up or down the street. This was the place alright.

"Any Sloppy Sevens around here?" Geth called from out in front of the inn.

Silence.

Then a shutter cracked. "Who's askin'?"

"A friend. Something like it, anyway. Not some watchman or bright-white, I can tell you that."

The front door to the inn opened and the same half-eared soldier that had accosted Geth on their way with Feru-Lea stepped out, hands on hips. "Well, if it isn't."

"You remember me, drunk as you were?"

"Remember?" Half-ear spit. "I never forget a Sixer. And I never turn my back on one either."

Geth snorted.

"Better speak quick and keep moving. You can see things are a little nervy around here."

Geth nodded. "I need to find my brothers. Truth be told I haven't worn white in years, I didn't come in with them. I need to know where the Sixth Host is staying though. My bet is it's not too far from our brothers from the Lows, Vorda's Own."

"Sixes and Sevens." Half-ear snorted a laugh. The old soldier stepped all the way into the street to look Geth up and down. Behind him, grim faces crowded the door.

Vriana shifted at his side, but Geth squeezed her hand, held her still.

"Huh," the old scratch said. "Now that I stand a little closer, I reckon I know you twice over. I saw what you did to Palladine—or tried to." He spit again. "You may not know it, but that one was Vorda's Own, through and through. Until he sold us out for the glorious First."

"He's done me worse than anyone," Geth said. "I promise I'll kill him if I get the chance. But I need to find the Sixth before any of that."

The soldier flicked his chin eastwards. "About a block down, in some rat's nest called the Odd Man Out."

Geth grunted his thanks and left Half-ear and the rest eyeing him and Vriana thoughtfully as they hustled past. They found the Odd Man Out right where the sevens had said it would be. The shutters and door were locked up even tighter than those at the Lamb's Tail.

But a couple lads of ten or twelve sat in a doorway across the street scratching the cobbles with sticks. Geth knew a lookout when he saw one. He walked straight up to them.

"Toss a rock at a window or whatever. Tell em I'm looking for Urian. I'm a friend."

The first lad shrugged, but the second looked Geth and Vriana up and down. "You don't look like friends."

"We don't look like Eleventh Host either, do we?"

"Look like foreigners."

"You gonna' throw a rock or what?"

He didn't have to. The door opened to admit a long-limbed scratch with a thick black beard and a red rag on his sleeve.

"You got some cherries on you, showing up around this place."

Geth just frowned at the man, but Vriana made a show of setting her stance, resting one hand on her hilt. "Too much talk. If you want to fight, we are ready."

"Looking for a fight, are ya?"

Geth stepped in front of Vriana, hands raised. "I'm looking for Urian. That's all. There's only one more day of the Games, I know you'll be leaving soon. I don't reckon you'll be sticking around for the feasts as things stand."

There was some hushed discussion behind Black-beard. Gods be praised, he stepped aside finally, but Geth didn't miss the curses he muttered.

"You can see him. They say you owe him a sword. I don't see one at your hip, but maybe some coin will see him to a proper burial."

Geth didn't like the sound of that. He flicked a glance at Vriana and followed Black-beard through the door.

Inside, a few lamps lit a low-ceiling common room. At first, all Geth saw were eyes looking back at him, the glint of a weapon or two, the glow of candle flame reflected off a tin tankard. As his eyes adjusted, he got a better look at the grim, scarred faces of the men of the Sixth Host. The *Bloody* Sixth. More than a few had the deep bronze complexion of the Mog. A few Dragonlanders looked back at him and at least one ebony-skinned Southlander. Geth wasn't the only man with tattoos among this lot either. The Odd Man Out couldn't have housed an odder bunch, even if they were some of the hardest damn soldiers in all the Sworn Realms.

But there wasn't more than a couple dozen of them. Geth cursed inwardly. He wasn't sure yet if the Sixth would even help him, or what they could accomplish if they did.

"C'mon." Black-beard led them upstairs with a wave. He stopped outside the door to the first room. "You wanted to see Urian, you can see him. But he may not see you."

Black-beard pushed the door open and there was the captain, laid out on a bed. The light was scarce but there was no mistaking the blood-stained bandages around one arm and across his middle. Despite Black-beard's word, Urian lifted his head at the sound of their entrance.

"You again," he managed, voice raspy. "Thram's left nut." He let his head rest back down on the pillow, still muttering curses.

Geth hesitated halfway across the room. A putrid smell wafted to his nose and he realized Black-beard hadn't exaggerated. Urian had one foot in the grave already.

"What happened?" Geth breathed.

Black-beard entered behind Geth, followed by Vriana. The Sixer shook his head. "Magicks."

"Damn."

Black-beard moved past Geth to settle onto the room's only chair. He took a cup of water from a stand and lifted it to Urian's lips.

"Bloody magicks," the tall lily went on after Urian had drunk. "Something drifted over us, like a sleep, only it was a nightmare. A waking nightmare. Wasn't the captain's fault. Nobody could move. We just...stuck."

Geth felt his stomach tighten. Only one man could conjure a spell like that.

Black-beard wasn't done though. "That bastard Palladine came with them. They just marched straight in. Captain here was the only one that could move his lips to curse 'em. They ran him through for his troubles."

By the placement of that bandage, and the smell, Geth figured they'd punctured his gut, left him to die slow. Gods but they had so much to answer for!

Urian's hand lifted before Geth could imagine more than a few ways to get even though. He beckoned him closer. "Half-breed."

This once, Geth stood straight, offered a crips salute. "Yessir, Captain. I'm here."

"Where's my sword?"

"Lost it. But the last place I put it was in and out of Hicrates's liver."

An appreciative murmur sounded from the door. Geth frowned at the crowd of soldiers looking in on them. Urian hacked a long, drawn out cough though. Geth turned his eyes back down to the wounded soldier. It was a second before he realized Urian was laughing.

"He's dead then, eh?" the captain asked.

"Dead as dirt."

Urian waved him closer still. Black-beard kicked his chair out of the way and Geth leaned in over the dying man. Gods but it reeked. The captain licked his lips, met Geth's eye.

"They were looking for you," he said, voice no more than a whisper.

Geth blinked. "They what?"

Then it hit him; by throwing Urian's sword at Ceter, he'd given the witch a path right back to the old Sixer, using the same finding magicks Feru-Lea had used to find Weeping Willow a season before. They'd hoped to find Geth more than likely, but that blade had only sent them back to its rightful owner.

Geth swallowed a curse. "I'm sorry, Urian." He couldn't think of anything else to say.

Urian reached up with a trembling hand, like he was going to touch Geth's cheek. He grabbed his throat instead. "Kill that bright-white bastard, Half-breed. You hear me? And his warlock."

"On my life."

Urian nodded. He closed his eyes, waved Geth weakly away. He had some dying to do.

Geth straightened up. He exhaled a long breath. Vriana met his eye. She would have taken his hand, he was sure, if there weren't a half dozen eyes watching them from the doorway.

Not to mention Black-beard, right there in the room. "Time's up, Half-breed."

Together they marched back out into the hall and down to the common room. Geth turned to face him as they reached the lower level.

"I needed to ask the captain for a favor. Seems like you're holding the honors now though, so I'll ask you."

"You want a favor from *me*?" Black-beard sneered, "after you poisoned my cup and stole my glory?"

Geth blinked. "You're Barand, the champion of the host?" He would have laughed if the joke had been on somebody else.

"That's right. I earned my spot on the fighting stage, and you came and took it."

"Or maybe I saved your life."

"Just speak your piece, Half-breed, if that's what its gonna' take to be rid of you."

Geth grimaced. "Fine. I want the help of the Sixth. I know you boys have a score to settle with the Elevens, and so do I."

Barand shook his. "I don't know if you've been paying any mind, but we're only twenty men here. The rest left out already and were the wiser for it."

"You've got me now." Geth hooked a thumb at Vriana. "And my wife. That's twenty-two."

Behind the big warrior someone snorted a laugh. "His wife, he says!"

Vriana swore in Ilar. She took one step toward that voice and her leg swung straight up, the way only a woman could swing it. Her boot caught the fool bastard right under the chin in the same knock-out blow that had dropped Raeg an age ago. And so many others besides. The soldier's eyes rolled up in his head and his knees went out from under him before the men to either side could even catch him.

"Thram's balls," someone in the back breathed.

"They did kill the commodore," someone else muttered.

Barand rolled his eyes. "That still only brings us to twenty-one men. And this one...*woman*, I reckon she calls herself."

"Do you want to fight me?" Vriana asked. "Do you think any man here can beat me?"

"Well..." Barand flashed a wide smile, but the chieftess has already turned to eye the others. A few spit or swore. Most of them looked away. But not Barand.

"Listen, sister, you don't need any more trouble than you already got. If you—"

"You will fight me. You want to, I can see it, mmmm? And if you win, we will leave."

Geth didn't know where Vriana was going with this, but he reckoned she had a plan. "If my wife kicks your ass though—and she will—you help us with the Eleventh. Deal?"

"Ha!" Barand shook his head. "Never thought I'd agree to thrash a woman. But if that's what it's gonna take for you to leave, I guess I've got no choice."

The men of the Sixth Host hooted and cursed and jeered. Tables were pushed back. One of the Dragonlanders started taking bets. The odds were split.

"Vriana," Geth said, voice low. "This man is the champion of his host. I'm not saying you can't take him, but he's no ordinary fighter. He—"

"Don't worry, Gethe." Vriana rolled out her shoulders, threw a few practice punches. "I will find his weakness."

Before he could say anything more, she stripped off her cloak, pulled her tunic over her head so that only a thin shift covered her torso. Her breasts pushed against the fabric, nipples clearly visible in the lamplight. She had great breasts.

"Uh..." Geth started.

But Vriana stepped out toward the center of the cleared space before Geth could say anything else. Barand snorted, shook his head, stepped out to meet her. The men hooted and cheered.

Barand squared the chieftess up, fists raised and ready. Vriana, crossed her arms as if to stretch them one more time, smashing her breast together and almost out of her shift. Barand started to grin, until Vriana lashed out with a kick so swift and sudden Geth hardly saw it.

He grimaced as if he could feel it though, watching with the shake of his head as Barand went down, both hands at his groin.

"Oh...gods!"

But his men only laughed. "Ha!"

"She did it!"

"Pay up, you bastards!"

Coin changed hands and Geth stepped over to kneel down beside Barand. "You alright? I tried to warn you."

"Thram and Awer! You said she was gonna' kick my *ass*!"

The men of the Sixth only laughed harder hearing that. Someone had poured Vriana a drink, which she downed in one go. Setting the cup aside, she extended a hand to Barand.

"Don't be angry, mmmm? I have beaten men far less handsome than you."

Geth scowled, but the flattery seemed to work. The Sixer took her hand, rose with a groan. Geth turned full circle to face each man in turn.

"Is it settled then? Is this the Bloody Sixth or not? Are you ready to get your revenge?"

More than a few soldiers grunted their approval. The black-skinned Southlander raised a finger. "Revenge? Sure. But how are twenty men going to do that against the great Eleventh?"

"Well—"

A frantic knock drew all eyes to the front door and more than a few hands to their hilts. One of the lads from outside was let in. A familiar voice echoed in from out on the street.

"Hey, you Sixer bastards! I know you're angling for a dust up! Well, how's about it? You gonna' let the Seventh in on the action or what?"

CHAPTER TWENTY-SEVEN

Half-ear was a grimy sonofabitch, but Geth was happy to have him. Judging by the reception of light-hearted curses, Barand's men were happy to have his dozen as well.

The leader of the Sevens marched straight up to the bar to pour himself a drink. He sucked it down before turning back to face Geth. "So," He wiped his mouth on the back of one white sleeve. "How we gonna' get back at that horse's ass Palladine? That's what we're after, isn't it?"

"Well—" Geth started to explain about the ships, but Vriana stepped past him.

"Yes."

"Good," said Half-ear. "We're in."

Geth called more drinks. And any food that could be had. He took a seat with Vriana, Half-ear, and Barand, and relayed the plan he'd come up with.

From the rooftops of the buildings surrounding the Great Harbor, they'd rain down flaming arrows on the warships of the

Eleventh. With any luck, a few of those ships would burn. The rest would cut ties and make for the safety of open water.

"We just need to hold the rooftops," Geth said. "They'll send swords to root us out, but with a dozen men to hold the ground floors, I think we can manage to hold three separate buildings—east, center, and west."

Half-ear shook his head. "Not sure how this gets back at Palladine."

"He's on one of the ships," Geth lied. "I just don't know which."

Half-ear didn't look convinced.

Barand spoke for Geth though. "We can't burn them all," he said. "But we can try."

Half-ear shook his head again. "Gods all be damned but this is a strange plan you've got."

Geth licked his lips. "Truth is, we expect Palladine to put up on a little island offshore. Provided we drive these ships out of port. That's where I get even with him."

Barand nodded but Half-ear raised a gnarled finger. "Do we have any bows?"

"Well..."

"And how do we get the arrows to burn? Got any pitch?"

Barand grimaced. "You haven't even got a sword, Half-breed."

Geth swallowed a curse. They brought up good points. But mention of a sword reminded him of Urian's lost blade and the finding magicks that led Palladine and Ceter to the Sixth. Those magicks gave him an idea.

"We may not have pitch, but we've got White Adus behind the bar. And as for bows, well, I reckon I know where we can find some."

It should have been a longshot, Geth supposed, but something told him he wouldn't be disappointed. He took Vriana, Barand, and Half-ear and started toward Neyna's Square. Night had settled over the Golden City, just as it had the first time he'd left in search of Weeping Willow's lair.

He found the enchantress's spice shop tucked among the other buildings like he remembered. His heartbeat quickened, but not from doubt. Weeds grew out of cracks out front and a pull at the door and shutters proved they were locked tight, just like he and Ratcher had left them.

"This is a bad place," Vriana muttered.

"You don't know the half of it," Geth said.

Half-ear grunted a curse. "Where are we?"

"The lair of an assassin," Geth told him. "And a sorceress besides."

"Feels like her spells are still on the place," Barand said with a shiver.

Geth suppressed the urge to shiver as well. The Sixer was right. Perhaps that's what Geth's gut had been telling him, that an evil like Weeping Willow's would discourage intrusion, even after several months. It didn't hurt that Ratcher had insisted they lock up behind themselves, covering their tracks.

"Me and a friend had a score to settle with the witch that lived here," Geth explained. "This woman, you could say she had a thing for bows."

He left it at that. With a well-placed kick, the door smashed inward. Geth waved the others to follow.

It didn't smell, not like he'd thought it would. And there were no flies either, no mice or rats scuttling for the cracks as they entered. Barand was right: somehow, after all that time, a measure of Weeping Willow's fearspell still hung on the place. A shiver ran through Geth as he started up the stairs toward the assassin's arsenal.

He shrugged it off best he could, one hand on the wall to feel his way through the dim light to the second floor. Vriana cursed in Ilar as they reached the first room, weapon's gleaming in the faint moonlight that filtering through the window. Half-ear croaked a weak laugh. Barand started pulling bows off the wall.

They took them all, bowstrings and arrows too.

"You can have whatever you want," Geth told them. "The previous owner doesn't need them anymore."

"Mmmm." Vriana examined a dagger, stuffed it through her belt. "It is good that you killed this evil woman, but why did she have so many weapons?"

"She was an assassin. We cornered her here, Ratcher and I."

Vriana frowned. "Is it not the assassin that is the hunter? Maybe I do not understand this word."

"She was hunting us too," said Geth. "A bunch of other assassins as well. But Ratcher and I..."

He trailed off, not sure what everyone knew about Ratcher's
past. And not sure what the man wanted them to know. But
Vriana just hummed again.

"Look," she said. Half-ear and Barand had gone to check out
the room across the hall, but the chieftess found something
leaned up in the corner, hidden in the shadows. "A sword."

She picked up the sheathed weapon, drew a few inches of
steel. Thumbing the edge, she nodded, satisfied. She waved
Geth over, leaned down to slip it through his belt.

"You go through swords like others go through boots," she
muttered.

"Er..." Geth didn't know what to say. But the weight of the
blade at his hip felt right.

Vriana dusted off her hands. "Now we are ready."

Armed with bows, lanterns for fire, and liquor-soaked rags
wrapped around their arrows, they set out onto dark streets.
Armbands and insignia of any kind they stowed, even if it was a
formality. With southies and half-breeds among the ranks, there
was no hiding who they were, but at least they could deny it.
Justice wasn't likely to follow them all the way back to the Lows
anyway.

They split into three groups. Geth and Vriana headed one while Barand and Half-ear each had a band of their own.

"Alright," Geth told them as they neared the port. "I'll take the west, Sixth Host can take the center, and Seventh takes the east. Find a building with some height and make sure you've got the ground floor well defended. You want my opinion, send all your arrows at one ship. If we each do that, we'll get three galleys burning. The rest will head for open water."

Half-ear looked from Geth and Vriana to Barand and back. "I'm not sticking around after," he said. "Tomorrow's the races, but we've had enough of the Games. And as for the feasts, Familae Leyai can choke on it."

Barand growled his agreement. "We'll have a feast of our own, to Urian's memory, when we get back to the Lows."

"Then this is it." Geth clasped hands with each of them. "See you in Vorda's hell. If not sooner."

They split up. Geth flicked a glance over his shoulder. Besides Vriana, he had a motley crew of Paellians, half-Mog, a Dragonlander, and the one Southlander. They numbered twelve in total. Geth smiled grimly, thinking of the Dead-man dozen back home.

These men, safe to say, had plenty of experience on the battlefield though. The Dragonlander took one of their two bows, a determined gleam in those eastern eyes of his. Vriana took the other.

"Tonight we get Ethen back," she told Geth.

He picked a building within bowshot of the westernmost galley, a merchant's warehouse from the looks of. They smashed in the back door, rousted the merchant and his family, along with a few stunned bodyguards and serving folk. Vriana and the Dragonlander hustled up to the third floor with their bows while Geth and the others secured the front and back doors.

"Your friend any good with an arrow?" Geth asked the Southerner.

The man snorted, white teeth bright in his dark face. "If they still had dragons where he comes from, he could take one out of the air with one bolt."

Geth liked the sound of that. And he already knew what Vriana could do.

He eyed the quiet port, moonlight glittering on a dark sea. A few doors down, sailors caroused at a tavern, but other than that, the only sound was the ripple of wind against furled sails, the slap of water against piers and hulls. The merchant would be running to the watch though, it wouldn't last long. Before the big warrior could get too anxious, a single red streak crossed the sky off to his left as Half-ear's gang began the assault.

"That's it, be ready!" he said.

More arrows cut across the dark sky. Down at the tavern, sailors cried the alarm. A horn sounded but it felt like an eternity before the first Elevens came for them.

"There!" a lily in the short tunic and breeches of the navy cried, pointing at the doorway where Geth and that southern scratch waited.

"Mind the back door!" the big warrior called over his shoulder.

A Sixer with a curled mustache grunted and took half the men that way. Ahead, a throng of sailors charged, weapons jangling, curses flying. Geth spared one final glance at the ships beyond them. A few bright spots gleamed here and there, but nothing like the fires they needed.

"Arrrggghhh!"

The first sailor arrived, swinging a sword in a tremendous arc at Geth's middle. The big warrior stepped into it, parried firmly, flung out a fist to stun the man. The southerner darted out from behind him to run the man through.

A second attacker was already coming at Geth from the other side, but he struck first this time and another man fell. The pair of them writhed on the ground, tried to crawl back the way they'd come. They didn't get far.

The next Elevens came more warily, even with the advantage of numbers on their side. Geth and his new friend stood outside the door to their building, flicking their blades at anyone that came within range. Behind them, three more Sixers crowded the entry, weapons ready. The arrows kept flying from above.

But it wasn't as easy to set a ship on fire as Geth thought, not without pitch or kindling or some other starter. And the seamen rushed with buckets to extinguish most of the arrows anyway. Vriana, the Dragonlander, and the others needed time.

Fools that they were, the sailors ahead of them seemed happy to give it to them. They retreated all the way back to their ships, arrows flying all the while. Only after several minutes did they come back. But still, they refused to press.

"Craven sea-crabs!" one of the men in the doorway behind Geth jeered. "Always scuttling side to side, never into the fight!"

"We know what you do below decks!" another goaded.

"Filthy horse-humpers!" the Elevens shot back. "How many bounties have you got on your head? It's the lowest of the lows that sinks to the Lows. Ain't it, boys?"

Geth just watched the arrows arc toward the harbor, counted sharps, aimed his meanest glare at the seamen a few yards away. The watch would be on the way, but not with more men than the Elevens already had. So why delay? Geth muttered curses, tried to make sense of it.

A cry from behind reached his ears before he'd figured anything out for himself.

"Aggghhh!"

"Stoli's down!"

Before Geth could turn to figure out how they'd been flanked, the sailors ahead of him charged. The clang of steel on steel echoed into the night as his newfound sword deflected blows and sent them back. Beside him, that southern scratch fought like the fabled Nyx. Together they held the door. But the cries and clamor of melee behind them grew more and more desperate.

"Half-breed!"

Geth turned in time to see Mustache getting hacked down as he ran for it. The other two men crowding the door behind

Geth fared no better. A pair of seamen stood over the one, stabbing his motionless form over and over while the third lay against a wall, clutching his guts and quivering. The Elevens had found a way up through the basement.

Geth swore.

"Go!" the southlander said. "I'll hold the door!"

Geth had no choice but to leave him. He raised his blade, growled low in his throat. A room-full of hostile eyes swung toward him, glowing in the lamplight. Red blades swung toward him as well.

He crossed the space between in a few long bounds, crashed among them with flailing steel. The first screamed as he took a slash across the neck. The second chopped down at Geth, but the big warrior was already past him, shoulder down, barging over seaman in the second rank. Another sea-crab thrust at him from one side. Geth deflected this, corralled his own momentum to turn back the way he'd come.

That charge had done what he'd hoped. Two Elevens were down while the rest backpedaled away from the madman sworn to the Bloody Sixth. And up ahead, the black man still held the door.

With a roar, Geth launched himself at the nearest enemy. This one got his blade up in time to parry a swing, but the blow was strong enough to send him staggering to one side. Geth left him there, whirled to face the man that was coming at his back. That one thrust for Geth's stomach. A deft twist let the strike fly past. A thrust of Geth's own crunched through the sailor's neck.

Bulging eyes stared at Geth as the man clutched the blade stuck through his throat, but Geth was caught off guard as well as his weapon refused to pull free. The hilt wrenched from his grip as his enemy keeled over backwards, taking the blade with him. Geth would have cursed if he had the time.

He didn't. A room full of enemies faced him, standing there unarmed, right in the middle of them. The sound of swords clashing rang from the back of the building and the black man's form could be seen flashing back and forth through the door to the front. The closest thing to a weapon within yards was his own sword, standing up like an axe in a log, stuck fast in the dead sailor's neck. If he charged he'd take a blade in the front. If he stood, he'd take one in the back.

"Got you now, you dirty—"

"Aeeeiii!"

An animal shriek pierced Geth's ears and the thwak of a bowstring sounded. A man in the back fell to his knees. Vriana's footfalls boomed as she jumped down the last steps of the stairway behind him, her sword rasping out of its sheath to hack down a stunned seaman. On her heels, the Dragonlander loosed an arrow at the sailor nearest to Geth. The bolt squelched into the man's stomach, sent him staggering backwards and down.

"Ha!" Geth used the distraction to lunge for his weapon. Planting one boot on the dead man's chest, he twisted the blade free. The Southerner came flying through the front door at the same time, slashing a sailor along the way, and barging into another. Like that, the Elevens were scrambling any which way but toward the fight, leaving Geth, Vriana, and the Sixers a chance to make for the back door.

More sailors, along with several confused-looking watchmen, crowded the alley at the back of the building. One scream from Vriana put them all on their heels as she leapt over the threshold. Judging by the wide-eyes and gaping mouths, Geth reckoned they'd never seen a man-sized woman in furs, bloody sword in hand and howling like a demon. Who had? A few sword strokes parted them. Geth pulled the Dragonlander and the other surviving Sixes through while that crazy southern scratch hacked down one more enemy before sprinting after them.

They ran until they were breathless, down one alley then another. Only once they reached a cross-street leading back toward the harbor did Geth look back. Red firelight lit the night as ships burned.

CHAPTER TWENTY-EIGHT

Geth and Vriana made their goodbyes with the men of the Sixth Host before starting toward the Fisherman's Harbor. The Southerner just rested a finger beside his eye, a gesture meaning he'd seen and marked the occasion. Geth saluted Umbel-style, fist to heart.

"Come," said Vriana. "The night is not young anymore."

Geth watched them go. If every captain had been like Urian, and every dozen like these men, he might have been with the Bloody Sixth still.

He hustled off in the opposite direction beside Vriana, down darkened streets toward the Fisherman's Harbor. At this hour, the docks were quiet, a pair of chatting watchmen walking the piers, a few drunks, the odd beggar or cutpurse. No one looked too hard at a man with his woman beside the water at night.

Geth didn't know where to find Agrem and the rest, but the Seer found him. He appeared out of the shadows, face white in the moonlight, spikey hair gleaming.

"This way."

He waved Geth and Vriana to follow, leading them to an inn with no signage to speak of. He'd already booked a room. Hack and Asaac waited inside.

Geth closed the door to the little chamber behind him. "Where's the prince?" he asked.

"He's with the ship," said Hack. "He's got the others too. We'll get your boy back, Captain. And we'll get our friends healed too."

He said it as if it was already done. Of course he did. "Gods bless you, Hack," Geth told him.

With no chairs in the little room, the big warrior plopped down on the edge of the bed. Vriana sat beside him. Agrem, Hack and Asaac stood, the old warlock's thin shoulders drooped already.

"Don't worry," Geth told him. "Your chance to make amends is coming."

Asaac sighed. "She's just so strong."

That got Geth thinking. He didn't even know what they were up against. And they'd only spoken briefly about the plan to trade Assac for Ethen and escape the Garden on a fast ship.

Looking from face to face in that little room, Geth realized just how ill-prepared they were. None of them knew what to expect. Aside from himself, none of them had ever had dealings with the queen either.

Except for Asaac.

"Tell me about Lyanne."

Geth's stare must have been a cold one. Asaac shivered where he stood.

"Lyanne. Gods but she's a devil! And she's strong. Relentless. When she wants something, she doesn't stop until she has it."

"What about her magicks?" Geth frowned. "What are we up against?"

The old warlock slid down the wall with a groan to sit on his rump. He didn't meet Geth's gaze. His eyes went distant.

"These arts we pursue...who really knows anything about them?"

"Mmmm." Agrem agreed.

"But if there's one thing that's sure, Lyanne's talents suit her perfectly as queen. She rules you. With a mere touch, the wave of a hand, the offering of a gift, her will slides inside your head and you think it's your own. You do what you're told. You don't even question."

"Compulsion." Geth growled the word. "That's what Feru-Lea called it."

Asaac shrugged. "That's one name for it. But Feru-Lea, Catriona, myself—none of us wield it like Lyanne. Perhaps they can fight it better than I, but for most, under the queen's hand, you are nothing more than a puppet on a string. And she is the puppet-master."

Puppets and strings, magicks and witches, it all made Geth want to curse. Much as he hated the thought, he reckoned they could have used Feru-Lea's help now. Gods only knew what had become of her.

He stood, turned to faced everyone. "So, we've got Lyanne's witchcraft to be wary of, in addition to all the swords at her call. The hand-off will be the most dangerous part. But that's why I chose the Garden."

Geth looked from one face to the next. "We'll give her one hour's time to meet us. If she refuses or runs late, we leave. She'll be instructed to arrive on the island with Ethen and just two rowers to bring her. As long as we get there first, we can keep a look out, make sure she doesn't manage to land a shipload of soldiers behind our backs."

"She'll try it," Asaac said. "She'll try...I don't know what, but she'll try *something*."

His eyes went to Agrem. A look passed between them and the Seer nodded.

"I will protect you," he said. "But first, you must prepare yourself, mmmm?"

"Do we have something of hers?" Asaac asked.

Agrem reached into a pocket and drew out a ring—a woman's ring—and passed it over. "This came from the prince."

The Assac took it, closed his eyes, exhaled a long breath. A moment passed, not more. The little lamp in the room flickered wildly, like a wind had somehow snuck inside the room. Suddenly they were looking at the straight-haired girl, Talayne.

"Gods above and below," Hack murmured.

"Now it's your turn," Talayne told Agrem, voice nothing like Asaac's. "Lay your wards. The queen must not see through this guise, otherwise she'll try to take me back under her control."

Agrem walked a circle around the shifted warlock, hands rising and falling, muttering charms all the while. He walked the same circle backwards. He took something from his belt and smudged it on slender wrists, again on the back of her neck and under her chin. When he was done, he nodded.

"Will this protect me from her pull?" Asaac—now Ta-layne—asked.

"Some. But you will have to be strong."

"That's right," said Geth. "Because you're the knife up our sleeve."

"The what?"

"You said yourself Lyanne will try to double-cross us. Of course she will. We've got to strike first."

Geth looked from face to face. Agrem was stoic, Vriana and Hack eager. But the shifted-warlock looked back from under dark lashes anxiously.

"I've really only got this one talent," she said.

"You've got feet, don't you? When the time comes, you run. They'll have to send a body after you. Then we'll be three against two."

"And Lyanne?"

Geth opened his mouth, but Vriana spoke first. "I'm going to kill her."

"Agrem and I will deal with her oarsmen," Geth said. "One of them will be Palladine, no question about that. One of them will go running after you. Hack can rush in from the wings to help."

Vriana pushed off the wall. "Good. Let's go."

But there was one thing left to do. Geth looked to Agrem. "Can you...uh, call to Lyanne?"

The Seer hummed. "Mmmm."

"Do you need a bowl of water of something?"

"Bowl of water?" One of Agrem's eyebrows went up.

"You know, like Sythme and Pythelle used?"

The Seer shook his head, sniffed. "Bowl of water..."

Geth watched as Agrem closed his eyes. He opened them again, turned eastward, stared, right through the walls. His mouth moved ever so slightly but no sound came out. Around the room, all eyes watched him.

With a sudden blink, Agrem was back among them. He grimaced, mouthed a curse in Ilar. "She will be there."

They caught up with Gahalus out on the night-quiet port. He waved them over to the ship he'd procured for them. Her sleek bow and polished rails stood out sorely among the creaky tubs and trawlers of Fisherman's Harbor, but this was exactly the sort of vessel they needed.

Eora, Ratcher, and Phelan had been assembled, sat cross-legged like children on the deck, but vacant-eyed like senile oldsters. They'd be healed soon, Geth told himself. He rested a hand on the mast, happy for the speed the ship promised. The

Sparrow, black lettering on the hull proclaimed. Geth whispered a prayer she was a good as her name.

"I can't believe I'm going back," a voice said from over Geth's shoulder. He turned to find Gahalus standing behind him, eyeing dark seas beyond the mouth of the harbor.

"If I could," Geth told him. "I'd bury the whole island under the waves."

The prince nodded. "She may have abandoned it, but there's no washing the stain clean."

Gahalus's eyes floated to Talayne. Geth could see the ache in them, how the lad wanted to go to her, even knowing it wasn't her at all. The big warrior knew that ache now himself.

Vriana stepped toward him from across the deck, like the mere thought could summon her. She ran a hand over the smooth rail, flicked a glance from mast to decks, to the proud fore, carved with a beaked bird, inspiration for the vessel's name, Geth reckoned.

"There are wonders south of the forests," she said. "My people are fools not to see it. These ships—maybe these are the greatest wonders of all. And the sea..."

Geth reached out and took her hand. "I've always liked it as well. Especially when you can look out over it from a high place."

"Mmmm. You come from a great land, Gethe. Loud with noise and smells, but great."

Waves lapped against the Sparrow's hull. Moonlight danced over the water. Geth pulled Vriana close, and they stood there in silence. He breathed her in, thanked all the gods for the gift.

"I'm glad you're here, Vriana. I tried, but I couldn't get him back without you."

The chieftess said nothing, only hugged him back.

"We've still got plenty of work to do though," Geth went on. "She's crafty, Lyanne. She'll have a trick in mind, some way to outmaneuver us, to get Talayne and still get to you and me."

"Then we will have a trick as well."

Geth grimaced. "You can't kill her, Vriana. She's the queen of a sworn ally. If we kill her, it will touch off a war. I can't do that to King Hadean, not after all he's done for me."

"Then this is what she will not expect? That we will try to kill her?"

Geth nodded.

"Mmmm."

That hum could have meant a lot of things, but it made Geth nervous just the same. Then again, he loved that about Vriana. She never did anything halfway.

Oars dipped into the water and the Sparrow slid out of port. Her sleek hull cut the waves, pushing westward. Night sill hung over them, but the Garden appeared through the clear air ahead like a dark lump, outlined in grey moonlight.

Ethen would be back in their arms within the hour, Geth told himself. He'd hold the boy close, Vriana too. All would be well.

But when had a hand-off ever gone smoothly? What if they failed? What if...

He shook his head, couldn't bring himself even to think of those things. Would Vriana still cling to him then?

They disembarked beside the little beach, splashing through the shallows, dark walls shadowing over them. The Sparrow's sailors muttered curses, spit to ward off bad luck. But Hack started straight up the zigzagging stairway, fearless as ever. Agrem, Asaac—in Talayne's form—and Vriana followed close behind.

Geth lingered behind. "The far side of the island," he told Gahalus. "Drop anchor and wait for us there. This is the only entrance, but I'll take a length of rope so we can come down over the walls to meet you."

"We'll be ready."

"It shouldn't take more than an hour." Geth looked to the east where the first signs of daybreak lit the sky. "If it does, well, then it will be a red dawn."

"Be careful, Wolf." He didn't have to say anything more.

Geth threw a coil of rope over one shoulder and started up after his friends. He found them standing just inside the gatehouse, eyeing the manicured lawns, the flowerbeds, the graceful path curved through the center. Asaac's thin, female frame shuddered. Agrem and Vriana turned circles, muttered softly despite their deserted surroundings, like someone might hear them.

"Hack," Geth said, "I want you up on the walls. Hidden, so they can't see you, but both eyes on the water. If Lyanne tries to sneak a warship to the island, we need to know about it."

The green-cloak saluted, fist to heart. He started up to the parapets.

Geth pulled at his mustache, studying the battlefield. Except for a few low bushes and ornamentals, the space just inside the gatehouse was empty, no trees or walls to obstruct sightlines. Nowhere to hide, but close to the exit. This was the place.

With Hack up on the walls, Lyanne wouldn't be able to sneak an archer up there either. Geth nodded. He turned to face the opposite curtain wall, some fifty paces off, dotted by doorways and painted shutters. Gahalus and the Sparrow would be waiting below.

Geth hefted his rope and hustled in that direction. Through a doorway and up a stair, he reached the parapet. Good as his word, the prince and their ship sat at anchor down below. Geth tied one end of the rope to a column and threw the other end down toward the sea.

He propped the door open on his way back out and jogged to join his friends. "Our exit's right there," he told them, pointing across the ward. "Look for the door that's open, then up and over the wall. The rope is tied and the Sparrow's already waiting."

"We must hide her," Vriana said, flicking a glance at Asaac. The shifted warlock crossed thin arms, rubbed at her shoulders. The chieftess was right.

"We can't let Lyanne have you until we have my son," Geth told him. "No telling what she might try. If I were her, I'd take you alive to keep Ryrus in check, but no sense taking chances."

"Agreed," Talayne's high voice replied.

Geth rested a hand on the woman's arm, the arm that actually belonged to Asaac. "You're doing a brave thing. Whatever she made you do before, standing up to Lyanne now, this trumps it."

"I know." Her face screwed up and she nodded. "I know."

Geth sent the shifted warlock to hide in the orchard behind them, to the left. Once she was settled, he turned back to Agrem and Vriana. The chieftess drew her sword to check the edge. The Seer stood muttering something under his breath, charms or curses, who could say?

Geth stepped through the archway beneath the gatehouse to peer down at the water. A wind rustled the tortured scrubs growing out of the cliff face. Those zigzagging stairs creaked, all on their own. Moonlight washed the rolling waves, but Geth heard the slap of paddles before he saw the little boat draw near. A cowled figure sat at the center, accompanied by one silver head and one bald.

Lyanne, Ceter, and Palladine.

CHAPTER TWENTY-NINE

Geth swore. He didn't like the match-up. There was no one he'd rather have at his side than Vriana—they held the advantage at swords—but what hell could the queen raise with Ceter's magicks to add to her own?

Geth flicked a glance at Agrem. *Two magickers to our one.*

They did have Asaac, he reminded himself. And Hack. As the little boat scraped up on the beach, Geth's eyes found the basket in Ceter's arms. *So close!* To let anything scare them off now was folly.

He turned, signaling to the others that the enemy had arrived. Stairs groaned as the queen and her entourage began the climb from the beach up to the fort. Geth stepped out to make sure they saw him. He locked eyes with Palladine. It was the captain that came first, Ethen's basket held ahead of him like a shield. Lyanne followed after, Ceter last of all.

"I want to attack them now," Vriana hissed, arriving at Geth's side. "On the stairs. But my son..."

"I'm glad you're here, Vriana," He touched her arm. "Together, we can do this."

She smiled. His *wife* smiled. It was grim expression, but comforting, nonetheless. Magicks and witches be damned, they were going to get Ethen back, and they were going to sail away clean.

Geth waved his friends to follow back out into the manicured ward. They turned and waited until Lyanne and her minions arrived at the top of the stairway, visible through the arch of the gate. Moonlight gleamed off the queen's rings, Palladine's polished cuirass, and Ceter's silver mane. The two sides stared each other down like arena fighters from across the sand.

Geth licked his lips and spit. He would have laughed under different circumstances. Had there ever been a stranger stand-off than this? A gutter-born sellsword and two savages from the northern wilds against the queen of the civilized world, her Hand of Justice, and an ageless sorcerer from...well, the gods only knew where. Three wild savages against three civilized monsters. Which of the fabled playwrights could have dreamed up such a plot?

Lyanne and her henchmen stepped under the shadowy gate. They halted there. The way the moonlight fell, Geth couldn't see her eyes, but that perfect mouth tilted in the barest hint of a smile

"I'll come no further. You may have an archer hidden on the walls or among the trees. Yes, Lord Ceter told me what you did on your North River, you and your tribeswoman."

"Feet gone cold?" Geth snorted. "You're the one who started this, witch."

"But it was you who started this, in truth, was it not? You began as a stone in my shoe, waving Hadean's banner in my halls. And you've only cut deeper into my heel since, meddling in my family affairs, even bolstering the familae that count the Leyai as enemies. Can you blame me for wanting to be rid you? Wouldn't you do the same? Haven't you? Yes, countless times, I'm sure."

Vriana stepped past Geth, eyes bright, voice dripping with menace. "Give me my son."

"He's here." Lyanne gestured with a beringed hand toward Palladine, on her right. "I give him to you, as agreed. Now, where is the Lady Talayne?"

"Let me see my son first!"

Lyanne looked past them all, into the Garden. She beckoned with a raised hand. The noise of footfalls sounded and Asaac, in the girl's form, came out of the trees at a shuffle, eyes trained on the queen and nothing else.

But Geth caught the shifted-warlock and held her before she could cross the space. "First, my son."

Lyanne sniffed. "Take him. Gods how I tire of the thing. He's got an appetite like a lion—a wolf, I should say. He never ceases to cry except when his mouth is full."

Reaching over, Lyanne took the basket from Palladine, folded back the covers so that one little foot showed, then two pale arms, as the baby flailed and began to cry. Lyanne carried the basket to the edge of the threshold, set it down there.

"Here he is, my gift to you."

Agrem hissed a warning, but Vriana surged past him to take the basket, hauling it away, back behind them. She knelt down to fuss over the child, to coo and kiss, voice trembling with emotion. How Geth wanted to join her! Lyanne lifted a finger, however, and Asaac strained in his arms. Geth let the shifted-warlock go, straight to the queen's side.

Agrem's eyes were big and white. His fingers flexed at his sides. But Lyanne breathed in a deep breath, there in the shadows. She wore an easy smile, one gentle hand on the girl Talayne's arm, like she'd come across a wildflower on a walk, unexpectedly.

"Take her and go," Geth said. "It's over."

He wanted to go himself, to turn and run with Agrem, his wife, and their child. But his warrior's instinct made him think better. Despite his own words, he knew this wasn't over, not yet.

He couldn't turn his back on Lyanne now. Her strike was coming. Her ploy. They had to absorb the blow, whatever it was. They had to bear it first, then retreat in the aftermath once the queen had spent herself. He braced for it where he stood.

But the strike that fell wasn't one he could have ever expected. With a crooked finger, Lyanne gestured across at them.

Not at Geth, but at Vriana.

The chieftess trembled in place, shifted her feet, then drew her sword. Geth leapt back as she lowered it directly at him.

From the shadows of the arch, the queen trilled a laugh. "That's right. It is I who am master here. And I shall have what I want! Did you really expect me to believe this was Talayne?"

CHAPTER THIRTY

"Vriana!" Geth held up both hands.

The chieftess's eyes never blinked. She didn't attack, but a booming command from Agrem seemed to have no effect either. Geth backed warily away.

"It finishes now," Lyanne said. "And no one is more pleased than I. Do you think the queen of Pellon has nothing better to do than fret over the mischief-making of a whore's son and his rabble of outland barbarians?"

"He's much more than that, my queen," Palladine put in, speaking for the first time. "He's a dangerous beast. Vicious, lawless. A wolf, just like they say."

"True. And what is a wolf after all, but a wild dog? Bigger, with a stronger bite, but an animal, nothing more, skulking the hinterlands, away from the staves and bows of civilization.

"You have hidden in those hinterlands long enough, under the protections of your boy-king. It's been too long those lands drifted astray, whipped this way and that like some ragged banner in the wind."

"You leave King Hadean out of this!" Geth growled. "You hear me?"

"But did you know all these northern shores along Longsea once belonged to a great utopia? It stretched all the way to Urosea and to the great oceans beyond. Mithea, they called it, a golden civilization, ruled by an immortal king and his queen. We will have such an age again. Your barbarian scryer must have seen it. It is my destiny to unite the Sworn Realms, all Aturians, as they haven't been, since the days of Atuer himself."

A wind blew. A cloud passed over the moon and the lawn went as dark as the black under the arch of the gate. Lyanne, Palladine, and Ceter were like shadows except for those rings, that polished cuirass, Ceter's pale hair.

The ancient warlock grinned. Paladine watched Geth with a hunger in his eye. They'd won, or so they thought. Lyanne opened her mouth to speak again, but Geth had figured out her next move.

"You're stalling."

It was the only thing that made sense. She wasn't going to get Talayne and she knew it, but she had Geth in a corner. And yet she hesitated. They feared him that much, Agrem too, the big warrior reckoned. He didn't need to hear the splash of oars down below to tell him Lyanne had more swords on the way.

"Captain!"

Hack's warning arrived, a moment later. Geth swore. He had no choice but to do the one thing they wouldn't expect. He opened his mouth as if to start some speech of his own, then charged Vriana.

"Argh!"

A slap with his bare hand, turned her blade aside as he barreled her over.

"Aeeiii!"

"Oof!"

He landed on top of her with a grunt, pinned her sword arm down with one hand, tucked his head in so she couldn't head-butt his face.

He couldn't hold her there for long though, Palladine was sure to run him through from behind. Before Geth could think what to do next, Vriana's other hand tore a knife free from somewhere. He barely got a forearm raised to block her swing at the wrist.

"Shit!"

With his right hand, Geth fumbled for Vriana's knife, with his left he bore down on her flailing sword arm, all the while taking knees into his thighs as she aimed at the target in between.

Lyanne's spell on Vriana wasn't the only attack they launched. Ceter's voice cut the air and a wave of fear lapped over the big warrior, followed by a bellow from Agrem and something like a warm wind washing the other way. The rasp of a sword leaving its sheath could only have come from Palladine, just yard away. He'd be on Geth's back in seconds.

But another yell sounded from overhead.

"Yaaaaaah!" Metal clattered and a heavy thud rumbled through the ground, followed by Hack's cry. "Fight me, you bastard!"

He'd leapt down from the parapet above, right in the middle of the fray. The clang of steel against steel echoed. *Gods bless you, Hack!*

But there was no way the green-cloak could stand against a master like Palladine for long. With a heave, Geth rolled off Vriana, over her sword arm so she couldn't use its length. Even so, he narrowly avoided a swipe of her knife as he struggled to get clear. By the time he scrambled to his feet, she was on all fours, eyeing him like a rabid animal.

He raised both hands. "Vriana—"

She was on him again before he could speak, not a hint of recognition in her unblinking eyes. He scrambled backwards, sidestepped a chop, ducked under a swing. He faked a lunge forward, goaded a haymaker from her, then drew his own blade—the blade she'd given him—in the moments it took her to reset her stance.

"Vriana, it's me! I can't—"

She came swinging again. She was fast, technical, stronger than plenty of men, and showed no sign of tiring out. Geth couldn't fight back either.

Gods all be damned! Asaac was right; Lyanne was more than a clever witch. She was a devil.

She'd conjured Geth's worst nightmare into reality. Vriana pressed, came at him from every direction. The big warrior parried, sidestepped, backpedaled, and cursed. Thank the gods, he was equal to the task.

Even under Lyanne's pull, Vriana could still think though. Frowning, she changed tactics. Geth wasn't the only one with tricks.

A darting thrust turned into a flick at the leg, nothing lethal, but a painful cut if it had landed. She swung wide to invite a counter, dragged a leg in invitation, pretended to stumble to draw her enemy out.

But Geth didn't dared launch an attack of his own. This only earned a low growl from deep in Vriana's chest. She came at him even harder.

And somewhere in the background, Lyanne trilled that laugh.

"Run, Asaac!" Geth yelled.

He had no idea if the warlock heard him, if the man even could get himself loose from the queen's grasp. He had no idea what turn Agrem's duel with Ceter had taken either, though, by the sound of clanging steel, Hack still stood against Palladine. Geth might have counted it all a stalemate, no worse, if not for the tramp and creak of footfalls bounding up the zigzagged stairs.

"My queen!" a soldier called.

They were out of time. Geth's eyes searched left and right. The only thing within feet of them was Ethen in his basket, little arms waving, crying for all his lungs were worth.

Geth sidestepped toward the basket until it stood between him and Vriana. He lifted his blade over his own son, bellowed as loud as he could. "Drop your sword!"

Vriana faltered. Her lips moved but no sound came out. The tip of her blade wavered. A tremble ran through her.

"Vriana i Vather!" Agrem's voice called out. He howled some command in the Ilar tongue. The chieftess dropped her weapon. It wasn't a fraction of a second, however, before a wave of cold fear shot up Geth's spine, washed across the entire Garden.

Agrem wailed from somewhere off to one side. Vriana's back arched, stuck fast. Geth's experience with Ceter's magicks offered some resistance, praise the gods. He managed to turn his head as a whimper and a growl sounded back near the gatehouse.

The growl came from Hack.

"I...am...not...afraid!"

Across from him, Palladine stood wide-eyed, sword still bared but shaking wildly in his grip. Hack raised his own blade, dragged himself closer for the killing thrust.

But Ceter spied the danger. Like a weight from their shoulders, his magicks fell away.

CHAPTER THIRTY-ONE

Palladine was the quickest to react. His sword lashed out with deadly precision.

"Ahhh!"

"Hack!" Geth cried.

The blade, punctured Hack's stomach, came back out red. The green-cloak, clutched at his middle and collapsed. A troop of lilies charged through the arch of the gatehouse as he hit the ground.

But Vriana was back. She raised her weapon and loosed that shriek of hers, freezing Lyanne's reinforcements where they stood. "Aiiieeee!"

"I have him!" Agrem's voice called from behind Geth. Geth dared a glance, saw the Seer holding Ethen close to his chest. The Ilar's eyes looked sunken, his face pale as ash. Across the space, Ceter had retreated under the protection of the arch to huddle beside Lyanne.

With a better look at the sparse resistance ahead of them, the troop of lilies steeled themselves and advanced, Palladine at the fore. Geth and Vriana closed ranks, standing between them and Agrem, their son, clutched in his arms.

"Run!" Geth hissed over his shoulder. "Get him away!"

Ahead of the big warrior, soldiers piled into the ward, fanning out in either direction as he and Vriana inched backward, foot by foot. Palladine wore that hungry look again, his sword red with Hack's blood. Geth felt all the rage he'd ever known throbbing at his temples, begging him to attack. But that would have meant certain death. And he had so much to live for.

He looked to Vriana, side by side with him again, sword leveled. Triumph lit her face even as they faced their end.

"We have him, Gethe," she said. "We did it."

She was back alright. Gods, how he loved her.

But another voice jarred him from the moment, Lyanne's, calling out from behind the grim ranks of her soldiers.

"No man can stand in the way of destiny!" she said. "Much less a pack of stray dogs!"

Palladine barked a command, and his lilies fanned out even further, closed the circle. Best Geth could tell, Agrem had gotten away. Vriana's back pressed against his as they prepared for the onslaught.

But another voice spoke, directly into his mind.

They are coming.

"Oedelia?"

A startled noise sounded from the soldiers facing Geth, followed by a gasp from Vriana.

"Gethe..." she breathed.

The big warrior just laughed. "It's alright, Vriana. Our friends are here."

Around their ankles, like a ghost from the grave, a mist had begun to rise.

CHAPTER THIRTY-TWO

"Lyanne!" a woman called.

"Lyanne!" crowed another.

"Lyanne!" a final cried. "Answer for your crimes!"

That one, Geth recognized. The mist rose until he couldn't see farther than a few yards in any direction, but he knew Catriona's voice. The tramp of what felt like a thousand feet thumped up through the ground.

Could they have? No, it was some trick of their craft. But Geth would have sworn the witches had brought an army.

"Stand firm!" Lyanne commanded.

If she used her magicks, they failed her now. A man wailed. The sound of curses and retreating footfalls reached Geth's ears, dampened by the mist, but unmistakable. Other voices cut the veil like thunder through the night.

"Lyanne!" Feru-Lea howled.

"Answer us!" the voice of the fierce little witch screamed.

An actual peal of thunder shook Geth dizzy, followed by a flash of lightening that struck close enough to stand his hair on end. He swallowed hard, took Vriana by the arm.

"Get back to the ship!" he said. "It's that way, I think. Get Ethen and get out of here! I have to find Hack."

"We have to kill her, Gethe. We have to kill her now."

"Forget that! Find Agrem and get everyone on the ship!"

He didn't wait for an answer, just plunged ahead into the mist. Men and women cursed and screamed and cried out, in pain or in terror. Geth tried to move in the direction of Lyanne's voice, the direction in which Hack had fallen.

Faces appeared and disappeared, just as fast, through the fog. A lily materialized in front of him, sword raised. Geth ran him through. Another stumbled into his back before Geth could even turn, but the bastard just clutched at him, shrieking like a madman.

"Help me! I'll drown! Help me! Please!"

Geth torn the man off and shoved him out of the way. He turned in circles, all sense of direction lost. "Hack! Hack!"

"Captain..."

Thank the gods! There he was, on the ground. Geth rushed toward Hack's voice, slid to a stop on his knees at the green-cloak's side.

"Hack!" He took his friend's hand, squeezed, searched his wounds.

Gods, there were so many. A dark stain beneath the sternum marked Palladine's final blow, but by the cuts along the Umbelman's shoulders, legs, and one forearm, it was plain the queen's hound had found flesh more than once.

But Hack had refused to go down.

"We have healers," Geth told him. "Strong magicks. We'll get you sorted, don't worry. Don't you worry at all, you hear me?"

Hack turned his head, tried to meet Geth's eye, but his gaze was far away already. His lips worked like it took every scrap of strength he had left. "I'm...not...afraid."

He was gone. Geth screamed, a wordless noise of rage and desperation. He bellowed his pain up into the fog, into the last shreds of night, to join all the others shrieks and cries.

That's how Palladine found him.

CHAPTER THIRTY-THREE

There were no words. Hatred propelled one warrior against the other at first sight, sparks lighting the mist as Geth's first, massive blow struck Palladine's weapon, careening down the length and off to one side. Momentum took him past the captain. They circled, came together again in an exchange of force and anger and steel that reverberated through Geth's bones but only made him hate the captain more.

Palladine never let up either. He wasn't as big or as strong, but he was quick, faultless, deliberate, and unrelenting. His sword matched Geth's in parry and riposte. His feet threw kicks, his gloved hands punches. He was a hound alright, bred and groomed to match a savage wolf.

Geth tried a wide swing, parried a thrust, sidestepped a shoulder-barge. Palladine's feet flitted over the grass as he dodged and deflected, sending back cuts of his own. They could have been fighting in Holrain's Court again or on the platform in front of the Leonine Gates. They could have been the only two people in the world, wrapped in mist, hidden from everything.

But they weren't. A cry sounded over Geth's shoulder, and he turned in time to dodge the charge of a lily arriving through the fog like an apparition. A shove sent the man right into Palladine's path, thwarting the blow he'd lined up at the big warrior's back.

"Fool!" the captain hurled the soldier aside.

Geth used the distraction to launch another attack. He thrust hard and straight, aiming to puncture that pretty cuirass. With a backward step and a two-handed flick, Palladine's blade deflected the blow. They circled again, looked for weakness, opportunity.

Geth didn't really have to think, not after all those hours in the sword-yard, those bouts in the pits, those battles across every fold of Wide Eria. He attacked with force and speed, defended with precision, kept his feet moving, never let his guard waver. Sweat ran down his temples and Palladine panted across from him. But neither balked. They were two gods of war, sparring among the clouds.

"You can't kill me, stray," the captain sneered. "You can't stand in the way of destiny."

Geth spit. "Your only destiny is to wipe my ass in Vorda's halls."

"Ha! If you knew—"

A shape tumbled through the mist on Palladine's left, and his blade lashed out. His mouth dropped, however, as the interloper fell between them, rolled to her back. It was the fierce little witch, brown, child-like eyes wide and staring.

Geth sucked in a shocked breath. "Gods..."

Palladine staggered back from the dead witch, looked to Geth, clenched his jaw.

"Argh!" he growled. Those icy blue eyes beaded up, like it was all Geth's fault. He hefted his sword.

But another fight sounded through the fog nearby.

"Answer, wench! You'll answer me! You'll pay for what you've done!"

"Aaahhh!"

There was no mistaking Catriona's voice, Lyanne's whimper. Palladine disappeared in their direction through the mist. Geth followed after. Catriona had the queen by the throat, until Palladine's sword flashed.

"Eeehh!"

The witch went down to one knee. There was no sign of remorse this time as Palladine pulled his blade free. Geth raised his sword to start after the captain, but the mist dissolved almost instantly to leave them all blinking at the carnage of the field.

This Garden was no supposed den of tranquility any longer. Nor even a mere prison. It was a butcher-yard.

Lilies lay moaning and bleeding among the flowerbeds, or huddled and shivering under ornamental trees, still and lifeless in the bushes. A handful of dead witches joined them. And also Hack. Geth's eyes searched frantically for Vriana, for Agrem and

Ethen. Relief coursed through him when he didn't find them. They must have escaped.

That left him alone with Palladine, Lyanne, and what looked like a fresh troop of soldiers arriving through the arch under the gatehouse.

"Mother!" A man with a short coif of curly dark hair rushed to the queen's side. His soldiers looked up, Palladine too, but they weren't looking at Geth.

"What the..."

They *were* looking at Geth, but that man was across the lawn, waving his sword and cursing them roundly. The real Geth patted himself, wondered if he was dead for a split second, before recognizing Asaac at work. The real Geth ducked down where he stood lest they all realize their folly.

"Take him!" the dark-haired man, Prince Eachus, cried. The queen tried to call them off, but her voice was weak after Catriona's attack. Smoldering eyes burned into the real Geth, until they hauled her off with them.

A gentle hand came to rest on the big warrior's shoulder and he gasped. Oedelia's voice sounded in his head. *It's time to go.*

Feru-Lea came hand in hand at her side, humming softly. With all the queen's men charging off after Asaac, the space between them and the gatehouse cleared, leaving only trampled turf, the wounded and the dead.

"Hack."

Geth went to him. He knelt, groaned with the weight, but managed to lift the green-cloak up into his arms. Though the mist was gone, the magicks of witch-song cloaked them now. Oedelia led them straight to the gatehouse arch.

Geth turned to look for Asaac. Best he could tell, the warlock had led Palladine and the rest into the orchards, toward the inner citadel, Lucean's den. There was no way out from there.

"It's his choice," Feru-Lea said. She pulled at Geth's sleeve. There was nothing for it but to follow, down the zigzagged stairs. He clutched at Hack's lifeless form, tears sliding unbidden down his cheeks.

But those bitter tears turned to tears of joy as his eyes landed on Agrem, Vriana, and little Ethen in her arms, beckoning from the decks of the Sparrow.

"Gethe! We have him!"

CHAPTER THIRTY-FOUR

S pray arced over the bow of the Sparrow as her sail caught wind. Oars cut water and the speedy vessel lurched westward, away. But Geth's eyes looked behind them, east, at a red sun rising over the Garden.

"Gethe."

The big warrior exhaled. He turned to face his wife.

She pulled him into a tight embrace. "Mmmm."

He shook his head, snorted a bitter laugh. That hum about summed it up. They had Ethen and they'd gotten out alive. But they'd lost Hack, Asaac, and the other witches as well.

But that wasn't the only thing that weighed on Geth's mind. The sun battled a cloud bank behind them, tried in vain to warm the Sparrow's deck. The first cool of autumn in Pellon raised goosebumps on his arm. He shivered.

Lyanne. She wasn't done with them. They'd escaped, but they'd left a potent enemy at their backs. There would have to be a reckoning. Geth figured it would come sooner than later.

And what would she try next? Ominous words rang in his ear, of a supposed utopia, of divination, of an age to come.

It is my destiny to unite the Sworn Realms, all Aturians, as they haven't been, since the days of Atuer himself...

What exactly did that mean, for Umbel and King Hadean?

Geth reckoned she'd made that clear as well.

...too long those lands have drifted astray, whipped this way and that like some ragged banner.

Asaac had claimed Lyanne was relentless, that she'd never give up, and Geth had seen nothing to the contrary. Her ambitions were clear. Still, it was Palladine that had summed it all up.

Do you think you can stand in the way of destiny?

Geth heaved a sigh. "I love you," he told Vriana. "Do you know that?"

"I know."

He squeezed her tight.

At the same time though, his eyes drifted from his wife, back over the waves, to the shoreline and the Golden City beyond. They may have had Ethen, but how long before his enemies struck out at his family again?

No, the fight against Lyanne—against Palladine and the rest of her hounds—that fight had just begun.

A MESSAGE FROM THE AUTHOR

Thank you for reading LET SLEEPING DOGS LIE, I hope you enjoyed it! If you're hungry for more, join my newsletter at www.deankastle.com/newsletter.html and get a free short story about Phelan's infamous dice game and subsequent capture, told from Palladine's point of view. Subscribers will be first to know when new projects launch and will also receive exclusive content, bonus material, special offers, and more.

All the best!

DK

ABOUT THE AUTHOR

Dean Kastle is the author of SWORD SONGS, the DOG OF WAR Epic, and the forthcoming LEGACY Cycle. In addition to a love of 'story' in every medium, he's a rabid foodie, and soccer fanatic. As far as he's concerned, Pluto is still a planet, and the oxford comma is a matter of taste. He doesn't wear a beret or write with a fountain pen, but he does own a life-size replica of the Iron Throne. From that perch, he plots his next tale. Readers can connect with Dean by joining his newsletter at www.deankastle.com/newsletter.html on X, or on Facebook. He lives in fly-over country with his wife, three kids and—yes—a dog.